MW01449153

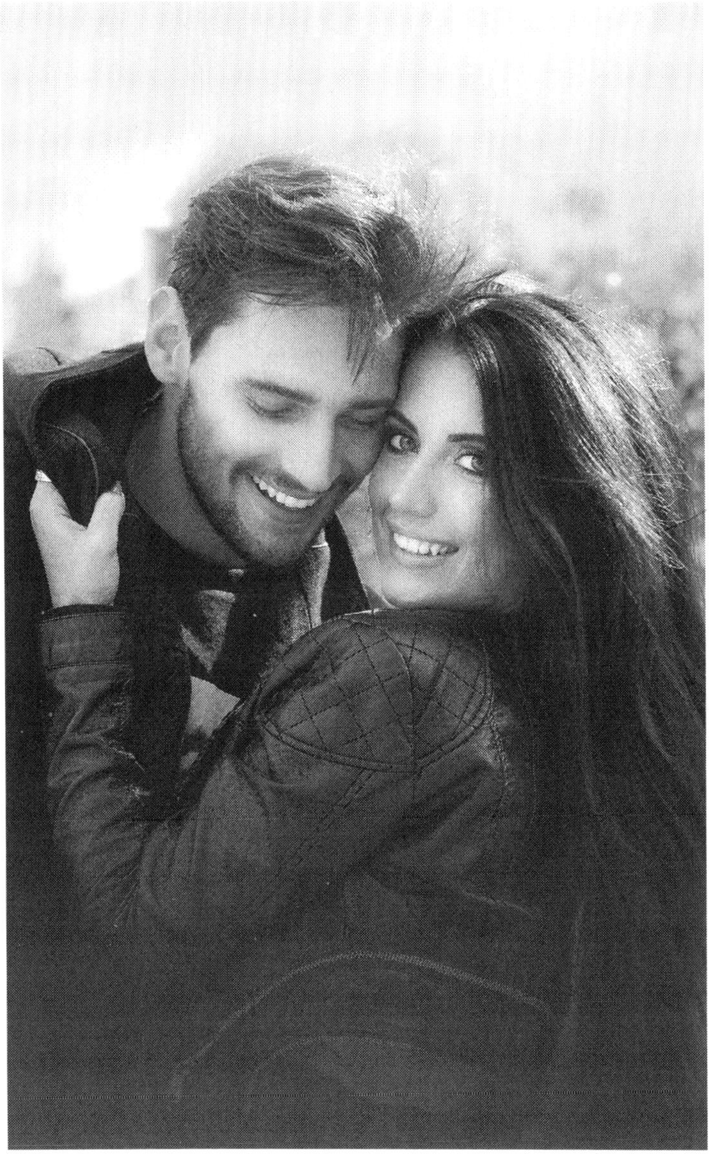

This is a work of fiction. Names, characters, organizations, places, events, and incidents are either products of the author's imagination or are used fictitiously.

Text copyright © 2018 Sandra Owens
All rights reserved.

No part of this book may be reproduced, or stored in a retrieval system, or transmitted in any form or by any means, electronic, mechanical, photocopying, recording, or otherwise, without express written permission of the publisher.

This book is licensed for your personal enjoyment only, and may not be re-sold or given away to other people. Thank you for respecting the work of this author.

Print ISBN- 978-0-9997864-6-8
E-Book ISBN- 978-0-9997864-6-8

Edits by: Melody Guy and Ella Sheridan
Printed in the United States of America

Cover Design and Interior Format

Still Savannah

Blue Ridge Valley

SANDRA OWENS

PRAISE FOR

SANDRA'S BOOKS

The Blue Ridge Valley series is Sandra Owens at her finest. Filled with Southern charm and a dash of humor, she had me churning through the pages. I laughed. I cried. This series has it all.
Heather Burch, bestselling author of ONE LAVENDER RIBBON

Take everything you love about a Sandra Owens novel—the dry humor, the hot alpha heroes—and transplant them into a quirky small town, and you have the Blue Ridge Valley Series. Charming, funny, and sexy.
Jenny Holiday, *USA Today* bestselling author

Snappy dialog, endearing characters, and a delightful plot . . . I loved, loved, loved Just Jenny!
Barbara Longley, #1 Bestselling author

Welcome to Blue Ridge Valley . . . A town you'll want to visit and never leave. You'll fall in love with the quirky residents who will make you laugh, and you'll cry tears for Jenny and Dylan—two hearts in need of healing—as they find forgiveness and love.
Miranda Liasson, Bestselling author of the Mirror Lake series

JUST JENNY, set in the picturesque Blue Ridge Valley, is just an all-around good time. It's got its share of colorful characters, juicy secrets, nosy neighbors, apple pie moonshine, and a romance that will touch your heart. Small town living at its best you

don't want to miss.
Tamra Baumann, Bestselling author

"*If you are a fan of this author or enjoy romantic suspense or just love your heroes to be swoon-worthy, Jack of Hearts is highly recommended.*"
Harlequin Junkie Top Pick

"*A heated romance is at the forefront of this novel, backed by a compelling story that will lure readers into Madison and Alex's world.*"
Publishers Weekly

"*I love this new series! It's filled with ongoing suspense and tension, then sexy hot romance, and relatable people that you want to spend time with.*"
Reading in Pajamas.

To sign up for Sandra's Newsletter go to:

https://bit.ly/2FVUPKS

Also by Sandra Owens

~ BLUE RIDGE VALLEY SERIES ~
Just Jenny
All Autumn

~ ACES & EIGHTS SERIES ~
Jack of Hearts
King of Clubs
Ace of Spades
Queen of Diamonds

~ K2 TEAM SERIES ~
Crazy for Her
Someone Like Her
Falling for Her
Lost in Her
Only Her

~ REGENCY BOOKS ~
The Dukes Obsession
The Training of a Marquess
The Letter

DEDICATION

This one is dedicated to Jim, who still makes me laugh.

CHAPTER ONE

~ Savannah ~

"I CAN'T DO IT. I WON'T do it." The mere thought of it made me sick.

Jackson's cold eyes roamed over me. "Who made you what you are today, Savannah?"

Me. I made me who I am today, I screamed in my head. It was my face, my body on the covers of all those magazines, not his. "You," I said, hating the sound of defeat in my voice.

He pointed the knife he held at his chest. "Exactly. If not for me, you'd still be modeling for catalogs."

That might or might not be true. I'd never know, but maybe I wouldn't be miserable. I eyed the carrots he was peeling—my evening snack—with distaste. I hated carrots. Not that he cared. Jackson controlled my food intake as closely as he did my career.

"I'm not hungry," I said when he pushed the three carrots across the counter. That was a lie. I was always hungry. But I wanted food, real food. I would just about kill for a slice of red velvet cake from Mary's Bread Company in my hometown of Blue Ridge Valley.

"Eat the carrots."

It was a command, and if I didn't obey, he would get angry, so I picked up one, nibbling on the end. I closed my eyes and imagined the moist, buttery taste of a Mary-baked cake. It was a trick I used to get the carrots down. Sometimes it still amazed me how good I'd become at tricking my mind. It also made me sad that I had to do that.

Once all the carrots had been chewed and swallowed, I tried one more time to make Jackson understand that he was asking the impossible from me. "I can't take off my clothes in front of a roomful of people. I just can't. Please don't make me do it."

Jackson sighed as if I were a contrary child who was annoying him. "I've already signed the contract, so you don't have a choice. Did you even pay attention to how much money they're going to pay for the nude spread?"

"I don't give a dang about the money!" Or the French magazine whose name I couldn't even pronounce that apparently thought it would be a grand idea for the world to see the famous model, Savannah, without a stitch on. That had been Jackson's doing, the one-name thing. I hated it. I had a last name, but Graham had been lost years ago, along with my identity.

My bio, the one Jackson wrote after my mother signed me on as a client at his agency, claimed that Savannah—no last name—was from Charleston, South Carolina. There was no hiding my southern accent, so he'd chosen that particular city because there were a lot of old-money families in Charleston. It was a city of expensive older homes and a culture steeped in prestige, tradition, and charm. A good place for a model to be from, he'd claimed. It was also big enough that it would be difficult to disprove my vague bio. I'd never understood why I couldn't just be me, a girl from a small mountain town in the North Carolina Blue Ridge Mountains.

"Yelling isn't attractive, Savannah. And I've told you repeatedly to stop saying 'dang.'" He sneered. "Makes you sound like a mountain hick."

"News flash. I am a mountain hick." And dang proud of it. I picked up the contract Jackson had set on the counter, glanced at his name signed at the bottom, and then tore it down the middle. It was the first time I'd dared to defy him, but the anger that had been simmering inside me since he'd told me that I would be posing nude had finally boiled over, impossible to contain.

Suddenly he was behind me. He wrapped an arm around my chest, holding me so tight that it was hard to breathe. He brought the knife up to my face, pressing the sharp edge against my cheek. I froze. Jackson was demanding and controlling, but he'd never physically threatened me before. Not that there weren't times when I thought he wanted to hit me, but my body and face were his meal ticket, so he used intimidation and manipulation to keep me in line.

"A few cuts to this pretty face and you'll never grace the cover of another magazine. Is that what you want, Savannah? To be a nobody again?"

Yes, that was exactly what I wanted, what I craved. "No," I whispered, my lips trembling as I told him what he wanted to hear. I didn't believe he would cut me. My face was too valuable. But his temper had been getting worse lately, and I was no longer sure of what he might do.

"Didn't think so." He let me go, put his hand on my butt, and gave me a push. "Go pack. Our flight to Paris is an early one."

And just like that, he acted as if he hadn't held a knife to my face. My knees were still shaking, and my stomach was churning as I turned to leave the kitchen. I couldn't go on like this.

"Oh, FYI. That was a copy of the contract you tore up, not the original."

I didn't answer, just kept going. In the bathroom I lost the contents of my stomach, all three carrots. After splashing cold water on my face, I spent a mere ten minutes packing, which I had down to a science since I traveled frequently. Even on location I wasn't free of Jackson. He always came with me. Not because he wanted to be with me, but to make sure I knew he was watching me.

Out of all the beautiful women surrounding him, I don't

know why he chose me for his girlfriend. I suspected it was because my mother signed over control of me—both my physical body and my money—to Jackson. The day she did that was the day he moved in with us and into my bed. By that time I didn't much care about anything, so I didn't even try to put up a fight.

Something had to change, but I didn't know how to make that happen. From childhood I'd been managed, first by my mother and now by Jackson. I hated myself for allowing my life to reach this point, but I'd never learned how to stand on my own two feet. The truth of that was pathetic.

Jackson had always intimidated me with those piercing brown eyes that seemed to constantly be watching me, just waiting for something he could criticize. He frowned and scowled more often than he smiled. At least at me. He had plenty of smiles for whoever's ass he was kissing. We were the same height, and I think it irritated him that he couldn't look down on me.

He was good-looking but not gorgeous. It was his confidence, intelligence, and success that drew people to him. Models and wannabes would openly flirt with him, even if I was at his side. Jackson Marks could make you famous if you were lucky enough to be signed by him. He was smart about that. He didn't sign anyone unless he was sure she had the *it factor*, which meant that he had very few failures.

As for the flirting, I didn't care. They could have at him. My greatest wish was that he'd leave me for one of them, but unless he could get control of their money like he had with mine, he wasn't going anywhere. But it was more than that. For reasons I'd never understood, Jackson had an unhealthy obsession with me, to the point he didn't always give his other models the attention they deserved. Recently he'd lost a few to other agents, and when I told him he needed to pay more attention to the others before he lost more, he got angry. Apparently I didn't understand business.

It was only ten, but that was usually my bedtime since I often had to get up early for a photo shoot. Jackson never slept more than five hours a night, so he would be up for a while. Having the bed to myself for two or three hours was one of my few blessings.

My stomach rumbled. Long used to feeling like I was starving, I could usually ignore the hunger pains and fall asleep, but for some reason I wasn't able to tonight. Maybe because a thousand thoughts were spinning around in my head. Contract or not, I just couldn't do a nude shoot. What if Adam saw it? He'd be so disappointed in me. Or maybe he couldn't care less anymore. Thinking of Adam made me want to cry, so I tried to think of how to get out of the mess my life had become. I was nothing more than a doormat, an empty shell. I'd lost myself.

I must have drifted off, because I startled when the bed dipped. Even being in the same room with Jackson, much less the same bed, was becoming torturous. Jackson was one of those people who fell asleep as soon as his head hit the pillow. My stomach was killing me, and I felt like bugs were crawling under my skin. If I didn't get out of this bed, I was going to scream. Inch by careful inch I slid out. When my feet landed on the floor, I crouched next to the bed, listening to Jackson's breathing. He was still asleep.

Jackson kept treats for himself in a locked drawer in his office, but I knew where he hid the key. I wouldn't take enough so that he'd notice, just a few chips from an opened bag or, if I was lucky, a bag of candy. A few bites to get something in my stomach, then maybe I could sleep.

The bedroom was pitch-black—the way Jackson liked it for sleeping—and I held my hands in front of me as I shuffled toward the closed door. Pain shot up my foot when I stubbed my toe, and I slapped a hand over my mouth, silencing a screech. I stilled until I was sure Jackson hadn't woken, and then I reached down to touch what

I'd walked into. It was my overnight bag, containing one change of clothes, makeup and toiletries, some jewelry, and my Kindle and its charger, along with my phone charger. Everything else for the trip was in my large suitcase. My hand seemed to separate itself from me as my fingers wrapped around the handle of my overnight bag without any instructions from my brain.

Time stopped, and I think my heart did, too. Did I dare? My heart started beating again but hard against my chest, pounding the same word over and over into my mind. *Go. Go. Go. Go.*

With no other plan than to escape, I picked up the bag and slipped out the bedroom door, closing it gently behind me. I wished I could have grabbed my suitcase, too, but it would have made too much noise rolling over the marble floor. Barefoot, I made my way to the living room, my gaze searching for anything I might want to take with me. There was nothing of me in this cold room of leather, chrome, and glass, and unless I wanted to carry a large abstract painting out with me to sell for cash… I shook my head at the foolish thought. My purse was on the kitchen counter, and I slipped it over my shoulder. The good news, I'd stuck my phone in my purse so I wouldn't forget it in the morning. And lucky me, I'd forgotten to put away a pair of running shoes—which irritated Jackson to no end when I left stuff lying around—and I grabbed them. I decided to take it as an omen that I'd left the shoes out. Normally I was careful not to do anything that would set him off.

Minutes later I was in the hallway. Was I really doing this? I stopped and reconsidered. Where would I go? I didn't have close friends in the city. Jackson had seen to that, isolating me from anyone who showed an interest in friendship. As for money, there was, at the most, two hundred dollars in my wallet, another Jackson thing. He controlled all my money and doled it out sparingly. Nor did I have a credit card. If I needed clothes or whatever, Jackson paid for them. Well, technically I paid since it was my money, but that was a moot point at the moment.

Where could I go with only the money I had on me? But I couldn't stand here outside the door to my apartment thinking about it. God forbid that Jackson caught me out here with my overnight bag. I ran down the hallway to the elevator. While I waited, I opened my bag and pulled out the black sweater dress, slipping it on over my camisole and boy boxers. I congratulated myself on my foresight to always stick one change of clothes into my overnight bag in case my luggage didn't arrive at my destination with me. The running shoes would look funny with it, but I was lucky to even have them. I wished I had the black knee-high boots I'd planned to wear tomorrow, though.

Our night doorman widened his eyes at seeing me. "I'll get you a cab, Miss Savannah. Where to?"

"Thank you, Frank." He was used to seeing me leave at odd hours, but Jackson or I had always given him notice when I'd need a cab standing by. And where to was the question, wasn't it? "Airport," I said. Not that I had any intention of going there, but when Jackson found me missing, he would question Frank.

Within minutes a cab pulled up, and I walked out of my building for what I hoped was the last time. A freezing blast of cold air hit me, and I rushed into the back seat. "Greyhound bus station," I said once the door was closed behind me and Frank couldn't hear. A Greyhound seemed like the fastest way to get out of New York with what little money I had.

I glanced out the rear window as we pulled away, wondering if I was crazy leaving a penthouse apartment in one of the most desirable sections of New York City and a hugely successful career. But as my neighborhood faded behind me, I didn't have any regrets, other than that I hadn't managed to bring a coat with me.

After paying the driver, I gathered my meager belongings and ran inside the bus terminal. Dang, it was cold. But I'd done it. I'd escaped. And with each block separating me from my prison, the heavy weight in my soul was a little lighter.

Now I just needed a plan.

CHAPTER TWO

~ Adam ~

EVERYTHING THAT COULD HAVE GONE wrong had gone wrong. Connor, my identical twin, and I were building three model homes and a sales office on a piece of property on the main street of our town. Retirees were discovering Blue Ridge Valley, North Carolina, and it seemed as if they all wanted one of the Hunter brothers' luxury log homes. Business was booming, and I wasn't complaining about that at all. But I was ready to kill the man standing in front of me, giving me a dozen excuses as to why the wrong kitchen cabinets had been delivered.

"Roy, we buy local as much as we can, which is why we ordered these cabinets from you," I said. "You just sent my schedule into the toilet."

After profusely apologizing and swearing that I'd have the right cabinets in four days, even if it meant overtime for his employees, he left. I tackled the granite counter problem next. The deliverymen had dropped the island countertop, breaking it in half. They'd called their boss, and the message back was that a new counter would be delivered in two weeks. That was not acceptable. I'd taken out my phone to deal with that issue when Connor and Autumn, his girlfriend, walked in.

Seeing the two of them holding hands and laughing, I had the urge to unbuckle my tool belt, drop it to the floor, and walk away. To where, I didn't know. Didn't care. Just somewhere far away.

Don't get me wrong. I was happy for my brother that he and Autumn had finally dealt with their issues and now seemed to be ridiculously in love. But every time I saw them together, I thought of Savannah and how we'd once been that happy. I shook my head, banishing thoughts of Savannah from my mind. She was my past, and that was where she would stay.

"Bro, what's with that sour look on your face?" Conner said.

Instead of punching him for smiling like an idiot, I settled for a glare. "Where should I start? With the wrong kitchen cabinets sitting over there?" I swept my hand out at the offending cabinets. "Or how about the delivery guys dropping and breaking the granite countertop for the island? Then there's the—" My phone rang. Hopefully it was one of the reasons for my problems calling to make things right. The number was an unknown, so probably not. I answered anyway, hoping it was someone with good news.

"Adam Hunter." All I heard was breathing. I frowned. Just what I needed, a prank phone call. "Hello."

"Adam?"

I stilled, certain that I was hearing things. That voice whispering my name couldn't be Savannah. "Who is this?"

"Savannah." She laughed, but it sounded brittle. "I guess you've forgotten… Never mind. I shouldn't have called."

"Don't hang up."

"Who's that?" Connor said.

I glanced at my twin, the only person in the world who could practically read my mind. Right now I didn't want him in mine. Without answering, I walked outside. After all this time why was she calling? I'd given her my number last year when she'd come to the valley for Jenn's wedding. It had been obvious that she wasn't happy, and in a moment of weakness I'd told her to call me if she ever needed anything.

"What do you want, Savannah?" I'd once loved this girl with every bone in my body and every beat of my heart.

As much as I kept telling myself I was over her, I wasn't sure I'd ever be.

"I… I, ah… I'm sorry. I shouldn't have called you."

"You already said that. Talk to me, Savannah. Are you in trouble?"

"Not exactly."

I sighed in frustration. "What does that mean, exactly?" I glanced up to see Connor standing outside the back door of the house, watching me. I turned my back on him. "Savannah?"

She hung up on me.

I hit call back. Her phone rang six times before she answered. When she didn't say anything, I said, "Where are you?"

"Allentown, Pennsylvania." A few beats of silence and then, "I ran away, Adam."

At those words my heart took a tumble to the pit of my stomach. "From Whatshisname?"

"From Jackson, yes. I didn't know who else to call."

"Seems like Jenn or Autumn would have been a likely choice." Jenny Conrad and Autumn Archer were her best friends in the valley. Connor and I had grown up with the girls, and they were tighter than bark on a tree.

"I know. It's just that the first place Jackson will look for me is there, and both of them will be at the top of his list to interrogate. I don't want them involved."

If there was a chance the schmuck would come here, I didn't want them involved either. But I would warn Dylan, Jenn's husband. He was our chief of police and one of the good guys.

"Okay, I get that. What kind of help do you need?"

"This is so embarrassing, but could I borrow a couple of hundred dollars? I'll pay you back as soon as I can access my bank account."

"When will that be?" I realized how that sounded. "What I mean is, a few hundred bucks won't get you far. How far are you going, anyway?"

She started crying. Hell, she didn't have a plan.

"Two questions. Has he ever hurt you, and will he really try to find you?"

"He... he put a knife to my face and said he'd cut me if I didn't do what he says." Another sob sounded over the phone. "And yeah, he won't stop looking for me until he finds me since I'm his meal ticket. I just need a little money until I figure out what to do."

The bastard had threatened to cut her? I paced the ground, wondering how fast I could get to New York and see how the man liked my fist in his face. Out of the corner of my eye I saw Connor still watching me. He probably suspected whom I was talking to. Although we'd all been friends growing up, after Savannah and her mother had left for New York to pursue a modeling career for Savannah, leaving me with a broken heart, he'd stopped liking Savannah. But he didn't know the whole story. It was the only secret I'd ever kept from him.

"Okay, here's the plan. I assume there's an airport in Allentown?"

"Why?"

"Go there. I'll have a ticket to Asheville waiting for you."

"No, Adam. The first place he'll look for me is Blue Ridge Valley."

I hoped so. "Savannah, there's no safer place than here. The entire town will protect you, you know that. Now do as I say. I'll call you back with your flight information." I disconnected before she could protest.

As soon as Connor saw I was off the phone, he headed my way. "What's going on?"

"Not now. Where's Autumn?"

"Inside measuring the rooms."

Autumn was an interior designer, a damn good one, and she would be doing the decor for our model homes. "Good. Find a reason to get away, then meet me at the police station in an hour. And Connor, don't give her any reason to be suspicious."

He frowned at me as I walked away. My problems with the building suppliers temporarily forgotten, I headed home to book a flight for Savannah and take a quick shower. I had a good crew, and they would continue on without my supervision for the remainder of the day.

I'd called Dylan on my way to the police station, so he was expecting me. Connor was already sitting in his office when I walked in, closing the door behind me. "Savannah called me."

Connor scowled. "I knew it."

Yeah, sometimes it was a pain having a twin who could pick up on things others couldn't. I ignored him as I sat in the chair next to him. "She ran away."

"So? What's that got to do with you?" Connor said.

"If you'd shut it, I'd tell you." He didn't want Savannah anywhere near me. I got that and understood. Connor had been there for me after Savannah left, even when I'd wished he'd get lost so I could be alone with my misery. He'd watched me struggle to get over her, had made sure I ate, and hadn't gotten mad when I refused to tell him exactly what had gone down between us. One of the problems with some twins was that they felt each other's pain, and it had always been like that for Connor and me. I hadn't been the only one who'd hurt.

"I gather this isn't a simple breakup between Savannah and Jackson?" Dylan said. "Considering you've got me and your brother here behind closed doors?"

"He held a knife to her face and threatened to cut her." What kind of man did that to a woman?

Dylan sat up, his eyes turning hard and cold, and beside me Connor hissed. She hadn't answered her phone when I'd called to give her the flight information, so I didn't know if she'd gotten the message I'd left or if my worst fear had come true. That Jackson Marks had found her.

"We need to bring her here where we can protect her," Dylan said.

Connor nodded. "I agree." He put his hand on my arm. "She's not my favorite person, but she's one of ours. No one hurts what belongs to us. Dylan's right. We need to get her home."

"That's my plan." I hadn't doubted that Dylan would be on board with however I decided to handle Savannah's situation, but I hadn't been sure about my brother. I glanced at him, and as often happened, a message passed between us without words. *Thank you*, my eyes told him.

I'll always have your back, he responded.

"I booked her on a flight to Asheville, but she didn't answer her phone when I called to give her the info. So the question is, will she be on the plane?"

"What time does she arrive?" Connor asked, then added, "If she is on the plane."

"A little before eight in the morning. It was the soonest I could get her out of Allentown to here."

"That gives us time to make a plan," Dylan said.

I had a plan all right. Make sure Savannah was safe and then wait for Jackson to show up. He was going to wish he'd never stepped foot in my town.

"We'll need to hide her," Connor said.

"If she's not on the plane, then I'll go looking for her. If she is, the last thing we should do is hide her." Both my brother and Dylan turned surprised eyes on me. "He'll know she's here, and from what she said, he won't stop until he finds her. You ever see the Clint Eastwood movie, *High Plains Drifter*?"

Dylan stared at me for a moment and then broke into a smile. I'd watched the movie on a cable channel a few weeks ago, and while showering earlier, I'd thought of the town that had joined forces to beat the outlaws. An idea had taken shape.

"Yeah, I have," Dylan said rather gleefully as understanding settled on his face.

"I watched it with Autumn, maybe two weeks ago." Connor glanced at Dylan. "She loves old movies." His eyebrows furrowed when he turned back to me. "We're going to paint the town red?"

"No, dumbass, we're not painting the town red, but the town is going to circle the wagons against the bad guy." After working out the details of our plan, I headed home to grab some sleep before I had to leave for the airport.

The next morning I was at the Asheville airport thirty minutes before Savannah's flight was due. She'd never called me back. As I waited in baggage—the closest I could get to where she would exit the terminal—I wondered if she'd gotten on the plane.

CHAPTER THREE

~ Savannah ~

COMING HOME TO BLUE RIDGE Valley had been a mistake. I would be bringing my troubles to the people I loved, and that was the last thing I wanted to do. I should never have stepped on that plane.

Adam had booked me a seat in first class as far as Charlotte, North Carolina, and from there, a window seat on the commuter plane to Asheville. Although I was used to flying first-class, I didn't like that Adam was spending that kind of money on me. As soon as I could get control of my bank account, I'd pay him back.

Since my face was recognizable, I'd bought reading glasses and a baseball hat to tuck my hair under at the Allentown airport. Between my meager disguise and the fact it was a red-eye and everyone was tired and sleepy, no one gave me a second glance. When they called for boarding, I almost walked out of the airport, but desperation was apparently an excellent motivator. I had nowhere else to go.

As I neared baggage, my heart beat an erratic drumbeat in my ears. I would be seeing Adam for the first time in over a year. There was no doubt in my mind that when I walked through security, he would be there, waiting for me. When I'd briefly talked to him at Jenn and Dylan's wedding, he'd asked if I was happy. I'd lied, telling him I was, but the tears I couldn't hold back had said otherwise. Adam was and would always be the man I loved.

The years hadn't dimmed what I felt for him, but he couldn't know that. By now he would have moved on, made a life for himself. Nor did I want his pity. On the flight I'd considered my options. They were too limited for my peace of mind, but my first objective was to get control of my money. Then I needed to decide if I'd continue to model. I didn't want to, but I didn't know anything else.

I'd led a sheltered life thanks to my mother and then Jackson. It was ridiculous that I didn't even know how to write a check since I'd never once done that, had never paid a bill. But that was going to change. By leaving Jackson, I'd taken the first steps to get control of my life. There would be no turning around now. Forward was my only direction from today on.

When I spotted Adam, he was looking directly at me. No smile greeted me, but I wasn't expecting one. With one phone call I'd disrupted his life. Yet he'd been there for me. That was Adam. A man his friends could always depend on. He was also a man who still stole my breath.

Tall with short black hair and blue eyes that had always made me think of a cloudless summer sky. Even in high school he'd had a hot body, but the man had filled out in all the right places. He built houses, so he probably had muscles from the physical labor that I'd never touched. My heart broke a little at seeing him and what I'd lost.

An attractive woman walked ahead of me, and as she passed Adam, she gave him the once-over. I couldn't blame her. It shouldn't matter that he didn't seem to notice her, but I would be lying to myself to claim otherwise. My steps slowed as I neared him, and I took a few extra seconds to compose myself.

One of the advantages of being a model was that I'd learned to project on command whatever image the photo shoot called for. Sexy, you got it. Girl next door, I'm her. Badass female CEO, all over it. So I formed an image in my head of a woman not in love with the man waiting for her, hiding what was in my heart. Composed, no love stars shining in my eyes, and no soft smile on my face, I stopped in front of Adam.

"Hello, Adam," I coolly said.

"I gave you a fifty-fifty chance of getting on that plane."

"Almost didn't. When I asked to borrow a little money, I wasn't hoping for a knight on a white horse."

"There's not even one white horse in my stable."

His eyes were as blank as I knew mine were, and I hated that it hurt not to see anything resembling fondness for me on his face. Either he was as good at hiding his feelings as me, or he really didn't think of me as more than a friend he was willing to help. My money was on the latter.

As far as his willingness to step into a messy situation and help me, that wasn't a surprise. Both the Hunter brothers had always been protective of Jenn, Natalie, Autumn, and me. We'd all been friends since elementary school, and the twins had even tolerated us girls invading their tree house. Of course Adam and Connor had soaked us with their water guns in an attempt to keep us out, but once they realized we thought that was fun, they'd decided we weren't so bad.

Natalie, Jenn's twin, was gone now, leaving a hole in all our hearts after she'd died of a brain tumor a few months after graduating high school. Jenn was married to Dylan Conrad, Blue Ridge Valley's new police chief, and Autumn was single again. I regretted that I hadn't been there for her when she'd caught her husband cheating on her. Since leaving the valley, I'd been a crappy friend to this group of people that I loved. I could blame that on my mother and Jackson, but that didn't ease the guilt.

"Your luggage should be coming out in a few minutes," Adam said, taking my overnight bag from me. He put his hand on my back, steering me toward the carousel.

"I don't have anything more."

He darted me a surprised glance but didn't comment. No doubt he thought a famous model would have a truckload of luggage when she traveled, and normally that was true. I usually had one case that held nothing but shoes;

then there was my makeup bag, larger than most women's. And I won't even start on my clothes. It wasn't that I cared much for those things.

Always looking perfect was in my job description, and there was nothing the paparazzi loved more than catching you at your worst. That had happened once before my mother died, when I'd slipped out without makeup, without my hair done, and wearing what she called *ratty* clothes. Within hours that photo had been popping up all over the place. All I'd wanted was a latte, something I wasn't allowed. Mother and Jackson had been furious, because of both the latte and the pictures. I'd never made that mistake again.

Fortunately it wasn't as cold as it had been in New York and Pennsylvania, but I still shivered when we stepped outside.

"Where's your coat?" Adam said, his gaze raking down me, pausing for a moment on my running shoes.

"Don't have one."

He slipped off his leather jacket, putting it over my shoulders. The inside was warm from his body heat, and I almost sighed with pleasure before I caught myself.

When we reached Adam's vehicle, I smiled at seeing the muscle car. Adam and his brother were classic car nuts, had been for as long as I could remember, something they got from their father. "What year is it?"

He fondly eyed the car. "She's a '68 Camaro SS. Took us a year to restore her to her original condition."

"She's beautiful." Because of the brothers I had an appreciation for classic cars. In high school they'd owned a 1970 Mustang Boss they'd restored to its original condition, and Adam had taken me on many dates in it. I had a special fondness for the back seat of that car.

"That she is." He opened the Camaro's passenger door and I slid in. I pulled off the reading glasses and watched him walk around the hood of the car. I could spend my life watching him, enjoying the fluid grace of his movements… truthfully, just feasting my eyes on him in general. When he got in, I blanked my face, hiding my longing behind my mask.

Adam didn't seem to be in the mood to talk, so I left him to his thoughts. He probably wished he'd never answered the phone when I'd called. As he drove up the entrance ramp to I-26, it occurred to me that I had no idea where I'd be staying in Blue Ridge Valley. Mother had sold the house when we'd moved to New York, and I refused to bunk with my friends, bringing them into Jackson's line of fire.

There were cabin rentals galore in the area, so maybe one of those. That would mean asking for more money, which I so didn't want to do. I was worth millions yet couldn't get to any of it. That fact made me feel stupid for meekly bowing to Mother's will. One thing I did know, I wouldn't take any more money from Adam. I considered my choices and decided I would ask for a loan from Autumn. After the twins she made the best living as an interior designer, and she wouldn't say no. Feeling a little better for having the beginnings of a plan, I settled back in the seat and stared out the window as I subtly inhaled the scent of Adam lingering on his jacket.

We merged into the heavy weekday traffic on the power of a car meant to run. He gave it even more gas as he moved into the passing lane, easily surging ahead of the slower cars. Because I had my face turned toward the window, I allowed myself to smile. He was showing off his pride and joy, and I was duly impressed.

We'd only traveled a few miles when he moved back into the right lane and then onto the exit ramp. "Where are we going?"

"Breakfast."

"I'm not hungry," I lied. As if it had heard the word *breakfast*, my stomach rumbled. Lying about my hunger was ingrained in me, and I wondered if I would ever be able to eat without looking over my shoulder to see if Mother or Jackson were watching me.

"Well, I am," Adam said as he turned into the parking lot of a Huddle House.

Oh God. Huddle House was Calorie Central. They had the best grits soaked in butter in the world. Adam had me out of his car and seated in a booth in less than three minutes. My stomach loudly rumbled again at the tantalizing smells of coffee and bacon.

"Not hungry, you say?" Adam said.

I chose not to dispute the obvious. When the waitress stepped up to our table, I said, "Coffee black, one slice of wheat toast, no butter."

After a brief glance at me, Adam turned his attention to our waitress. "She hates coffee black. Actually she doesn't like coffee at all. You have chocolate milk?"

The woman nodded. "We do."

"Bring her a glass of that and a bowl of grits with extra butter. I'll have two eggs over easy, hash browns, buttered toast, and bacon." His eyes darted my way, and then he said, "Two orders of bacon."

A storm of emotions threatened to drown me. He'd remembered everything I liked and didn't like, and that sent an unwelcome warmth through me. He'd also overrode my wishes without blinking an eye, just the way either Mother and Jackson had done every day of my life.

"Make that black coffee and one slice of unbuttered wheat toast"—I glanced at her name tag—"Stacy." I ignored Adam's scowl while trying to figure out how I could steal one piece of his bacon without him noticing.

CHAPTER FOUR

~ Adam ~

SAVANNAH WAS GOING TO EAT more than one damn slice of plain wheat bread if it killed me. She was a good fifteen or twenty pounds lighter than she'd been in high school. Maybe that rail-thin look was fashionable in her world, but she looked like she hadn't had a decent meal in months. And I'd heard her stomach growling the minute we'd walked inside the restaurant and the aromas of breakfast foods had hit us.

I wasn't a man who enjoyed forcing my will onto a woman, but I knew Savannah, understood that for all her life her choices had been made for her. Her breakfast order was what her mother, and I'm guessing Jackson, too, would have approved of. I didn't, but I did like that she'd stood up to me.

Savannah had always been extremely shy, conditioned by her mother to be afraid to speak up for herself. I hated that. Hated Jackson Marks, too. I definitely looked forward to dealing with him.

"How did you get away?" I asked.

"Snuck out in the middle of the night. I was supposed to leave for Paris this morning, but here I am instead."

With that one statement she'd driven the point home of just how far apart our worlds were now. I'd never been to Paris and had no desire to go. I had a thousand questions, but I shelved them for now. When we talked, I didn't want any interruptions.

Her phone buzzed from somewhere inside her purse. She pulled it out, frowned after glancing at the screen, and then placed it facedown on the table.

"Jackson?"

She nodded. "He wants to know where the hell I am."

I studied the girl I'd once thought I'd spend the rest of my life with. She had her black hair tucked under a baseball cap and zero makeup on. The last time I'd seen her, at Dylan and Jenn's wedding, her hair had reached halfway down her back. I wanted to snatch off that cap, see her hair tumble over her shoulders. She wasn't classically beautiful like some models, but her creamy pale skin, that raven-black hair, and the grayish-blue eyes made for a striking combination. The camera had always loved her.

"So what's the latest valley news?" she asked.

"Have you talked to Jenn or Autumn lately?"

Her gaze shifted away as she shook her head. "I'm a lousy friend," she whispered.

"Sounds to me like you've had a lot on your plate lately, so don't beat yourself up. Anyway, if you haven't talked to them, you might not know that Connor and Autumn are together now."

Her mouth formed an O, and her eyes lit up. "Really?"

I nodded. I also needed to stop staring at that mouth and remembering how it felt against mine. You'd think after nine years I'd forget how soft her lips were and how good she tasted, but apparently not.

"Finally."

I lifted a brow at that.

"They've always loved each other. They just didn't know it."

"If you say so."

"I know so."

A tiny spark had flamed in her eyes, the first real sign of life I'd seen in her since picking her up. My mind started working on ways to see more of that.

Our food arrived, and without saying anything, I slipped a piece of bacon onto her plate. As I ate, I watched her nibble on the toast while her eyes kept sliding over to the bacon. She wanted it. Lowering my gaze to my breakfast, I pretended to ignore her. After a few minutes she broke off the end of the bacon, ate it, then did it again. When it was gone, I put another one on her plate and went back to eating. I let another few minutes pass before I put a forkful of hash browns on her plate. Deciding not to push my luck and have her rebel, I ate the rest of my food. Her plate was clean by the time our waitress dropped the bill on the table.

Once we were back in my car, headed to Blue Ridge Valley, I said, "How long do you think it will take Jackson to arrive in the valley?"

She visibly shuddered, making me wonder if she'd told the truth when I'd asked her if he'd ever physically hurt her. I'd met him twice, first at Autumn's wedding to her ex-husband, and then at Jenn and Dylan's. I'd disliked him on sight, and at first I'd attributed that to him being with the girl I'd been in love with. But as I observed the control he'd exerted over Savannah, I'd had even more reason to dislike him. He hadn't made any effort to get to know her friends, had in fact kept her away from us. The second time they were in town for Jenn and Dylan's wedding, I'd wanted to shake Savannah, demand to know why she put up with that shit.

"I don't know," she said in answer to my question. "He'll spend today looking for me in New York, but since I don't have any friends to turn to, it won't take him long to realize that home is the only place I had to go."

She didn't have any friends in New York? It would seem that she'd know a lot of people, but I let that pass for now. "Why wouldn't he think that you might have taken off for some island or resort to hide?"

"Because…" She stared down at her hands as a blush spread across her cheeks. "Because he knows I don't have any money."

She was embarrassed, but I didn't get why. "You're broke?"

Her laugh sounded bitter. "Not even close. I have plenty of money, but I don't have access to it."

"Credit cards?"

"No."

The hell? I realized I was clenching my fingers on the steering wheel and relaxed them. I glanced at her. "How do you not have access to your money or no credit cards?"

She lifted her eyes to mine, tears swimming in them. "This is getting pretty personal, don't you think? Or are you just worried that I won't be able to pay you back for the ticket?"

"You know better than that. Don't insult me." I was insulted that she would even think I'd care about her owing me for the ticket.

"I'm sorry."

The tears welling in her eyes spilled over, and I felt like an ass. I bit back a sigh. "Savannah, I'm just trying to understand your situation so I can help you."

She glanced at me and then lowered her gaze to her lap. "I was thinking that I'd ask Autumn for a loan so I can rent a little cabin for the week or two that I'm here."

"No."

She jerked as if I'd slapped her. I wondered if she wasn't answering my question about her money because she was ashamed for whatever reason. And her reaction to my *no* made me think Jackson had been abusing her. I clenched my fingers around the steering wheel again.

"It's not up to you, Adam. In fact, I don't want you involved."

"Then you shouldn't have called me." She turned her face to the window. This time I let the sigh out. "Now I'm sorry. For being so brusque. But you're not going to hide out in some cabin by yourself. You have friends, and we're here for you. All of us."

She lifted her hand and swiped her fingers across her cheeks. *You made her cry, douchebag.* I reached across the console and put my hand on her arm. "It's going to be okay, I promise. I have some things to tell you as soon as we get home."

"I don't have a home," she softly said.

She sounded so sad that I found myself trying to swallow past a lump in my throat. We made the rest of the trip in silence, each lost in our own thoughts. I wondered what she'd have to say when I told her the plan Connor, Dylan, and I had come up with.

Savannah had wanted to shower when we'd arrived at my log home, so I showed her to the guest bedroom and attached bathroom. Now she was curled up at the end of my couch wearing a long-sleeved T-shirt, sweatpants, and socks I'd given her to put on after her shower. While she was in the bathroom, I'd gotten a fire going and had boiled some water for the cup of tea she'd asked for.

Savannah was tall, so the sweats almost fit her lengthwise, but she'd had to pull the drawstring tight around her waist to keep them up. With her hair down and still damp from the shower, and without any makeup, she looked younger, like the girl I'd fallen in love with.

Sitting at the opposite end of the sofa with the coffee I'd made myself, her with a cup of tea, and a crackling fire going, an image of us here by the fire on snowy nights with Savannah curled up next to me popped into my head. I pushed it away. That train had left the station the day she'd moved to New York. As soon as she got Jackson Marks out of her life—if that was what she really wanted—she'd hightail it back to her glamorous job.

"I'm surprised you had tea bags," she said.

"Autumn likes a cup of tea sometimes. I keep a box for when she and Connor are over."

"Oh. Do she and Jenn know I'm here?"

"No yet. They will soon." I set my cup on the coffee table. "I want you to hear me out before you say anything, okay?"

She stared out the window. "It looks like it's going to snow."

"We're supposed to get an inch or two this evening. Savannah—"

"Your house is gorgeous," she said, looking around.

"Thank you." It was. I'd built both my and Connor's log homes. They were similar, but with enough differences to set them apart. An entire wall of windows framed an amazing view of a fast-moving river at the bottom of my land with the Blue Ridge Mountains rising in the distance. Most days there was a soft blue haze across the tops, earning them their name. My stone fireplace was also floor to ceiling and was my favorite feature of the house.

"I have to leave shortly, so you need to listen."

She drained the rest of her tea, then set her cup on the table. "I'm all ears."

"I have to run by three jobsites this morning, make sure my crews are straight on what they need to work on today, then there's a meeting at Town Hall."

"No problem. I didn't expect you to babysit me." She turned her sad eyes away and stared out the window again.

A phrase I'd heard somewhere popped into my mind as I watched her. *Little girl lost.* I didn't want to feel something heavy in my chest, but it was there. I'd been friends with Savannah for most of my life, and then had loved and lost her when she'd been a girl on the cusp of becoming a woman. In all the years I'd known her, I'd never before seen defeat in her eyes or in the slump of her shoulders. But it was there now, and I wanted to ask her mother and Jackson Marks how they could have done this to her.

I remembered the gangly girl with braces who'd been made fun of by our classmates. String Bean and Bones had been their favorite names to call her. I'd been sent to the principal's office more than once for fighting some boy or other for making fun of her. Somewhere around the eleventh grade I'd started seeing her as more than just a friend.

The summer between our junior and senior year, I'd kissed her for the first time. After that we'd been inseparable until we'd graduated and her mother had paid me a visit. There had been many times after Savannah left for New York that I'd wished I'd done things differently.

Before I pulled her onto my lap and kissed the hurt out of her eyes, I stood, going to the window Savannah stared out of. What was she seeing? The view she'd grown up with, probably taking it for granted like most of us who were born and raised here? Maybe she was seeing Jackson, wondering why she'd left him. At that thought I stuffed my hands into my pockets to hide my clenched fists.

How different would my life be today if… If she hadn't left for New York. If I hadn't listened to her mother. If I had fought harder for her? Savannah wasn't the one to blame for our breakup. That was all on me. And her mother. But Savannah didn't know about Mrs. Graham's visit, and I'd never tell her.

Besides it didn't take her much more than a blink of an eye to get over me. Only a few months after moving to New York, pictures started showing up of her on the arm of a famous baseball player known for dating models and actresses. There was even talk of an engagement, although that never happened. Seeing how easily and quickly I'd been forgotten had not only hurt but had made me angry. I don't know. Maybe I still was. Where Savannah was concerned, my emotions were all over the place. And after nine years I wasn't happy about that.

"The Town Hall meeting I mentioned, we're going to talk about how to protect you." I faced her, wanting to see her reaction.

She blinked. Once. Twice. "A Town Hall meeting, like

where anyone can come? And you're going to talk about me?"

I nodded. "Yes, about how to keep you safe."

"You're joking, right?"

CHAPTER FIVE

~ Savannah ~

ADAM COULDN'T BE SERIOUS. THE town was going to get involved in my mess? I had a sudden vision of Mary throwing a pie in Jackson's face or Hamburger Harry, our infamous moonshiner, pickling Jackson in one of his backwoods stills. Laughter bubbled up, but it was hysterical laughter, uncontrollable, and I pressed my face against my knees.

"Are you okay?" Adam asked, coming to me and putting his hand on my shaking shoulders. I longed to lean into his touch, but I no longer had that privilege.

No, I wasn't okay, and I wasn't sure I ever would be. I nodded.

He moved away, and I felt the sofa dip as he sat next to me. I took a deep breath, and when I was in control again, I lifted my head. "I'm just tired and punch-drunk."

"Why don't you take a nap while I'm gone? I'll be back in a few hours, and we can talk more. You're going to need to give me more information about your situation."

"Why don't you cancel the meeting instead? I don't want people talking about me."

"Gossiping about you is not on the agenda. All we're doing is planning how to protect you." He sighed as he rolled his head and rubbed the back of his neck. "You should appreciate that, Savannah."

Well, I didn't, and I took a bit of perverse pleasure that I seemed to be giving him a headache. Served him right for making plans that involved me without asking first.

"You should have talked to me about this before you

invited the town into my business."

He sat back, propped a foot on the coffee table, and then turned those blue eyes I could still get lost in on me. "You're right, I should have. But it's too late to cancel now, and me, your friends, your town… we just want to help, okay?"

So used to Jackson refusing to listen to me, it took a moment for it to sink in that Adam had agreed I was right. He couldn't begin to understand how much that meant to me.

"Fine, and I appreciate it. I do. But if you're going to talk about me in a dumb meeting, I want to be there." I was done with letting people make decisions for me. There was no telling what the residents of my hometown would get up to. They'd been known to take things to extremes when they got riled up about something. I trusted Adam and my friends, but seriously, involve Mary and a few others and it was time to run for the hills.

"Are you sure?"

"Yes." No. I wasn't at all sure. I was the hometown girl who'd made it big, and now I'd come back with my tail tucked between my legs. The last thing I wanted was people I'd grown up with looking at me with pity in their eyes. But if I was going to take control of my life, then I had to do this.

His phone buzzed, and he picked it up from the table and glanced at the screen. "It's Jenn, and you can bet Autumn's with her." He put it to his ear. "Hey, Jenn." He listened for a minute and then said, "I'll tell her."

After disconnecting, he said, "They're on the way over. You can ride to the meeting with them if you're determined to go." He tapped his thumb on his phone's screen a few times, then looked up at me. "We really do need to talk, so don't make plans with them for after the meeting. And you can count on them wanting you to stay at one of their houses, but that wouldn't be wise. Jackson knows they're your best friends here, and he'll probably show up at both places, trying to find you."

He would, but did Adam intend that I should stay here? So not a good idea, especially for me. Just being near him was killing me. I wanted to touch him, wanted to curl myself up in his arms and let him make the world go away. I wanted to know all the differences between what the boy I'd loved had been and the man he was now.

"I still think I should find a cabin. Autumn will loan me the money to do that, and that way I won't be putting anyone in Jackson's line of sight." Including Adam. Not that I thought Jackson would hurt any of my friends, but if he thought they were hiding me, it would make him angry. An angry Jackson could cause a lot of trouble. I'd seen him ruin people, models and other agents, if they displeased him in any way.

"Already told you that's not happening, Savannah."

"You've gotten bossy in your old age."

He flashed a smile, the first one he'd given me since I arrived, and dang if a wave of warmth didn't rush through me. That was why I couldn't stay here. Adam Hunter was dangerous to my heart and other parts of me. I hadn't wanted another man, including Jackson, since the day I'd left Adam. All it took was one smile from him and my panties were ready to melt off.

"Let me take care of you until we're sure you're safe, and then you can go back to your glamorous life in the big city." He stood, his gaze going to the window. "I need to head out. The girls will be here in a few minutes." He glanced down at me. "I guess I'll see you there?"

"You will." I watched him walk away, and as much as I wished they didn't, my eyes loved looking at him. There was something about a man wearing a flannel shirt over a T-shirt, jeans, and work boots that was downright sexy. Or maybe it was just that it was Adam wearing them. I'd attended more galas and charity events than I'd ever wished to. Men looked great in their tuxes, but apparently flannel shirts did it for me.

Adam thought my life was glamorous. That was a laugh. Crack-of-dawn photo shoots, wearing bikinis in the middle of winter or dressed up as a snow bunny in August, photographers yelling at you for the goose bumps on your arms or the sweat rolling down your cleavage… I could go on and on. The bottom line, my life wasn't glamorous. Not for me anyway.

For sure, there were models who loved the whole shebang; the travel, the notoriety, all the parties that came with modeling. My mother had started on my modeling career when I was two, a commercial for a bedding company out of Asheville. I was the cute baby, giggling while bouncing on a mattress. Beauty pageants had been fast on the heels of the commercial, and I hated those with a passion. I think that was where I learned to be shy. My mother was never satisfied with my performance or my looks, and the other mothers could be vicious against anyone—even three- and four-year-olds—who might show up their own darling. I think it would surprise anyone not familiar with pageants how mean little girls could be to each other.

With each pageant my mother put me in, I withdrew a little more into my shell. It reached a point where I would get physically sick moments before having to walk out on the stage. That was the only reason she finally gave up on me building up a portfolio of wins. But the TV commercials for local businesses continued, and those I didn't mind as much.

In my teen years she started me on catalog modeling, and I liked that even better than doing commercials. I didn't have to talk to anyone. I could just stand there and follow directions—smile, tilt your head this way or that, put your hand on your hip. Turned out I was good at it, and my mother was finally pleased with me. Almost.

"You've gained a pound, Savannah." (Yes, I had to step

on the scales every morning.)

"Look at your fingernails, Savannah. When was the last time you manicured them?" (I kept my hands out of her sight as much as possible.)

"You spend too much time with those girls." (Meaning Jenn, Natalie, and Autumn, and that was the complaint from her that I both heard and hated the most.)

And then in my senior year I fell in love with Adam. My mother and I had some vicious fights because of him. He was going to wreck my life. He was going ruin everything that we'd—meaning her—had worked toward. He wasn't worthy of me. It was never ending, her condemnation of him.

Adam knew she didn't approve of him, but I never told him just how much she hated him. I finally reached my breaking point and told her that if she didn't shut up about him, the day I turned eighteen I was going to move out and never see or talk to her again. She must have seen in my eyes, heard in my voice that I meant it.

Regina Graham had just been making a name for herself in the modeling world when she became pregnant with me. She actually told me once, during one of our Adam battles, that she'd seriously considered aborting the pregnancy. She'd followed that up with, "I wish now…" Then she'd clamped her mouth shut and walked to her bedroom, slamming the door behind her, leaving me to wonder if she'd almost said she wished she had aborted me.

To hear my own mother say something like that had ripped my heart to shreds. But I'd had Adam, and he loved me. Or so I believed. I believed it until the day after we graduated and he broke up with me. I was so devastated that when my mother packed us up and moved us to New York, I didn't have the will to resist. Her goal had always been for me to live her dream of being a world-famous model, and she'd pushed and pushed me until she'd made it happen. I'd been on the cover of *Vogue, Elle, Cosmopoli-*

tan... well, you name a fashion magazine and I'd been on the cover. And even though I'd been miserable, I let her dictate my life because without Adam, I hadn't cared about anything. Not even when she'd picked Jackson as my ideal mate and moved him in with us.

As I sat here in Adam's beautiful log home, I felt like the most pathetic person in the world for letting my life get so out of control. But it didn't have to continue that way. Everyone had choices, including me. And although my mother and then Jackson had made decisions for me from the day I was born—had controlled my money, my food intake, and had scheduled my time, telling me where I had to be and when—those days were over. That was my promise to myself.

Adam walked back into the room.

"I thought you'd left."

"Getting there." A blue-eyed, black cat peered around the side of his neck, blinked at me, then climbed from Adam's back onto his shoulder. "This is Jinx. He's a monster, a thief, and will talk your ears off. Don't believe a word he says. A little advice, hide your socks and underwear."

"Oh," I breathed. "He's a beauty."

Adam snorted as he pulled Jinx from his shoulder and dropped him onto my lap. "Found him at a jobsite. Bugger was half-starved and wild. Should've taken him to the shelter but figured no one would want him."

I combed my fingers through the cat's soft fur. "Ah, you're a softie, Adam Hunter." I loved cats but had never been allowed to have one.

"No, just had a weak moment." He glared at the cat purring sweetly in response to getting a massage. "Oh sure, make her think you're a little gentleman." Adam lifted his gaze to mine. "Believe me when I tell you he lies."

There was fondness in his voice when he spoke of the cat, and I smiled at him before I caught myself. Our eyes locked on each other and a return smile seemed to start;

then he gave his head a little shake. His face closed up, and he stepped away, leaving my heart beating hard in my chest.

So not good, Savannah. I had to keep my feelings for him shut down while I was here. No gazing into his eyes or giving him soft smiles. No crying over what might have been. And especially no more wondering how his man body would feel under my fingers.

"If he gets too rambunctious, there's a playpen in the utility room. And if you do come to the meeting, make sure you put him in it and close the door. You can't imagine the trouble he can get into if left loose."

"Aww, this little angel cause trouble? I don't believe you." I brought Jinx up to my face and buried my nose in his fur.

Adam scoffed. "Trust me on that."

I listened to the sound of his work boots striking against the wood floor, but I didn't raise my eyes to watch him walk away. A few seconds later I heard him coming back, but I still didn't look up, too afraid he would see the longing in my eyes. Something that looked like a toy fishing pole with a feather on the end of the line fell onto my lap.

"You can entertain him for hours with this."

Then he left. The room suddenly felt empty and lonely without his presence. Being here with Adam was breaking my heart. I needed to get this business with Jackson taken care of so I could leave.

He was right. Jinx loved trying to catch the feather as I bounced it around. We played for a good twenty minutes before he seemed to get tired. He was hilarious, arching his back and leaping up in the air.

"Silly thing," I said. Jinx froze at the sound of my voice, and then he made a drawn-out noise, something between a meow and a whine. He climbed onto my lap and made three circles before curling up and sticking his nose under his tail.

I heard a car and glanced out the window. Jenn and

Autumn were here. My heart bounced with joy. The last three times I'd seen them—at Autumn's wedding to her ex, at Jenn and Dylan's wedding, and when they'd paid me a surprise visit in New York—I'd been under Jackson's thumb. I'd hardly spent any time with my best friends because he was always there, a wall between us, keeping me separated from them. I pulled down a throw from the back of the sofa, settled Jinx on it, then scrambled up and raced to the door.

They both jumped out of Jenn's Mustang and ran toward me, arms outstretched. I headed for them, meeting them halfway up Adam's sidewalk. We ran right into each other, tumbling onto the grass, laughing and hugging. I plastered kisses onto both their cheeks, getting the same back from them.

"God, I'm so happy to see you both," I said, pushing onto my knees.

Jenn stood, then offered a hand. "Right back at ya," she said, pulling me up.

"You're home to stay, right?" Autumn asked.

"I don't know." Probably not, but I wished the answer was yes. The only life I knew was modeling, though, and that meant I'd be returning to New York.

Autumn stood, narrowing her eyes. "Well, we'll just have to see about that. We also need to fatten you up. You're way too skinny."

That was so Autumn, opinionated and absolutely no filter. I laughed, incredibly happy to be with the only people I believed had truly loved me.

"It's freezing out here. Come inside." We walked in with our arms around each other. "You both look great," I said. "You look happy." And they did. I'd only met Dylan, Jenn's husband, twice, so I didn't really know him, but I was thrilled that Connor and Autumn were together.

"Life is great," Jenn said. She took my hand and pulled me to the sofa. "Oh, Jinx!" She eased onto the seat next to him. He lifted his head, looked at her, yawned, then snuggled into the throw and went back to sleep.

"He looks so sweet when he's sleeping," she said, scratching his head.

Autumn chuckled. "A true case of looks being deceiving."

"Adam said he's a monster, but I don't believe it." He'd been a perfect little gentleman for me.

"Believe it," Autumn said. She sat on Adam's leather chair and curled her feet under her. "Adam found him at a jobsite. I thought he'd take him to the shelter or find a home for him." She looked at me, a sly look in her eyes. "He tries to hide it, but he has a soft heart."

"You mean by taking in strays like me?" I hadn't meant for that to come out sounding bitter, and I had no reason to be mad at my friends, especially Adam. It was just that seeing my two besties happy and in love was bittersweet. I was truly glad for them, but it felt like the world, the one I'd grown up in and loved, had moved on without me. There was nowhere I belonged anymore.

"So life is great for you both," I said, wanting to get back on solid ground.

"For us, but it's not been so great for you, has it?" Autumn said.

Tears pooled in my eyes. "Not so much." I hated that I was envious of them.

"What happened?" Jenn asked. "All we heard was that Jackson threatened you."

"Can we postpone talking about this? Maybe have a girls' night with wine and I'll tell you my sad story?" Lack of sleep on top of my problems had me feeling like a walking zombie. If I started talking about Jackson and my life, I'd end up a hot mess.

"Okay, but you need to let us in." Autumn gave me an I-mean-business stare. "You've shut us out long enough."

"I know, and I'm sorry for that. I'll explain everything, I

promise. In the meantime I understand there's a meeting this afternoon, and I'm the subject of discussion. I want to be there, but I have a problem, specifically, no clothes."

Autumn's eyes lit up. "Pffft. Give me a hard problem to solve." She stood. "Let's go."

"Where? We don't have time to go shopping." Nor did I have money to spend on clothes.

"My house."

"Oh, okay. I have to put Jinx in his playpen."

I scooped him up, and when I found the utility room and the playpen, I glanced down at the cat who was now voicing his displeasure at his nap being disturbed. "Wow, he built you a kitty mansion." It was actually a child's playpen with a litter box, food and water, a pet bed, and a pile of toys inside. When I set Jinx in it, he seemed right at home. He nosed around in his toys, picked up a stuffed mouse, and took it into the pet bed with him.

"Be good, sweet boy."

"It's cold out. Where's your coat?" Jenn said when I returned and headed for the door.

"Don't have one." My two friends frowned at me, and I shrugged. "I left in a hurry."

We piled into Jenn's Mustang, and after a short ride across a bridge, we pulled up in front of a log home much like Adam's. "This is your house?" Last I knew, she was still living in the home she and Brian had owned.

"Technically it's Connor's, but we're living together now."

It hit me just how out of touch I was with my friends. "I'm sorry. I should have known that. Adam told me you were a couple, but he didn't say you'd moved in together."

Jenn turned the key, shutting down the engine, then reached across the console, putting her hand on my arm. "No saying I'm sorry, okay? You're here now, and that's all that matters."

From the back seat Autumn tugged on my hair. "What

she said. Let's go get you dressed."

"Can I say thank you?" I said, my voice trembling and my heart filled with love for these two women.

Autumn laughed. "You can after you see how gorgeous I'm going to make you."

I knew she believed that would excite me, but being gorgeous was my job, one I had grown to hate. All I wanted were some decent clothes. But I wouldn't spoil her fun.

"Awesome. Let's do this."

CHAPTER SIX

~ Adam ~

WE HADN'T ANNOUNCED A FORMAL town meeting, instead only asking a select few to attend. Ten minutes before we were due to start, everyone was here except for the girls. I scanned the faces of those waiting to hear why Connor, Dylan, and I had asked them to come.

Our mayor, Jim John Jenkins, was busy eating a slice of the cake Mary had brought to the meeting. Mary—the best baker for a hundred miles—held a mirror up to her face, fussing with her green hair. My mouth curved up in a smile. The barely five-foot-tall woman's hair color changed on a regular basis. Each ear boasted a row of earrings, her green turtleneck sweater said *The Bomb* in silver glitter, and her boots had a row of green fur at the tops. She called to mind an outrageous cartoon character. We wouldn't want her any other way.

When Connor, Dylan, and I had made a short list of who to bring into our plan, we'd had a spirited debate regarding our infamous moonshiner, Hamburger Harry. But I'd had an idea how he could contribute to keeping Savannah safe, so his name had gone on the list.

The only other person in the room was the owner of the Mountain View Bed and Breakfast, Harvey Bowen, who knew every one of the valley's hotel, motel, and rental cabin owners. We'd included him because if Marks did show up, he'd have to stay somewhere, and Harvey could help us get up to no good.

Dylan had warned me that we couldn't break the law,

but we could make Jackson Marks's life miserable for as long as he was here. We obviously wouldn't paint the town red like in the Clint Eastwood movie, but we sure could make the man wish he'd stayed in New York.

Before Savannah got here, if she decided to come, I wanted to warn everyone so they wouldn't make a big deal when she arrived. She would hate that. "We have a possible situation. Savannah Graham is back home, and trouble might follow her. Her agent threatened her, and she ran away."

Mary bounced on the edge of her seat. "No one messes with our girls."

"I agree. Savannah might show up in a few minutes, and right now she's both scared and embarrassed. If she does come to this meeting—"

"Autumn just texted me," Connor said, eyeing his phone screen. "They'll be here in a few minutes."

"Okay, when she does get here, just be cool. Don't overwhelm her with hugs or whatever." I looked at Mary.

Mary glared back at me. "If you think I'm not gonna give that girl a hug, then you don't know me, Adam Hunter."

Dylan chuckled. "She has a point."

"Can I hug her, too?" Hamburger asked.

I sighed. "Fine. Smother her with hugs." Maybe that was what Savannah needed. Some love from those who cared about her.

"Why am I here?" Harvey Bowen said. "I don't think I've ever met her."

He hadn't, having moved here six years ago after buying his motel. "We'll get to that."

The door opened, and Savannah walked in flanked by Jenn and Autumn. When I'd left, she had been huddled up in the corner of my sofa, her hair in a ponytail and wearing clothes too big for her. Now she had on a blue and white print skirt, boots, a white sweater, and a wool coat. Had she gone shopping?

"She's wearing some of Autumn's clothes," Connor said, reading my mind.

"Ah, okay." With a second glance I saw that the clothes were a little baggy on her slim frame. I made a mental note to take her shopping. And feed her.

Mary jumped up and ran to Savannah with outstretched arms. Savannah's gaze shot to mine, panic in them, but all I could do was shrug. Mary was an unstoppable force of nature. I wasn't sure why Savannah was so tense. I knew she was shy, but she'd grown up with these people. Maybe she'd been gone too long and didn't think of us as her friends any longer.

She'd left nine years ago, lived in the big city, hobnobbed with the rich and famous, and had led a glamorous life. We were just common, small-town people and couldn't compare to what she was used to. There wasn't a person in the room who cared about any of that, but maybe she did.

For years the girl I'd fallen in love with had lived in my heart even though she was gone, but sitting in this room, watching her awkwardly pat Mary on the back, it hit me that I didn't know her anymore. She wasn't the girl I loved. I didn't know how to process that.

Connor put his hand on my shoulder, picking up on my confusion. Sometimes it was comforting to know your twin could pretty much read your mind, but other times it was damn annoying. Like now, seeing the concern in my brother's eyes, I wished I could close off my thoughts.

Mary finally released Savannah, and once everyone was seated, I said, "Do you want to explain the situation, Savannah?" She shook her head, which I'd expected. She'd been flanked by Jenn and Autumn again—her protectors—as they took their seats, and by the way she seemed to fold in on herself, I thought that she wished she were invisible. It bothered me that her eyes were downcast, as if she were embarrassed.

Where was the self-assured, glamorous model that graced

the magazine covers? Yeah, I'd seen them. They were impossible to miss standing in line at the grocery store. My deep, dark secret? I had a stash of *Vogue*, *Cosmo*, and other magazines featuring her on the covers hidden at home. I didn't look at them much anymore, but sometimes I'd take them out and try to see the girl I'd known intimately in the cover model's smile and eyes.

Mostly that girl was missing in the photos, but every once in a while I'd see one that showed a glimpse of the Savannah I'd known. A shy smile, a certain turn of her lips, something in her eyes. Those were the ones that gutted me.

I glanced around the room at the people sitting in a circle, my gaze lingering for a moment on Savannah. When she'd stepped off the plane, a part of me had dared to hope that she'd come home to me. But it was sinking in that we couldn't go back to what we'd once been. The best thing to do, the only thing to do, was take care of her problem, then send her on her way. I didn't regret that she was here because I thought I'd finally be able to accept that we weren't meant to be, and I'd put that part of my life to rest. I hoped so, anyway.

"Savannah has a problem that we can help her with. You never met him, Harvey, but the others here have, and that's Jackson Marks, Savannah's"—I looked at Savannah—"agent? Manager?"

"Both those things."

"You poor dear," Mary said. She shot Savannah a smile. "I didn't like him. Sorry, sugar, but I can't lie about that."

Savannah lifted one shoulder in a shrug. "That's okay. I don't like him either."

"Back to the problem," I said. "He's threatened Savannah, and she believes he'll show up here, looking for her."

Mary pointed a finger at Dylan. "You'll arrest him, right?"

"I can't, not unless he breaks the law. But we'll be keeping an eye on him, that I promise."

"I cain't cotton to him hurting our Savannah," Hamburger said. "Whadda we gonna do about that?"

Mary huffed. "Time to get my gun out."

"I got me ah huntin' rifle," Hamburger said.

Dylan groaned. "Do not even think of it. Either one of you."

Before things got out of hand, I said, "Our plan is to make his life miserable if he shows up here." I paused, making sure I had their attention. "Without any of us breaking the law or strapping a gun on our hips." I looked at Mary when I said that. She humphed. "He'll be going around town looking for her, asking people if they've seen her. We're going to send him on wild-goose chases. He'll probably fly into Asheville and rent a car. Once we know what he's driving, we'll pass the word."

"What does he look like?" Harvey asked.

"Dylan will give you a printout of his photo before we leave. Pass it around to the motel owners. If he wants a room, have everyone tell him they're booked. Anything y'all can think of to do that will make his time here miserable without—and again I repeat—without breaking the law, do it. Jenn, you know the restaurant owners. Pass the word that he gets lousy service."

She grinned. "I can totally do that. His food won't be so good either."

"What can I do?" Autumn asked.

"Stick close to Savannah when I can't. Once he arrives, we'll adjust our plan as necessary." Although our plan seemed a bit juvenile, I had the feeling that Jackson Marks would only be able to take so much from a hick town that didn't treat him like royalty before he gave up and hightailed it back to New York.

"Where's Savannah going to be staying?" Mary asked.

"With me."

Jenn glanced at Savannah. "Does Jackson know you have a history with Adam?"

My gaze landed on Savannah, waiting for her answer.

Her eyes met mine for an instant; then she looked down at her lap. "Yes. My mother told him."

I didn't know how to feel about that. Was I not important enough for her to tell him about that part of her life?

"Then you can't stay with him," Jenn said. "That's the first place he'll look."

Connor glanced at me. "She can stay with us. I'm around the house if I don't have a listing, same for Autumn if she doesn't have an appointment. He doesn't know Autumn and I are together, does he?" he asked Savannah.

Considering how he felt about Savannah, that was generous of him to offer. I gave him a dip of my chin in gratitude. He answered with a slight upturn of his lips.

Savannah shook her head. "I'm sure he thinks she's still married to Brian, but I don't want to inconvenience anyone," Savannah said. "I still don't see why I can't rent a cabin."

"And if he somehow learns where you are and shows up, catching you alone?" I shook my head. "That's just stupid." As soon as those words were out of my mouth, I wanted to snatch them back. She did her imitation of a turtle retreating into its shell. I wanted her to tell me to shut up or even go to hell.

"He's right, Savannah," Dylan gently said. "Based on what he did before you left, you can't predict what he might do if he found you alone. At the very least he might try to force you to go back to New York with him."

Autumn put her arm around Savannah. "I want you with me, okay? I've missed you."

"And I'll come over for girl nights," Jenn said.

"What can I do?" Hamburger asked.

"When he shows up, I want you to follow him around like a lovesick puppy." Jackson would never suspect someone like Hamburger of being something other than a good ole mountain boy. I grinned at Hamburger. "Play your fiddle for him, tell him you want to go to Hollywood and make a movie, beg him to be your agent. Don't take no for an answer. Keep up with him as much as possible and report on his whereabouts."

Hamburger's eyes lit up. "Like ah spy?"

"Exactly." Off to my left, I heard Dylan quietly chuckle at Hamburger's enthusiasm. "That's it for now. If anyone sees Jackson Marks, call me and I'll spread the word to the others."

Harvey took several of the printouts of Jackson's photo. "I'll start showing this around to the motel owners. But I'm thinking that instead of making sure he doesn't have a room in town, it's better if he does so we can keep an eye on him."

I thought about it for a moment. "You're right. That way we can keep a watch on his comings and goings."

"Wherever he stays, I doubt he'll much like the maid service." Harvey winked, then headed out.

Mary and Hamburger left together, each talking over the other about their plans to make Jackson's life miserable. I wondered for a moment just what I'd unleashed with those two.

"By the time they're done with him, Jackson Marks will probably say he'd rather face a zombie apocalypse," Connor said.

I laughed. "Let's hope it's enough to run him off."

"Jenn and I are going to take Savannah shopping. After that we'll swing by your place and pick up her stuff," Autumn said.

"Yeah, she needs some clothes, but later, okay?" I needed to know exactly what we were dealing with. Although I almost invited everybody left in the room over to hear what she had to say, I reconsidered. Even though we were all her friends, she probably wouldn't be as forthcoming with that many ears listening.

"I'll bring her over to your house this afternoon." Savannah didn't look at all happy about me overriding Autumn, but she didn't say anything.

CHAPTER SEVEN

~ Savannah ~

ADAM HAD STOPPED BY MARY'S Bread Company on the way to his house, picking up lunch for us. I'd stayed in the car. I loved Mary, but after being smothered when she first saw me and being embarrassed that there had actually been a meeting to discuss my private life, I was on overload. One more loving hug or, "You poor dear," and I'd have a meltdown.

I stared at the food Adam had spread out on his kitchen island. I'd missed Mary's food so much, and my mouth watered at the sight of the egg salad on a fluffy croissant and homemade chips. Adam had remembered my favorite Mary sandwich. I lifted my eyes to Adam's to tell him I wasn't hungry.

"You don't have to eat it all," he said before I could speak, as if reading my mind.

I lowered my gaze to the food, hiding the tears burning my eyes. I was used to being fed carrot sticks and salads with lemon juice for the dressing. But I couldn't relax on being careful of my food intake. I would probably return to my career as a model. I knew nothing else, and I still had a few good years left in me before the younger girls pushed me out. Besides, I had a dream for my future, one that would cost a lot of money over the years, so I needed to earn as much as I could while I still could.

Still, it touched me that, unlike Jackson, Adam didn't seem to care if I gained a few pounds. He had, in fact, said I was too skinny. Little did he know that my up-and-coming competition made me look fat, something Jackson drilled into my head at least ten times a day.

"Savannah—"

"I'm eating." To prove it, I tore off a fourth of the sandwich and took a bite from the end. Oh my God, it was so good. Maybe just this time I could eat the whole thing. A treat I would allow myself before returning to rabbit food. I'd eaten half when Adam put his hand over mine.

"Save a little room. Mary sent you a surprise along with your lunch."

He let go of my hand, and I had the crazy urge to snatch it back. That was a stupid thought. Adam had hurt me beyond repair when he'd broken up with me, refusing—even though I'd begged him—to stand up with me against my mother. I had loved him to the depth of my soul and hadn't wanted to move away unless he would agree to come with me.

"If you won't come with me, I'll stay here. I don't care about being a famous model. That's my mother's dream," I told him.

His answer, "We're just a high school romance, Savannah. Two kids having some fun. Nothing more than that. Go be famous. I'll see your face on magazine covers in the not too distant future and think, I knew she'd do it."

Then he'd walked away, out of my life, leaving me too devastated to fight my mother. Since that day I'd been numb, too broken to care what happened to me. But I was done being a doormat.

Adam took something out of the bag from Mary's, put it on a plate, and then held it behind him as he returned to the island. He stopped in front of me and whipped out his hand. My eyes fell on what he held, my breath letting out a puff of air as I stared at the treat.

My eyes devoured that decadent slice of heaven. "You're evil, Adam Hunter." Mary's red velvet cake was my weakness.

"I had nothing to do with it, so take it up with Mary." He set the plate between us, then handed me one of the two forks in his hand. "Pretty good," he said after taking a bite.

"Hmm." I closed my eyes, letting the bite of the most delicious cake on the planet sit on my tongue as the flavors exploded in my mouth. I swallowed, licked my lips, and then opened my eyes. One more bite and I'd stop. I glanced up at Adam, my breath freezing in my lungs at the heat in his eyes. As soon as our gazes met, he looked down, shielding his eyes. The brief exchange puzzled and unsettled me, but then I decided my imagination was working overtime. That I was only wishing he would look at me the way he used to.

"Good, huh?"

"The best." I couldn't resist a third bite, but after that I set my fork down. If I kept it in my hand, I'd finish off the cake.

"Done?"

"Yes. If you see Mary, tell her I said thank you."

"You tell her." He took the cake to the counter, then from the pantry he took out a roll of plastic wrap. When he brought the remaining half back, he said, "Take the rest with you when you go to Connor and Autumn's."

I started to say that I didn't want it. I did, but I couldn't go on eating binges. At the determination in his eyes I held my words. Autumn could have it.

"Ready to talk?"

"No." I'd rather not talk about the past nine years. Ever.

"Let's go sit on the back deck." He handed me the coat I'd borrowed from Autumn. "The sun's out and there's no wind, so we won't be cold." He slipped on his jacket.

As I followed him to the French doors, my gaze strayed to the living room. Adam's home was beautiful. I loved the tall windows and the stone fireplace that extended to the ceiling, and that whole wall was logs. The beautiful dark wood floors were a perfect contrast to the cream paint on the walls. Jinx streaked by with something blue in his mouth. I squinted, but he passed by too fast to see what it was. Probably one of his toys.

"Coming?"

"Yeah." I followed Adam outside, pausing for a moment to take in the view. I'd grown up in these mountains and had taken the beauty for granted as a kid. Each time I'd come back since leaving, though, I was struck by how beautiful the landscape was and how much I missed the valley.

There were things I liked about New York. The energy in the air, the display windows in the stores at Christmas, Central Park, things like that. But it was the mountains of Blue Ridge Valley that lived in my heart. Some people built their houses on the mountains, their views looking down on the valley, which could be spectacular. Adam's home sat on the valley floor with the mountains rising up around him. His grounds sloped down to a fast-moving river, and I could hear the melody of the water as it moved over rocks. I could live on this deck.

"This is beautiful," I said after we were seated.

"Thank you. It was one dream that came true, anyway."

What did he mean? There was a time I would have asked, when I felt I could talk to him about anything, but I didn't know this man. Not really. I still loved him. He still made my heart beat faster and still made me feel like I had butterflies in my stomach. He'd been a crazy cute boy, but the man was just downright hot. I'd always loved his blue eyes, especially the way they used to grow warm when he looked at me, and in high school I'd thought it was cool that we both had black hair.

How would he look in the summer when building one of his houses, his shirt off, his jeans hugging his hips, and a tool belt strapped around his waist? I coughed to cover the hitch in my breath at that image in my mind. If he'd come with me to New York, I had no doubt that he could have made it as a model. I imagined him in a Calvin Klein underwear ad. Women would've torn that ad out of their magazines and stuck it on their bedroom walls; they'd have posted it on their Facebook pages and on Twitter and Instagram. On second thought, I was glad he hadn't become a Calvin Klein underwear model.

"It's nice that your and Connor's homes are close," I said, pointing at the beautiful log home on the other side of the river. The twins had always been tight, and it didn't surprise me that they'd built their houses near each other. "If Jackson does find out where you live and comes here looking for me, do you think he'll check out Connor's place, too?"

"You have to pass my house to get to his, and the bridge we built over the river isn't visible from my front yard. If he does find the bridge, there's a remote-controlled gate that we'll keep closed once you're over there."

"I didn't mean for this to get out of hand, for the whole town to get involved. Maybe I overreacted." All I'd wanted was to borrow a little money until I could get my hands on mine. How did it go from that to some kind of comedy movie with a cast including a woman with crazy hair and a moonshiner?

Adam turned an intense stare on me. "Did he really hold a knife to your face and threaten to cut you?"

I nodded as a shudder passed through me.

"Then you aren't overreacting. Where was your mother in all that? Why didn't you go to her?"

"She died last year." It was jarring that Adam didn't know about my life anymore, but I hadn't even told Jenn or Autumn when it had happened. My friends hadn't liked her, and I hadn't seen the point in letting them know.

"I'm sorry."

"Thank you, but not necessary. She was my mother. I loved her, but I didn't like her much." I glanced at him.

"Does that make me sound awful?"

"From my perspective, not at all."

A laugh escaped me. Of all my friends, Adam had disliked her the most, and I couldn't blame him. She had hated him, believing that he could steal my dream—her dream—of the future she'd planned for me. She would have been right if he'd really loved me as I'd believed.

"Start from the beginning, Savannah."

I hadn't thought I wanted to talk about this, but suddenly I wanted him to know. "The beginning... You have to know that everything she wanted for me happened." He nodded but didn't say anything. I wouldn't tell him how much I'd been hurting, how much I didn't care what was happening to me. How I let my mother dictate my life. How I'd missed him every damn day.

"Two years ago she was diagnosed with stage four breast cancer. She'd never had one symptom, and then one day she didn't feel good. The next day she felt worse. On the third day she went to the doctor."

"She didn't go for regular mammograms?" Adam asked.

"No, she'd never had one. Until that diagnosis Regina Graham thought she was invincible. For the next year we spent a fortune on treatments, even going to Mexico because she'd found a doctor there who swore he had a magical cure." I turned my face to the river, my gaze on the little white splashes as the water tumbled over the rocks.

It had been crushing watching her reach out for any doctor, treatment, shaman who could save her life. She'd said to me a few months before she'd died, her mind not all there because of the drugs, "I used to be young and beautiful like you. I had a brilliant future ahead of me. And then he came along, swept me off my feet. As soon as I told him I was pregnant, he vanished." She'd flicked her fingers at me. "Like a poof of smoke."

"Who was he?" I'd asked, dying to know my father's

name. She'd laughed as if my question amused her. I never asked again, even though I knew my father's name would die with her.

Adam shifted his chair toward me. "Why didn't you tell Autumn and Jenn when she died?"

I shrugged. "Why? They didn't like her any more than I did." What I didn't tell him was that Jackson had taken over all the arrangements, ignoring my wishes. I'd wanted a simple service, but he'd made it an event, and the several hundred people who'd attended had been mere acquaintances, not her friends or mine. My friends had been here in Blue Ridge Valley. If I'd told Autumn and Jenn, they would have come to New York to lend me support, and although I desperately wanted that, Jackson wouldn't have been happy to see them.

"I assume you and Jackson live together?"

Now there was a story.

CHAPTER EIGHT

~ Adam ~

SAVANNAH SEEMED TO FIND GREAT interest in the river after I asked my question. I waited, and finally she said, "Lived. Past tense."

I don't know why her answer pleased me. As I'd told Connor once, my and Savannah's time had passed. She wasn't the same girl I'd loved. Although shy, that girl had been warm and loving, had cared about her friends, and was funny once you got to know her.

The woman sitting on my deck was distant, the warmth in her beautiful gray eyes gone. This new Savannah was everything I'd expect a famous model to be. Even in her borrowed clothes that didn't quite fit, she was elegant and untouchable. As if she weren't quite real. Her black hair was up in some kind of fancy twist, her fingernails perfectly manicured, and her makeup flawless. I'd liked her better this morning when she'd been wearing my sweatpants and T-shirt, her hair in a messy ponytail.

"Do you love him?" That question had slipped out, and I don't know why I asked it. Her answer didn't matter one way or the other.

She turned her face toward me and gave a bitter laugh. "Not even."

"Then get a restraining order."

"It's complicated."

I held in my sigh. "Look, I know it's your private life, but you're the one who called me. Now you're here, and you seem to think he'll show up. I need to know what we're dealing with."

She studied the river again for a good minute, then leaned her head back against her chair. "Okay, it's like this. My mother always controlled my money. Well, pretty much controlled my entire life, as you know. When we arrived in New York, she opened a bank account in her name, and my income got deposited in it. One of the first things she did after we got there was to sign Jackson as my agent, and the two of them managed my career, told me where to be and when. She paid all the bills." She glanced at me. "I've never written a check."

Wow. I couldn't help comparing her to Connor and me, forced to be responsible for our finances when our parents had died. "Go on."

"I should have insisted on being more involved with all those things. I know that now, but that was just the way it had always been from the time I made my first commercial at two years old."

"Why did you need to borrow money from me now that she's gone? I mean, you do have money, right?"

"I have a healthy bank balance... at least, I think I do. The New York apartment is mine and in my name, thankfully. But here's where it gets complicated. Before my mother died, she put Jackson's name on my bank account."

She glanced at me, and the tears pooling in her eyes gutted me. "Why the hell would she do that? Did you give her permission?"

"No, and I wouldn't have. She didn't tell me. Jackson did after she died, after I told him I wanted him to move out."

"Christ, Savannah."

"Yeah, tell me about it. He said that she was afraid I'd quit modeling if I had control of my money, that I'd come back here. So he was my new jailer, and he had no intention of giving up his access to me or my money."

"What's to stop him from stealing your money now that you've run away?"

"Oh, he won't. He too arrogant to even consider that

he won't get me back where I belong. Under his thumb." She shrugged, as if that admission was a minor detail. "And why should he worry? My mother saw to it that he's the only one with access to my money."

I didn't even know what to say. Regina Graham had always been a cold and domineering woman, but to do that to your own daughter?

"Will you do me a favor?" She tilted her head and looked at me. "Keep this to yourself? It's embarrassing enough telling you all this, but I don't see any reason anyone else needs to know. I'll tell Jenn and Autumn, but that's all."

"It's not my story to tell." I still couldn't comprehend her mother doing something like that, although it probably shouldn't surprise me. "You need a good lawyer."

"I know."

"One last question. Why did he threaten to cut you?"

She stared down at the hands she had clasped on her lap. "Because I told him I wasn't going to do a nude photo shoot."

My rage was growing with every revelation. There were so many things I wanted to ask her, but I could tell she was drained. And if I heard much more right now, I was going to lose my cool, and she didn't need that. I had what I needed to know. Jackson Marks wasn't going to get near her.

My phone vibrated, my foreman's name showing up on the screen. "I have to take this. Why don't you gather your things, and I'll take you over to Connor's when I finish." I walked inside and headed for my office. After a ten-minute conversation about several issues concerning the newest log home we were building, I called Connor to let him know I was bringing Savannah over. I'd expected to find her in the living room, waiting to go, but she wasn't there. She wasn't in the guest room either, nor was her overnight bag waiting by the door.

I found her sitting on the floor in the utility room, having a tug of war with Jinx. At seeing the blue panties they were fighting over, I grinned.

Savannah lifted her eyes to mine, a soft smile on her face. "I always wanted a kitten."

That smile. "I remember." She'd asked her mother for one every Christmas until she turned eleven and gave up. What she got instead were designer clothes, which she could have cared less about.

"Apparently I left my overnight bag unzipped, and this bad boy helped himself to a pair of my panties."

"Told you." I squatted and pried Jinx's jaw open. It was the only way to get something from him that he wanted. I grinned when she held the panties behind her back, as if hiding them from Jinx. Or maybe from me. "We're both males. We're not going to forget you have a pair of sexy panties behind your back."

As if to prove the point, Jinx voiced his displeasure at losing his treasure as he made a beeline for the hand she was hiding.

Savannah patted his nose, then stood. "When I get my life straightened out, I'm going to get a cat."

"You should get two. That way they'd have each other to play with when you're working."

"Two's even better. I'm going to name one Never and the other Again."

"A statement? As in you'll never again let anyone control your life?"

"You always did understand me, Adam."

She walked past me, leaving me leaning against the doorframe and with more regret than I wanted to feel in my heart. Mrs. Graham had told me that Savannah would eventually resent me if I stood in the way of Savannah's dream, and that one fear had been the reason I'd let her go. Had I done the right thing, or had I made the biggest mistake of my life?

Savannah seemed to relax after we arrived at Connor's. Autumn had greeted her with an enthused hug, as if she'd hadn't seen Savannah only a few hours ago. At the moment she and Autumn were on the floor, laughing as Beau, Autumn's dog, tried to lick the two of them to death.

"How's she doing?" Connor asked as we sat at his kitchen island, watching them.

"Sad. Scared. Confused. Embarrassed. Take your pick." Like mine, Connor's home had a great room, the kitchen, dining room, and living room all open and spacious.

"And how are you doing?"

That was the question, wasn't it? "I'm fine."

"Mm-hmm." He twirled his beer bottle on the granite countertop.

I knew what was going to come out of his mouth. "Don't."

His gaze lifted to mine, concern in his eyes. "Don't tell you to guard your heart? You've never gotten over her, bro, no matter how much you might try to convince yourself otherwise. She's your kryptonite. You know she'll leave again as soon as we get her problems fixed."

"I do know that, and you can stop worrying about me. The only thing I have for her now are some good memories."

"Uh-huh."

Sometimes my twin was annoying, especially when he was right.

"You staying for dinner?" Autumn asked, walking up behind Connor and wrapping her arms around him. "I'm making spaghetti." She glanced over at Savannah, still playing with Beau. "I need to fatten her up."

"Good luck getting her to eat it. Just put a small amount on a plate and maybe half a meatball, then pretend you don't see her eating it if she does. She's used to having her food intake watched. If she thinks you're aware of what she's eating, it makes her nervous."

Connor's eyes narrowed on me. "Kryptonite," was all he said.

Ignoring him, I stood and took my empty beer bottle to the recycling bin. "Thanks for the offer, but I think I'm catching a cold. My head's stuffy and my throat's starting to feel sore." I really was feeling lousy. "I think I'll just go home and call it an early night."

Anyway, that was better than spending the evening enduring Connor's concerned looks or worrying about how little Savannah ate.

Autumn put her hand on my forehead. "You do feel warm. Want me to bring some dinner over to you later?"

"Thanks, but I'm going straight to bed." I stopped next to where Savannah sat on the floor with Beau. "Jinx isn't going to like smelling dog on you."

Her eyes—have I said she had beautiful eyes?—widened. "Oh, dang. I never thought of that."

"I'm teasing you," I said, then winked. "Maybe." Jinx and Beau were actually good friends. I glanced at the door, suddenly not wanting to leave. "I'm heading home. See you sometime tomorrow."

"Okay. Good night, Adam."

"Good night, Savannah." I walked out, doing my best to push away memories of how I used to kiss her each time we parted for the day.

CHAPTER NINE

~ Savannah ~

"NO MORE," I SAID, PUTTING my hand over my plate when Autumn tried to give me a second helping.

My friends meant well, I knew that. But they didn't understand. I already had one strike against me—my age. Younger, fresh-faced, beautiful girls wanted my life. They wanted the magazine covers, the travel, the parties, the glamour. As far as I was concerned, they could have it. But I needed another year or two to put more money in the bank.

I had a secret dream no one knew about. I'd done a free shoot two years ago as a favor to my favorite photographer. It took me two weeks of whining and begging Jackson to agree to let me do it. He finally gave in only because it was great publicity for the model Savannah to have the ugliest animals in the world clothe her body. They were the ones no one else wanted because they were missing ears or tails or a leg or an eye because of human abuse.

It looked like I was naked underneath all that fur, but I had on a flesh-colored body suit and none of my private parts were visible. Nothing like what Jackson had in mind for me for the French magazine shoot. Neil and his wife took those animals in, gave them love and safety. Sometimes they were able to find homes for them, mostly with older people whose kids were grown and gone. Most stayed on the farm with Neil and Clarissa, living out their life being cared for and loved liked they never had been before.

The shoot was for photos to include in their donation

requests, showing some of the animals, along with my endorsement of their cause. I wanted to do something similar but take it a step further, eventually training some of them as therapy animals. But I needed to earn as much money as possible, not only to make it happen but so that it was something that would last beyond my lifetime.

"I've got a contract I need to write up," Connor said. He took his plate to the sink, rinsed it, then put it in the dishwasher.

"You have him well trained." I grinned at Autumn. "Or is he just on his best behavior because I'm here?"

"Hey, I'm the ideal boyfriend. I not only clean up after myself, but I give awesome foot massages."

"Truth," Autumn said, her eyes turning soft as she looked at him.

Connor returned to the table and gave Autumn a lingering kiss. "When I get that done, I'm going to watch a game in bed. Take your time. I know you two have a lot of catching up to do." He nodded at me, then left.

"He doesn't like me anymore." He hadn't been rude, but he only talked to me if I asked him a direct question. No smiles even though we'd once been good friends, no warmth in his voice when he did design to talk to me. I had no clue what his problem was with me.

Autumn hesitated. "It's not that he doesn't like you. He's just afraid that you're going to hurt Adam again."

"Again?" I hadn't hurt Adam. Quite the opposite. He'd broken up with me.

"Do you still have feelings for Adam?"

"No, of course not. We were kids. You know, first love and all that." Except that after Adam I'd never been able to love another man. I had mourned in silence for nine years and would continue to do so. If I told Autumn I still loved him, she'd round up Jenn and the two of them would get up to no good in their effort to see me and Adam together.

She started to say something, stopped, then said, "So you

need to go clothes shopping?"

That wasn't what she'd first started to say, but I let it go. "The thing is, I need to borrow a little money." I hated asking for money, especially when I had plenty in the bank.

"Not a problem, but I don't understand why you don't have any money. I mean, you have to be one of the highest paid models in the world."

"It's a long story, and I said I'd tell you and Jenn. I'd rather do that when the three of us are together. Okay?"

"Tomorrow then. We'll meet for breakfast, and then we'll go shopping."

"Thanks. Now catch me up with all the valley gossip." I sat back, smiling as she told me who was seeing who, and who'd married or was having babies.

"He actually held a knife at your face and threatened to cut you?" Autumn said, her eyes bugging out.

I nodded. My appetite gone, I pushed what was left of my breakfast—dry wheat toast and fruit—aside.

Jenn had gasped when I'd related that part of what had happened. "Good God, Savannah, you can't go back."

"Not to him, no. But I do have to return. I have contracts to fulfill." I also needed to find a new agent, but that wasn't going to be easy. They wanted the younger girls, not a model approaching the end of her career.

I was scared. Ever since sneaking out of my apartment in the middle of the night, I'd felt lost. It wasn't that I regretted walking away. I'd do it again in a minute, but I'd always had people telling me what to do, where to go, and when to be there. Because of a rash decision, I was now on my own. Every time panic tried to seep in, I pushed it away, telling myself that I could do this, be an adult and make my own decisions. One minute I was sure I could pull it off, and in the next I wanted to slap a paper bag over my mouth and suck in air so I didn't pass out.

"Have you told Adam all this?" Autumn asked.

"Yeah. That's why he came up with his insane plan."

Jenn set her coffee cup down. "Why do you say insane?"

I decided not to roll my eyes, although I was sorely tempted. "You don't think involving Mary and Hamburger is just plain crazy?"

Both Jenn and Autumn laughed. "Well, you have a point there," Jenn said. "Speaking of Adam, how does it feel to be with him?"

"I'm not with him. And it's fine." I didn't want to talk about Adam. "Either of you know a good attorney?"

Jenn sighed. "You're avoiding the question. Do you still have feelings for him?"

Yes. "It's been nine years. All either of us feels for each other is… I don't know. We're not exactly friends anymore, not like we used to be. But we don't hate each other."

I had gone through a period of hating him for months after he'd told me what we had was just *fun*. I blamed him for everything wrong in my life. It took a good year to warm up to New York, and I'd been homesick for my friends and the mountains. Auditioning calls had intimidated me, and like in my pageant days, I would get physically ill on the mornings I had one scheduled.

My mother had grown more demanding and controlling, more determined that I would make a name in the modeling world. She'd gotten stricter with my calorie intake and my workout regime, even hiring a personal trainer who spent three hours every day torturing me to make sure I stayed fit (translate: skinny). She and Jackson had dragged me to any event they could get an invite to so I'd be seen. That had been my personal hell. I'm terribly shy and get tongue-tied around people I don't know, especially the ones they were introducing me to—the *beautiful and in* people. We'd return home after this gala or that, and she would be so angry with me because I'd blushed too much and hadn't chatted like she thought I should have. I could never make her understand that I didn't know how to make small talk.

All of that was Adam's fault. If he'd meant what he'd said, that he loved me and we would be together, whether in the valley or New York, I wouldn't have been so unhappy. Toward the end of our senior year, when the prospect of my having to leave loomed, he'd promised that he'd come with me. And even though I knew he had no desire to live in New York, I adored him for loving me enough to leave his home. It was all a lie, and I'd felt justified in blaming him for my misery.

If he'd meant the things he said, I would have stood up to my mother and refused to leave him. I'd approached graduation day excited about my future, because whether we stayed in the valley or moved to New York, we'd be together. And then the day after graduation he'd ripped my heart out of my chest. I'd arrived in New York, hurt, angry, scared, and miserable, and that was how I'd spent my first year there, numbly letting my mother and Jackson take over my life completely.

The funny thing was, even though she'd get furious with me for my shyness around strangers, I'd inadvertently created a persona of mystery. People started to take notice of the girl they couldn't get a handle on. Jackson had me drop my last name, created my fake bio, and made sure I was seen at all the right places by the right people. He chose my wardrobe, my hairstylist, and along with my mother, kept an eye on the foods I ate.

Another model with his agency was assigned to teach me how to walk a runway, how to pose, and any other modeling tips I needed to know. Jackson was also clever in recognizing how my shyness set me apart from other models who actually wanted to be noticed and worked hard at getting attention. He encouraged me to cloak myself in an air of mystery. Because I was untouchable, everyone wanted to touch me, and the job offers began to pour in.

I didn't care. I was just along for the ride. It took over a year to get over being angry with Adam, and after that the sadness settled in. It hadn't ever left, nor had my heart felt the slightest stirring for another man.

Maybe you can make him fall in love with you, for real this time. I blinked. Where in the world had that thought come from?

"You're like a hundred miles away." Autumn snapped her fingers in front of my face. "What're you thinking about?"

"Hmm?" I gave myself a mental shake. That last thought was just crazy. "I was just thinking how happy I am to be here with both of you."

Jenn smiled. "It's been way too long, and you have to promise that you'll never shut us out again."

"I promise." And it was one I intended to keep.

"You swear you're not going to go back to Jackson? Because if you do, I'm going to kidnap you and send you to brainwashing deprogramming or whatever you call it," Autumn said.

I laughed. "I wouldn't put it past you. Seriously, though, that is never going to happen, and I say that knowing I mean it."

She grinned. "Awesome. Now let's go shopping."

We went to the mall in Asheville, and I had the most fun I'd had since I'd left for New York. It was like old times, the way we laughed, tried on clothes, made fun of each other, and oohed and aahed when something really looked fabulous on one of us.

Jenn bought a sexy dress and shoes to match; Autumn went for some new jeans, leggings, and lingerie that was going to make Connor's tongue hang out. Since Autumn was buying my clothes, I tried to keep it to necessities—a few casual things suitable for cold weather, underwear, one pair of winter boots, a pair of flats, and a coat—but both Jenn and Autumn insisted I needed at least one dress and heels to go with it.

"Just in case," Autumn said.

I raised a brow. "Meaning?"

"You never know. You might get invited out to dinner or something while you're here. Might as well be prepared."

Jenn nodded. "She's right, and besides, you know it's useless to argue with her."

"True." And I did love the dress Autumn had picked out. I was careful to tuck all the receipts into my wallet so I could pay her back.

We were driving back to the valley when my phone rang. Again. Jackson must have called and texted a hundred times already, demanding to know where I was. I would have turned it off, but then Adam wouldn't be able to call me. Not that he would, but I still kept it on for that reason. I almost didn't look at the screen, sure it was Jackson, but I did check it, and this time it actually was Adam.

"Hey," I said, wishing my heart wasn't fluttering at seeing his name come up.

"It's Adam."

Like I didn't know that. "You don't sound good."

"Stupid cold. Where are you?"

Well, so much for small talk. "We're about halfway back to the valley."

"Jackson's here. Go straight to Autumn's and stay there with her. Connor's home and is waiting for y'all."

"Okay." He disconnected before I could question him on what Jackson was doing or saying. The *Adam heart flutters* morphed into rapid panic beats. *And so it begins.*

CHAPTER TEN

~ Adam ~

SOMETHING WAS TICKLING MY NOSE. I peeked out of one bleary eye to see Jinx's tail twitching across my face. After calling Savannah to warn her Jackson had arrived, I'd tossed a couple of cold pills down my throat, then stripped down to my briefs and fallen face-first onto my bed for a few minutes, hoping the pounding in my head would ease up. Groaning, I pushed the cat off my pillow, rolled over, and checked the time on the bedside clock. I'd slept for five hours, but between the pills and the nap I was feeling a little better.

Jinx jumped onto my chest, digging his claws into my skin. "Ouch." I picked him up and held him above my face. "Learn some manners, dude. Why are you in my room, anyway?" I'd gone to the jobsite this morning, but my crew had mutinied when I kept sneezing on them and they'd kicked me off the site. Usually I freed him as soon as I arrived home, but my head had been so stuffed with cotton that I hadn't even thought of him.

"There he is."

I glanced up to see Savannah standing in the doorway. As soon as I'd heard Jackson was in town, I'd gone to my brother's house to wait for her and Autumn to return. After sneezing on Connor one too many times, he'd pushed me out the door with instructions to go home and take care of myself. The only reason I'd agreed was that he'd promised to keep an eye on Savannah. So why was she here?

I jerked the sheet up, covering the lower half of my body. Her gaze fell to my chest, her lips parted, and when her eyes strayed farther down, as if she wished she could see through the sheet, arousal stirred.

Not good, Adam. I wasn't about to go there with her again. She'd already said she was going back to New York. And even if she were staying, we had too much hurt and too many years between then and now.

"I made you some soup."

"Huh?"

"Chicken noodle soup. I made you some."

"Thought you said newt. My ears are stopped up." She laughed, and I remembered how much I loved her laugh when we were together.

"Yeah, I went out and gathered a bucket of newts and frogs to make a witch's stew. Guaranteed to cure anything."

The three times I'd seen her in the past nine years, she'd always seemed sad. To see a little bit of sparkle back in her eyes had me wanting to keep it there. "Come get your familiar, witchy woman. He's a skin-clawing demon." She laughed again, and I pulled my pillow over my head to hide my smile.

"Come on, my precious baby," she said, taking him from my chest. "Do you feel like coming down, or should I bring your soup up?"

I lifted the corner of the pillow. "I'll be down in a few minutes."

After she left, I sat up and stretched my aching muscles, then dressed. As I slipped on a pair of sweatpants and a long-sleeved T-shirt, I tried to remember if I had any cans of chicken soup in my pantry. Canned soup wasn't something I ate, but I must have picked some up at some point.

Halfway down the stairs, an aroma filled the air, one I hadn't smelled since my parents had died in a house fire when Connor and I were away at college. Our mother had always made chicken soup if one of us was sick. That scent drifting up the stairs couldn't possibly be from a can.

At the entrance to my kitchen I paused and took in the

woman busy wiping down the counters. She had on a pair of leggings and a hoodie pullover. Her hair was pulled up in a ponytail, and she wore socks with what looked like kittens on them.

Savannah was only a few inches under my six-foot-two height, something I'd always liked about her. I hadn't had to bend down to kiss her. We had been a perfect fit. She was too skinny now for my taste, but I still found her downright hot. Wished I didn't. Also wished I didn't like seeing her in my kitchen.

"I see you've been shopping."

She turned, then stilled when she saw me leaning on the doorframe. "There you are." She smiled. "Yep, with Autumn and Jenn. Sit. Soup's ready to eat."

I walked to her, my gaze homing in on her hood when a pair of blue eyes peeked over the hem. "Your hoodie is wiggling."

She craned her neck to look behind her. "He was trying to climb up my leg, so I put him there. I think he smelled the chicken."

"That would do it." I scratched Jinx on his nose. "Snuggly bed you have there, dude." He let out a loud wail. "Yeah, jail sucks, little man." It was an effort to keep my attention on the cat, being this close to Savannah. How would she react if I kissed her? The urge to do so was so strong that I almost did, but my better sense stopped me from so much as touching her. Obviously I had leftover issues where this woman was concerned.

"How'd you get in?" And why?

"Oh, Autumn let me in." She turned and lifted her eyes to mine. "I told her I wanted to make you some feel-better soup, so she ran me by the store. Now here I am. You don't mind, do you?"

"You didn't have to cook for me," I said after taking a seat at my kitchen island where she had two place settings. As for minding, all I minded was how much I liked her here. She ladled soup into two bowls, then pulled one grilled cheese sandwich out of the oven, cutting it in half, and then putting it on the plate. I got the plate with the grilled cheese.

"Don't get used to it. My cooking repertoire consists of what you see and a few things to do with eggs. I can scramble them and boil them. Anything more and you're on your own."

"Well, it's good," I said after tasting a spoonful of the chicken soup.

"Thanks."

The barely there smile she couldn't hide told me that I'd pleased her. I eyed her bowl with displeasure. There wasn't much in it besides broth. It couldn't be healthy to weigh next to nothing. I dropped one half of my cheese sandwich onto her plate, then went back to eating.

She studied me for a moment. "You look better than you did earlier today."

"Just a head cold, and I do feel better."

She tore the crust off from one side and nibbled on it like a damn rabbit. I made a vow right then and there that by the time she left, she'd weigh at least five pounds more.

"Are you okay?" I asked.

"About what?"

"Jackson being in town."

"I don't want to talk about him. Not tonight."

"Okay, but when you do need to… Autumn or Jenn will be there for you." I'd almost said I'd be there for her. I seemed to keep forgetting I couldn't be that man anymore.

Jinx climbed out of the hood onto her shoulder, and she reached up and grabbed him, setting him on the floor. "Go play with your mouse, stinker."

"He's a handful." The first day I'd had him was a disaster. I came home that evening to shredded toilet paper scattered all over, one electrical cord chewed—amazing that he hadn't been fried to a crisp—and Jinx stuck behind the fridge. Something had to be done but sticking him in a cage where he'd be confined to a tiny space all day hadn't seemed right. The renovated playpen seemed to be working great, though. I still wasn't sure why he was still here or why he had more toys than he could play with.

Savannah watched him for a moment as he batted a mouse around, then lifted her eyes to mine. "Can I ask you something?"

That kind of question was never one a man wanted to hear. "You can ask. I might not answer."

"Are you seeing someone now? I mean, I don't want your girlfriend to get upset that I'm playing nurse."

"That's nothing you have to worry about." I didn't know why I didn't tell her that I didn't have a girlfriend. Never had after her. Sure, I dated. A lot. But Savannah was the only woman I'd ever been serious about. Maybe I wanted her to be jealous. I knew I hadn't liked seeing her picture in the paper with that ballplayer or with Jackson the first time she'd come home, bringing him with her.

"There's something else I've wanted to tell you for a long time," she said.

"What's that?"

"I never got a chance to tell you how sorry I was to hear about your parents. Jenn called me when it happened." She made circles on the table with her finger. "I wanted to come to the funeral, but my mother refused to allow it. I was going to come anyway, but she caught me sneaking out."

"Thanks for that. At first I was hurt that I didn't hear from you, not even a card, but then I figured it was something like that."

She frowned. "I sent a card."

"Never got one."

"I'm sorry, Adam. I wanted you to know I was thinking of you and Connor. Mother said she'd mail it for me." Tears pooled in her eyes, and she blinked them away. "I should have guessed she'd do something like that and mailed it myself."

Although that had been eight years ago, it had always hurt that she hadn't even bothered to get in touch. I knew Jenn or Autumn would have told her about the house fire, and hearing nothing had seemed like a sign that she'd moved on. At the time it had only reinforced my belief that I'd done the right thing in breaking up with her. Now I didn't know what to think.

When more tears shimmered in her eyes, I put my hand over hers. "Thank you. I'm glad you told me." At her smile—the shy one I remembered she would give when she was unsure of herself—something shifted inside me. I pushed the bar stool back, needing to break this connection between us that felt too familiar.

"Want to watch a movie?" Where had that come from? Spending time with Savannah was not a good idea, especially when my defenses were down. Whether it was her making me soup because I was sick, or learning that she had tried to contact me when my parents died, or the tears for me after all this time that had shifted my perception of who she was now, I didn't know. Maybe it was all those things that had me wanting to wrap my arms around her, hold her close, and promise I'd do whatever it took to make her happy. Instead I stuffed my hands into my pockets as I waited for her answer.

She glanced at Jinx playing on the floor. "No thanks. I'll call Autumn to come get me and let you get back to bed."

I was both relieved and disappointed.

CHAPTER ELEVEN

~ Savannah ~

"I'LL TAKE YOU," ADAM SAID.

For a long time now I'd managed to put Adam on a low burner, but being close to him again, all the feelings I'd once had for him were bubbling to the top. For all the good that would do me. Adam had moved on. But when Autumn said he was sick, I couldn't stay away.

I couldn't cook worth beans. Jackson and I always ate out because he liked to be seen with a famous model on his arm. But I could make a dang good chicken noodle soup. I'd learned how when my mother couldn't eat anything else. She'd refused to move to hospice, demanding that I take care of her to the end. Of course I would. She was my mother. Not once did she thank me for being by her side, but I didn't blame her. She was dying and in a lot of pain.

So those were my two talents, taking care of a sick person and making chicken noodle soup. That I was photogenic was by chance, not a talent. Adam probably couldn't wait to have me out of his hair. But he'd seemed to like that I'd made him the soup.

He pulled up in front of Connor's house. It was maybe a five-minute walk between the twins' log cabins, and I could have easily walked. But it had grown dark, and I knew it was fruitless to even suggest to Adam that I was capable of getting to Autumn's by myself.

"Thanks for the soup, Savannah," he said after coming to a stop. "I really do feel better."

How ridiculous was it that my heart thought it should melt over his faint praise of my soup? "You're welcome.

It was the least I could do after…" I put my hand on the door handle, anxious to get away before I said too much.

"After?" Adam said, his voice rougher than I'd ever heard it before.

"After everything we used to be to each other." I glanced at him, and I don't think I'd ever seen such a mix of yearning and resentment in a man's eyes before. I didn't know what to make of it. I opened the door, intending to get out. Adam's hand clamped down on my wrist, stopping me as I was halfway out of his car. I fell back onto the seat, pulling the door closed.

"Adam?" That was all. One word, the one name that meant everything in the world to me.

"If you don't want me to kiss you, Savannah, say so right now."

I should. I totally should say so. I didn't.

His mouth covered mine, and I was sucked back to a time when I had loved this man… except he'd been a boy then. He'd kissed so good back then, but now? Oh God, now. His lips on mine stripped away all my objections, as if he had a superpower I couldn't begin to resist.

"Adam," I whispered, maybe begged.

He tore his mouth away from mine and shot out of the car. I got my door open, but before I could step out he was there, offering a hand. As soon as my feet were on the ground, he put his palm on my back, giving me a push toward Connor's door. Obviously Adam couldn't wait to be rid of me. I picked up my pace, wanting to be away from him before the stupid tears burning my eyes dripped down my face. I walked inside, and Adam left without a word being exchanged between us.

What just happened?

"How's Adam?" Autumn asked from the sofa where she was curled up next to Connor.

"Better," I said, walking right past them and heading for my room. I couldn't talk right now, especially with Connor there. Looking at him was as good as seeing Adam, and I just couldn't be around Connor tonight.

Not two minutes passed when there was a knock on the bedroom door. "Savannah?"

I sighed. Of course Autumn had picked up on something being wrong, and of course she couldn't leave it well enough alone.

"Yeah?"

"Can I come in?"

"If you must."

"You know me. I must," she said, giving me a grin after entering.

She sat on the edge of the bed, watching me remove the clothes I'd bought this morning from the shopping bags. I'd been in a hurry to get to the store and get the ingredients I needed to make Adam soup, and I hadn't bothered putting the items away when we'd returned from the mall.

"What happened?"

"With?"

She shook her head, letting me know she wasn't buying it. "Spit it out."

Fighting Autumn was like trying to stop the force of a tsunami with your bare hands. Useless.

"Adam kissed me." I sank onto the bed next to her.

"Yeah? That's not such a bad thing, is it?"

"It is when he suddenly realizes what he just did and can't wait to get rid of you." I shrugged. "Besides, Adam and I are old news. Nothing to talk about."

She put an arm around my shoulder and gave me a hug. "I'm not so sure about that. Was it good kissing him? Was it what you remembered?"

"It was more," I whispered. And it had been. A streak of jealousy raced through me, thinking that he kissed even better as a man because of all the practice he'd gotten in after me.

"Aw, hon. You do still have feelings for him. I knew it."

"Doesn't matter. He has his life now, and when I get the problem named Jackson taken care of, I'll be going back to New York."

"Is that what you really want?"

No, but what I wanted didn't matter. Never had. "Of course. I have a life there, a career."

"Why can't you model from here? We do have an airport less than an hour away, you know. When you have a job, you just get on a plane." She waved a hand in the air. "Simple."

I laughed. "No, it isn't that simple."

Connor poked his head around the open door. "You coming to bed soon, Beautiful?"

"Be there in a sec, babe," Autumn said.

Her seconds could easily turn into minutes or hours if she got to going. Although I wasn't sleepy, I yawned. "It's been a long day. Bed sounds good to me."

She squeezed my hand. "We'll talk more in the morning."

No, we wouldn't. Not about Adam. "Sure. Go to your gorgeous boyfriend."

"If you think he's gorgeous, then you think Adam is." She waggled her eyebrows, then twirled out of the room.

I smiled to myself after she was gone, wishing I had a fraction of her personality. After a shower, I slipped on a pair of boy boxers and the long-sleeved T-shirt of Adam's that I'd kept. Hours later I was still awake, my mind going in a thousand directions at once. My life, how it had come to this, what I was going to or could do about it. But mostly I thought of Adam kissing me.

"Why did you, Adam?" I whispered into the dark as I touched a finger to my lips.

CHAPTER TWELVE

~ Adam ~

I KISSED HER!
The hell of it was that I didn't regret it. I totally should. But there had been something in her eyes when she'd made that comment about everything we used to be to each other. A glimpse of the shy girl I'd once loved, a vulnerability? I don't know, and it bugged me that I didn't. Until she'd returned, I thought I'd put her in my past where she belonged. Now? All the feelings I'd had for her were surfacing like a secret that couldn't stand to be hidden.

"Kryptonite," Connor's voice whispered into my ear.

"Shut up," I answered, then felt like an idiot when I realized I was talking to myself. To get my mind off *The Kiss*, and since I couldn't fall asleep, I turned my mind to planning Jackson Marks's demise. Okay, that didn't sound right. I wasn't going to kill him, much as I might like to, but the man needed to be taught a lesson on how not to treat a woman.

Harvey Bowen had called yesterday to tell me that Jackson Marks had shown up at the Vistas, our nicest hotel, demanding their best room. I'd had to laugh when Harvey told me that they put him in a smoking room, which resulted in Marks storming back to the lobby and raising hell. They then put him in the room next to the elevators and ice maker. That got the registration clerk another dressing down and a demand to see the manager.

The manager had appeared and took offense at his hotel being called a "shit hole" and told Marks that he'd probably be happier at the Mountain View Bed and Breakfast, coincidentally owned by Harvey. Apparently Harvey had taken it upon himself to get the hotel and motel owners to agree to herd Marks to Harvey's bed-and-breakfast.

"I got him where I want him," Harvey said. "I didn't give him my best room but not my worst either. I didn't want him to go to another place where I can't keep an eye on him for you. He's right demanding, though, so it's doubtful he'll be happy with our slower pace of doing things."

My town was the greatest.

The next morning, and feeling much better, I made stops at the three jobsites I had going and gave my construction crews their instructions for the rest of the day. Then I went on stakeout duty.

Harvey had given me the make and model of Marks's rental car, and I parked a few spaces away from it, pulled my ball cap down on my forehead, and slouched in my seat. While I waited for him to make a move, I called Dylan to update him, following that call up with ones to Mary and Hamburger. Mary cryptically said that she had a special treat for Marks if and when he showed up—and even not knowing what she planned, a shudder traveled up my spine. Mary was not to be trusted.

Hamburger said that he was biting at the bit to "go a'spying," and I swallowed a laugh, not wanting to hurt his feelings. I told him to head into town and wait for further instructions.

Marks didn't show his face until after lunchtime. I should have packed a sandwich. I followed him to Fusions, the closest restaurant to Harvey's bed-and-breakfast. As soon as he entered, I got out of my car and walked in. Leah Ann, the hostess, jerked her chin toward the bar, and I winked at her, thanking her. There probably wasn't a person in the valley who hadn't seen Marks's picture or who wasn't watching out for him by now.

"This isn't what I ordered," Marks said as I walked into the lounge. He pushed his glass back across the bar.

Greg, the bartender, picked up the drink and sniffed it. "You said Chivas and water. That's what I gave you."

"I said, Chivas and soda. How does soda sound like water?" He lifted his face to the ceiling. "Jesus, is everyone in this hick town an idiot?"

"Sorry, man. Pretty sure you did say water, but a scotch and soda coming up."

"Not any scotch. Chivas!" Marks yelled.

Greg glanced over his shoulder as he dumped the scotch and water into the sink. "Dude, no need to yell. I got ears. Little early to be drinking, dontcha think?"

Stifling a laugh, I slipped onto a stool at the opposite end of the bar, took out my phone and called Hamburger, telling him where Marks was. When Greg saw me, I mouthed, *Club soda on ice with a lime.* He nodded, then put the new drink in front of Marks.

The man stared at it a moment, then said, "Who the hell puts a cherry in scotch?"

Greg lifted his hands in the air. "Dude, obviously you're having a bad day. I was just trying to make it better, ya hear?"

I wished Savannah could be here to see how those who loved her, and even the ones who didn't know her but had been told that an outsider was out to hurt one of our own, had got on board to circle the wagons.

Marks plucked the cherry out of his drink, dropping it on the bar. He pulled his phone from his pocket, scrolled through it, then held it out to Greg. "Have you seen this woman around?"

"Yep," Greg said after peering at the photo. "Saw her just last night at the grocery store."

"Which one?" Marks asked.

"We only have one. I was standing in line and there she was, on the cover of a magazine."

I quietly chuckled.

"Idiot. I meant have you seen her in person?"

"Hey, now," Greg said, puffing out his chest. "No need to call me names. You asked if I'd seen her and I had."

Hamburger must have been close when I called him, because he walked into the lounge, fiddle in hand. "I herd there's ah Hollywood agent in town," he announced, his gaze zeroing in on Marks. He eyed the cherry Marks had set on the counter next to his glass. "Ya gonna be eatin' that, Mister?"

Marks slid a stink eye Hamburger's way. "Eating what?"

"That cherry." When Marks shook his head, Hamburger grabbed the cherry and popped it into his mouth. "Fruit's good for ya, boy." Hamburger set his fiddle case on the bar. "This be yer lucky day."

"Excuse me?"

"Hollywood. Din't ya hear me say that? Yer ah agent, right? Just listen."

Hamburger was really laying on the hillbilly accent. There were enough people at the bar for me to blend in, and I couldn't resist taking out my phone and videotaping him playing for Marks. Hamburger played fast and furious, his feet doing their shuffling thing. The people sitting at the bar and at tables in the lounge all stopped their conversations to watch him, most of them clapping to the rhythm of the music.

Everyone was loving it except for Marks. Halfway through Hamburger's song, Marks threw a five-dollar bill on the counter, then stormed out.

"Hey, dude," Greg called after him. "That drink was six dollars."

Marks stopped, spun on his feet, stomped back, and slammed another dollar down next to the five.

"Guess I don't get a tip," Greg said.

"Hick town," Marks muttered on his way out the door.

"But ya din't finish hearing me play for ya, Agent Man," Hamburger hollered, grabbing his fiddle case. Hamburger glanced at me and winked before following Marks out.

Our moonshiner was having the time of his life already, and we'd only just begun to mess with Savannah's nemesis.

I chuckled as I put a ten on the bar for my three-dollar club soda. "Keep the change," I told Greg, tipping him for both Marks and me, and for the trouble he'd given the man for Savannah's sake.

"Thanks, man. Hope he comes back. That was fun."

Yeah, it was. I nodded, then hurried to catch up with my prey. I found him pulled over on the side of the road with a police cruiser parked behind him, blue lights flashing. Hamburger sat in his truck behind the cruiser. Laughing, I turned into the parking lot of a gift shop next to them, and while I waited, I took pictures of Tommy Evans, one of Dylan's cops, talking to Marks.

Ten minutes later Marks drove away with Hamburger following close behind. I got out and walked up to Tommy.

"Afternoon, Tommy," I said. "What'd you stop him for?"

Tommy grinned. "Speeding. He was two miles over the limit."

"Bet that didn't make him happy."

He snorted. "Gave me an earful. I don't think he appreciates our lovely town."

"He hasn't seen nothing yet. You ticket him?"

"Nah, saving that for when I stop him tomorrow for driving too slow. Wrote him a warning, though. He showed me a picture of Savannah on his phone and wanted to know if I'd seen her. Told him that as far as I knew, she lived in New York City now." He'd drawn out New York City in a slow southern drawl, and I could just imagine Marks gritting his teeth.

Tommy glanced down the road, and we both watched as Marks turned into the parking lot of Mary's Bread Company, Hamburger following faithfully behind him. "He's gonna wish he'd driven right past Mary's."

"No doubt. Call me if you run into him again."

"Will do."

I returned to my car and headed to Mary's. Marks would recognize me from the weddings, but I was too curious not to go inside. Besides, I was ready to have a face-to-face with him. When I walked in, Marks was trying to talk to Mary over the noise of Hamburger's fiddle.

"Would you shut the hell up," Marks yelled at Hamburger.

Hamburger gave him a toothless grin and kept playing. Marks hadn't noticed me yet, and I leaned back against the door, making sure the man would have to go through me to get out.

"Have you seen this woman?" Marks said, raising his voice as he held his phone out to Mary.

Mary put a hand to her ear. "Sorry, can't hear you." She picked up a chocolate cupcake that had been sitting off to the side. "Eat this. It's on the house. When he finishes, we can talk."

I narrowed my eyes on the cupcake. Mary was up to something, but I couldn't figure out what. Marks snatched the cupcake out of her hand and ate it in about two bites. Meanwhile Hamburger played on.

When he finally finished the song, he said, "Whadda ya think, Agent Man? Cain't ya just see me in one ah them musicals"—he pronounced it *muse-a-cows*—"like that Elvis Presley movie, *Jailhouse Rock*? I'm gonna make both'n us famous, boy, just ya wait and see."

A laugh escaped, drawing Marks's attention. At seeing me, Marks wadded up the paper cup his treat had been in and dropped it on the counter, then aimed straight for me.

"Where is she?" he said, getting in my face.

"Who?" For a second I thought he was going to put his fist through my face. I wished he would. It would give me all the excuse I needed to rearrange his.

"You know damn well who. Where. The. Hell. Is. She?"

And then I came within a breath of doing exactly what I wanted. Would have if Mary hadn't come tottering over in purple four-inch heels, putting herself between us.

She tugged on Marks's sleeve. "I remember you from our girls' weddings. You were with Savannah. Have you misplaced her?" She poked a finger into his stomach. "Because if you have lost our dear girl, I'm going to get my gun out and shoot you for dereliction of duty."

Marks's face turned red. "You people are not only idiots, you're all crazy."

Hamburger started playing his fiddle again.

Turning back to me, Marks said, "You think this is a game? I know she's here, and I'll find her. Without me, she's nothing, and she knows that. I know all about your past with her, but that's old history. It's me she spreads her legs for now." He smirked. "If you think you can keep her, think about this. You're just a country bumpkin who will bore her out of her mind before it's all over."

"Get the hell out," Mary said, her eyes shooting fire.

Marks peered down at the woman with bright green hair as if she was no more than a bug under his foot. "Oh, I'm going, but just one more thing." He looked back at me, his eyes filled with a challenge. "She's mine. I created her, and I own her. She's just having a little snit, but she'll come back to me, mountain boy, as soon as she realizes you can't give her what I can."

There was only one word in my mind. *Kill*. I went for him, but Hamburger put his arms around my chest, holding on to me for dear life.

"Stupid hick town," Marks said. His face twisted as if he were in pain. He jerked open the door and ran to his rental car. Hamburger followed him, talking a mile a minute, probably about Hollywood and movies.

Mary peered out the window, watching as Marks closed his door in Hamburger's face and then tore out of the parking lot. "Poor man."

I unclenched my fists and took several deep breaths. "Why do you say that?"

Mary beamed up at me. "Oh, I might have accidently mixed some laxatives into that cupcake. He won't bother anyone for the rest of the night."

I snorted as I leaned over to catch my breath. "You're a little devil, Mary, but I love it." It was actually better than my intention to beat the crap out of him. "Thanks. Since he's in for the night, your work for today is done."

She rubbed her hands together with a little too much glee. "Can't wait for tomorrow."

For a millisecond I felt sorry for Marks. I headed home, curious to learn what Savannah would think of today's events.

CHAPTER THIRTEEN

~ Savannah ~

"OH MY GOD, SHE DIDN'T?" I wiped tears of laughter from my eyes after Adam finished telling us what Mary had done. "I wish I could have been a fly on the wall to see Hamburger playing his fiddle for Jackson."

Jackson couldn't stand anyone who wasn't rich and famous, and I could just imagine what he thought of a coverall-wearing moonshiner following him around like a lovesick puppy, playing his fiddle, or having to deal with Mary, with whatever color her hair was today, dressed in her outlandish clothes, and her body loaded down with jewelry.

"Figured you'd say that," Adam said with a smirk. I knew that look. He was pleased with himself. He picked up his phone from the coffee table, fiddled with it, and then handed it to me.

Autumn and Connor leaned over my shoulder as I watched the video of Hamburger playing for Jackson. Jackson's sour-lipped expression was priceless. Hamburger played a mean fiddle, and how could Jackson not see that, not see the talent in those aged fingers? I glanced at Adam to see an amused smile on his face that mirrored mine.

We were at Connor and Autumn's, and I don't think the three of them could begin to appreciate what it meant to me to be with my friends. I was free to enjoy myself without Jackson looking over my shoulder, scowling because I was laughing or saying the wrong things. I wished Jenn were here. Then it would really be like old times.

Autumn laughed. "Jackson doesn't seem to be enjoying

Hamburger's talents."

"No, he wouldn't." And that was what was so great about Hamburger following Jackson around.

"What's the plan for tomorrow?" Connor asked.

"More of the same." Adam glanced at me. "Since Jackson's in for the night, thanks to Mary, would y'all like to get out? Go somewhere for dinner?"

"If it means I don't have to cook, definitely," Autumn said.

"Do you feel like going out?" I asked Adam.

"I'm good. The chicken soup healed me." He winked, which I wished he wouldn't do because it made my heart act silly.

"Can we call Jenn, see if she and Dylan want to meet us?" I hadn't been around Dylan much, but the little I'd seen of him, he seemed like a cool guy.

"Great idea." Autumn looked around. "Where'd I leave my phone?"

Connor handed her his. "Use mine."

"They're in," she said after talking to Jenn. "I have to call her back when we decide where we're going."

"How about the Brewery?" Connor said. "It's casual, and the cheeseburgers are great."

I grinned. "So you haven't gotten over your love of cheeseburgers?"

"Never." He widened his eyes as if shocked I'd even think such a thing.

Autumn chuckled. "He'd have one every night for dinner if I let him."

"They also have a wild rice bowl that's good," Adam said, glancing over at me. "It's got asparagus and mushrooms in it."

That was something I'd eat. "Sounds perfect."

An hour later we were sitting at a round pub table made from oak casks. The stools were cool, too, the seats cork and the seatbacks made from tin beer cans. I glanced around, taking in the decor. A long copper bar ran the length of the back wall, potted hanging spider plants were scattered around, and the floor was covered in peanut shells.

"This place is awesome," I said. "Is it new?"

Adam, sitting next to me, nodded. "Been here a little over a year."

The waitress took our drink orders, all but Jenn and me ordering the beer flights, a sampling of locally brewed beers. When Jenn ordered water, the same as me, I narrowed my eyes. I was watching my calories, but Jenn enjoyed a beer or glass of wine as much as the rest of us. She returned my stare with a secretive smile.

"You have something to tell us?" I asked.

Dylan's wide grin confirmed my suspicion.

"What?" Autumn said, her gaze darting between me and Jenn.

I picked out a peanut from the bucket in the middle of the table and tossed it at Jenn. "Name one reason a woman who would normally have a beer or glass of wine orders water?"

Autumn's mouth fell open. "You're pregnant?" At Jenn's nod, Autumn screamed as she jumped off her stool and raced around the table, smothering Jenn in a hug.

"Think she's excited?" Connor muttered, making us laugh.

I slid off my seat and joined in the hug. It made me happy that I was here to rejoice with my friends in this awesome news. But it also made me sad, knowing I'd leave again as soon as I got Jackson out of my hair, and I wouldn't be here when the baby was born. At least I'd be free to come for a visit since by then I would be deciding my life, not him.

The waitress brought our drinks, and after she left, Adam raised one of his beers. "Congratulations to both of you. Seems like just yesterday we were all hanging out in my and Connor's tree house, and now we're talking babies.

How did that happen?"

Connor clicked his glass against Adam's and Dylan's. "If it's a boy, we'll build him a tree house. Maybe he'll let us play in it."

All three guys gave a man grunt of approval for that idea.

Later, after Connor had devoured two cheeseburgers and the rest of us had finished our meals, we sat around the table telling Dylan stories about the five of us growing up together. Most of the funniest ones were all on Autumn since she was both the troublemaker and the instigator of our exploits. We also talked a little about Natalie, Jenn's twin, and how happy she would have been about being an aunt. Then we all got teary-eyed, even Dylan who'd never had a chance to meet her.

"I heard Mary put a little present in the cupcake she gave Marks," Dylan said, changing the subject, probably because he realized we were all on the verge of bawling.

Adam laughed. "Remind me to never get on her bad side. Between Mary and Hamburger, he's not a happy camper." He pulled out his phone and brought up the video. "See for yourself."

"That's priceless," Jenn said with tears of laughter in her eyes.

"Have I ever said how much I love this town?" Dylan grinned as he handed the phone back to Adam.

"At least once a day," Jenn said.

He smiled at his wife. "Mostly because you're here."

They were so sweet together. I was glad to get to spend time around them because it was obvious how much Dylan loved her. I glanced over at Connor in time to see him give Autumn a quick kiss. My best girlfriends—my only girlfriends—were the happiest I'd ever seen them, and I was glad for them. But I was envious, too, because I didn't see myself ever having my own special someone.

Adam reached under the table and squeezed my knee, and when our eyes met, I saw understanding in his. I quickly glanced away. Adam had always been able to read me, and I didn't want him to see how lonely I felt, even here among my friends.

"Is Marks still calling and texting you?" Adam asked.

"Probably, but I blocked his number, so I don't really know." It hadn't taken long to tire of hearing my phone ring or buzz with an incoming text every five minutes demanding to know where I was.

"What's the plan for tomorrow?" Jenn asked.

Adam shrugged. "More of the same. Our town doing its best to drive him out of Dodge."

"I'm going to have to face him at some point." As much as I wished to never see Jackson again, I couldn't hide from him forever. Taking control of my life meant standing up to my bully, and I'd rather do it here where I had my friends at my back over New York where I'd be alone.

"You don't have to see him," Autumn said.

"She needs to do it for herself." Adam smiled at me.

I smiled back, warmth spreading through me that he understood. "I also need to find a good lawyer." It was time to start the process of getting control of my bank account and evicting Jackson from my home.

"You need one who specializes in this kind of thing," Autumn said. "I have a friend who will know who to recommend."

Connor raised a brow. "Who's that?"

"Lucas."

"Thought so."

She punched him in the arm. "Thought you were over that."

"I am. Mostly." He wrinkled his nose as if he'd smelled something stinky.

Next to me, Adam chuckled. "You better play nice to him, brother. We're about to build him the most expense log cabin we've ever done before."

What was that all about? "Who's Lucas?"

"Lucas Blanton," Autumn said. "The—"

"Senator?" She nodded. How did I not know one of *People Magazine's* Sexiest Men Alive was a friend of Autumn's? "I've met him." The man was drop-dead gorgeous.

This time Adam wrinkled his nose. "Is he a friend of yours, too?"

I got why Connor had done that. He was jealous that Autumn was a friend of someone like Lucas. But what did Adam care if I knew the man? "No, not a friend. I've met him at some events a few times. He seems nice." And he'd always had a stunning woman on his arm.

"He'll be here in the morning to look at the plans for his cabin," Autumn said. "We'll talk to him then."

Adam made a growling noise.

"Sure." Although I wasn't sure I wanted Senator Blanton to know about my problems. And what was with the weird noises coming from Adam?

CHAPTER FOURTEEN

~ Adam ~

CONNOR AND I WERE DUE to meet with Blanton this morning at ten to show him our preliminary plans for his log cabin. The house was going to be magnificent, and we both hoped that the senator would allow us to use photos of the finished result in our brochures. Autumn seemed to think he would.

What I didn't understand were the vibes under the surface between her and my brother whenever the man's name came up. I hadn't thought much about it, though, until Savannah had said she'd met the man a few times. I didn't much like her knowing some dude who was on a damn list of sexiest men. Now I got where Connor was coming from, and I was seriously not happy about that.

When my phone rang, Connor's name appearing on the screen, I was sprawled out on my sofa, drinking coffee and watching the sunrise through my east-facing windows while Jinx tried to steal sips out of my cup. For my brother to be calling this early, something was happening.

"Sup?" I said, answering while holding my coffee high above my head, trying to keep it out of reach of the little demon, now clawing his way up my arm.

"Autumn called Blanton last night and arranged for her and Savannah to meet with him before our meeting."

I sat up. "What time and where?"

"Nine, at our model home."

"See you there." The brat was still clinging to my arm. "I can still take you to the shelter, you know." Apparently he knew an empty threat when he heard it since he didn't let go. I pried him off my T-shirt sleeve, finished the last of my coffee, and then carried the little monster upstairs with me, dropping him on my bed. He had this thing about darting around on and under the sheets like a deranged idiot. Leaving him to it, I showered, shaved, and dressed.

After a quick breakfast I put Jinx in his playpen, then headed to our model home. Although I was early, I wanted to get everything ready for Blanton's arrival. Connor and I planned to build two more model homes on the land we'd purchased last year. Interestingly enough, Blanton had wanted the property for a dinner theater, but Autumn had talked him into letting us have it. There was a story there, but both Connor and Autumn were tight-lipped on how she'd convinced the senator to let us buy the land.

Autumn had done a fantastic job on the model home's decor, what she called contemporary rustic and perfect for a mountain log home. The colors were warm deep reds and dark greens, with a few accents in gold, reminding me of fall in the mountains. Most of the accessories were from local artisan shops. Having Autumn on board with the interior designs for our model homes was proving to be a brilliant move on Connor's part.

By the time nine rolled around, I had a fire going in the massive stone fireplace, soft music playing, and a pot of coffee brewed. One of the bedrooms had been set up as a conference room, and the plans and artist renderings for the senator's home were spread out on the table. I glanced around with a sense of pride for what Connor and I had accomplished. We'd only finished our first model home last week, and Blanton would be our first client here. Floor and countertop—granite, marble, quartz, and stained cement—samples were mounted on one wall of the conference room. On another were cabinet and hardware options, and on the third were exterior log choices. The fourth wall was tall windows that let in light and would offer great views when the log home was built on the owner's property. Right now the view was our parking lot.

One of the coolest ideas Autumn had come up with were the monitors at each place of the conference table. We would be able to bring up plans and renderings for our clients to see from their seats without everyone crowding around one computer the way we used to do it.

Satisfied I had everything ready, I made a cup of coffee and went next door to check on my crew. We'd started on the second model home a month ago, and it was coming along on schedule. The foundation was in and the walls were up.

The completed model home was five thousand square feet. The second one would be thirty-five hundred, and the third one two thousand, a good mix of sizes for our clients to get a feel of space. But we built whatever size they wanted.

"Morning," I said after walking inside.

"Morning, boss," my crew sang.

"Any problems I should know about?" I asked Tim, my foreman.

"Yeah, the electrician was supposed to start today, but he's got the flu. Said he hopes to be back on his feet in a day or two."

"No much we can do about that." A day or two wouldn't kill us.

"That's not all. Someone walked off with the AC."

"Shit. That was delivered just yesterday." I pulled him out of hearing range of the rest of the crew. "Think it was any of our boys?"

"I hate to think so, but who else would have known that fast it was here? I had the delivery guys put it up against the wall on the back porch where it wasn't easily seen."

"Or it could have been someone nosing around the property who saw it. I'll file a report with the police and ask them to keep an eye on the property on their rounds. We don't have a choice but to order another one. Security cameras and motion sensor lights around the property are scheduled to be installed in two weeks, but I'll call and see if we can get that date moved up."

"Sounds good, boss."

At hearing the arrival of a car, I glanced out the window. Connor and the girls were here. "I have meetings this morning, but I'll check back this afternoon. Call me if anything else comes up."

Tim turned his gaze from the window to me after Savannah got out of the car. "Is she the woman we're protecting?"

And that was my town for you. Everyone knew everything, and no one wanted to be left out of anything. "Yeah, that's her."

"She's real pretty."

Yes, she certainly was. "Yo, get to work, guys," I said when I noticed my crew crowding around the opening where a window would go.

"He's sweet on her. Don't want us looking at her," I heard one of the men say as they scurried to do my bidding.

No, I wasn't sweet on her, not anymore, even if I didn't like them looking at her. So if that was true, why had I kissed her? Good question, and one I didn't have an answer to. "Morning," I said, coming up next to Savannah as she followed Connor and Autumn up the porch steps.

She darted a glance at me, giving me one of her shy smiles. "Hi."

"Coffee's made if anyone wants a cup."

"Not for me," she said, looking around the great room. "Wow, this place is awesome."

"Thanks. We'll be glad to build you one."

A smile played at the edges of her mouth. "I'm sure you would be. I'd love a tour."

"You bet." Another car pulled up. "Blanton's here. He'll probably want a tour, too."

"I can't believe I'm going to air my dirty laundry to a senator. This is going to be humiliating," Savannah said, edging over to stand on the other side of Autumn.

"This is all on Marks. He's the one who should be humiliated, not you." My gaze roamed over her. She was looking better than she had the day I picked her up at the airport. The light was returning to her eyes, her cheeks seemed a bit fuller now that she was eating a little, and her complexion had a glow to it that had been missing. Whether she realized it or not, being home was good for her.

With her knit cap, quilted jacket, jeans, and fur-lined boots, she was far from the glamorous woman I was used to seeing on magazine covers. Still beautiful in a hometown-girl kind of way, and closer to the Savannah I used to know. I liked her much better.

"I'm so ready for spring," Autumn said, holding up her hands in front of the fireplace.

Connor walked up behind Autumn and wrapped his arms around her. "I know how to warm you up, Beautiful."

Savannah grinned at me and rolled her eyes. "They're just too cute."

"If you say so." Something tugged at my heart at sharing an amused glance the way we had back in high school over something our friends said or did.

"Good morning, everyone," Lucas Blanton said as he entered.

"Senator." I held out my hand.

"Just Lucas," he said as he shook my hand.

Connor let go of Autumn and exchanged a handshake with the senator. Autumn got a kiss on the cheek. I was probably the only one in the room who caught the flash of annoyance in my twin's eyes.

"Savannah, nice to see you again. It's been a while," Lucas said at seeing her. "Autumn didn't tell me her friend's name when she called last night."

"Um, sorry," she whispered, her eyes downcast.

"No reason to be. It's a nice surprise."

Savannah was slipping back into her shell. She'd never been at ease with people she didn't know well, and there had been a time when I was her buffer. Guess I still was. I walked over to her, and as soon as I stopped next to her, she leaned against my arm.

"Thanks for coming early, Lucas," Autumn said. "I'm hoping you can give Savannah some advice about the situation she finds herself in."

"If I can."

The gentle smile he gave Savannah told me that the man was good at reading people and had picked up on her discomfort. I had to respect him for that. "Would you like a cup of coffee?"

"Thought you'd never ask." He slipped off his jacket and hung it on one of the hooks on the coat stand in the entrance.

"Follow me," Connor said. He glanced over his shoulder at me. "We'll talk in here since Autumn will probably refuse to disconnect herself from the fireplace."

Autumn gave him a ridiculous grin. "Got that right, hot stuff. Make me a coffee while you're in there."

"Adam?" Connor asked.

I held up my cup. "I'm good."

Coffees made, we settled in, Connor and Autumn snuggled up on one corner of the massive sofa, Savannah hugging the other side, me in the chair closest to her, and Lucas in the chair opposite of me.

"Tell him, Savannah," Autumn said when Savannah turned mute.

The story came out in convoluted bits and pieces with her studying her hands as if they were the most interesting thing she'd ever seen. Christ, I hurt for her, wanted to take over and tell Lucas what he needed to know. But she had to do this herself.

CHAPTER FIFTEEN

~ Savannah ~

TELLING LUCAS MY STORY WAS as difficult as I'd thought it would be. It would have been easier if I didn't know him, if he was a stranger. But jeez, the man was a senator, one I'd met on several occasions. Halfway through I realized I was speaking in that bumbling way I had when Jackson would critically judge my every word.

You're not that person anymore, Savannah. I sat up straighter, took a deep breath to calm the erratic beat of my heart, and lifted my gaze from my hands to Lucas. "What I need is an attorney who can help me get control of my bank account and get Jackson out of my home," I said after explaining why my mother had moved him in with us and put his name on my account.

Something between a grunt and a growl sounded from Adam, and I glanced at him. His lips were pressed together in a tight line, and anger flashed in his eyes. When he caught me looking at him, he smiled and reached over and squeezed my hand.

"You definitely need an attorney," Lucas said. "And I know just the one. Her name is Jill Thornwood. She's a shark, as smart and tenacious as they come. Write down your phone number for me, and I'll have her call you to set up a meeting. She works out of Raleigh, but the two of you can arrange a meeting either there or here if you prefer."

"Thank you. Jackson is in the valley looking for me, and the sooner I get this started, the better."

"He's here?"

Adam nodded. "Yeah, and we're doing our best to annoy the hell out of him."

That led to telling Lucas what had occurred so far. Drained after telling my story, I sat back and let my three friends tell him the shenanigans they'd gotten up to. Adam whipped out his cell phone and showed Lucas the video of Hamburger playing his fiddle for Jackson.

"God, I love this town," Lucas said through his laughter.

I wished people would stop saying that. Each time I heard it, I was reminded that it was no longer my town, that I'd be leaving soon. The longer I was here, the more I didn't want to return to New York. I fished one of my personal cards from my purse and handed it to Lucas.

"This is my cell number." I glanced at Adam. "Are we finished?" If I sat here much longer, I was going to climb right out of my skin. At his nod I said, "Is it okay if I play with Jinx this afternoon?" For some reason the little fur ball soothed me, and all the stuff crowding my mind, making it feel like it was about to explode, faded away when I played with him.

"Of course. Autumn can let you in. Just keep the doors locked and the alarm on." He looked at Autumn. "Give her your code."

"Will do." She gave Connor a quick kiss, then stood. "Lucas, when you're ready to go over some ideas for the interior of your log home, let me know."

"I will." The men got to their feet. "Savannah, again, it's a pleasure seeing you," Lucas said. "I'll call Jill this afternoon. You can expect to hear from her very soon. I wish you the best and that everything is quickly taken care of. No person, man or woman, should be treated the way you have been."

"Thank you. I really do appreciate your time and the referral." He was a nice man, nicer than I'd thought from the few brief meetings at parties. There he had been the consummate politician with a beautiful woman on his arm, leaving me with the impression that he was a carbon copy of most of the men I came in contact with. Good-looking, entitled, and a player.

It made me wonder what impression I left on the people I met who didn't know me. If I had to guess, I'd say beautiful but aloof and unfriendly, probably not a person they cared to get to know unless there was something in it for them. In the world I lived in, that last one was the rule most of the people I met lived by.

So why was I determined to go back?

"You okay?" Autumn asked as we drove back to her house.

"Yeah. No. I don't know." What a hot mess I was. If my friends shipped me right back to New York, I wouldn't blame them.

"Ah, hon, everything's going to be okay."

I wasn't so sure of that, but I hoped she was right. "If not, it won't be from lack of trying from all of you. You can't know how much I appreciate everything y'all are doing. Honestly, I don't know why you're even bothering. I haven't been much of a friend since leaving here."

She scowled at me. "Stop that right now. We've been friends, all of us, for what seems like forever. It's what we'd do for any of us." She sighed as if exasperated with me. "I get that you're feeling sorry for yourself right now. I would be, too. But Savannah, so many things were out of your control. You never really had a chance to be your own person, not from the day you were born."

That was sadly too true, but somehow I should have found the strength to stand up for myself, first with my mother and then with Jackson. "Well, thank you anyway."

"You're welcome anyway. Why don't we call Jenn, see if she wants to come over for lunch? She can stop at Mary's and pick us up some sandwiches."

"Sounds like a plan."

Jenn was free for lunch and arrived around noon with a big bag from Mary's Bread Company. I'd asked for a vegetarian sandwich on rye, but when I peeked inside, I found a few slices of turkey.

Jenn slapped my hand when I started to pull them off. "Mary said you'd do that. She also said I had to spank your hand and tell you to just eat the damn thing. You're lucky she didn't pile a load of Black Forest ham and cheese on it like she wanted to."

"Fine, I'll eat it." Or half of it. "I can't believe you're going to be a mommy," I said to Jenn to get the attention off me.

"He's going to look just like his daddy." Jenn's dreamy smile was the sweetest thing. "Imagine a little Dylan running around."

"You're having a boy?" Autumn asked.

"Well, Dylan's positive the baby's a girl, but he's wrong. It's a boy." She patted her tummy.

That glow on my friend's face was beautiful. Would I ever have a baby, a family? I'd never told anyone this, not even my friends, but I'd never seen children in my future. Even as a teenager I'd understood that my life was screwed up, that my mother had messed with my head to the point that I couldn't take care of myself. It would be irresponsible of me to bring a child into my life. That didn't used to bother me, probably because I'd been too numb to care, but I'd begun my transformation and merely existing from one day to the next no longer worked. I had possibilities, choices that were mine alone to make. That didn't mean I planned to run out and have a bucketload of babies, but I let the idea of it happening someday creep into my mind.

Autumn kicked my foot. "Stop looking so serious. This is supposed to be fun girl time." She turned her attention to Jenn, and from the glint in Autumn's eyes I braced for whatever was about to come out of her mouth. "Did

Savannah tell you that Adam kissed her?"

"Autumn," I groaned.

"Well, he did, and since when do we have any secrets from Jenn? Since never, that's when."

"Whoa!" Jenn set down her sandwich. "Details."

"That's all there is to it. He kissed me. End of story."

Jenn rolled her eyes. "When? Where? What happened afterward?"

It was useless to refuse to answer. She'd just sit there and stare at me until I confessed all my secrets. "The when was he dropped me off back here after I made soup for him. The—"

"You made soup for him?"

"She did," Autumn chimed in. "He had a cold, and she insisted on taking care of him."

"Stop looking at me like that," I told Jenn when she smirked, as if making soup meant I still had a thing for Adam. So what if I did? Nothing could come of it. "It was just soup, not my undying devotion carved in stone."

Autumn snorted.

"Both of you, it was just dang soup!"

"Seriously, Savannah, you still say 'dang' for"—Autumn made air quotes—"'fucking'?"

My cheeks heated. "No, I just say 'dang' for 'dang.'" When we turned sixteen, Autumn had decided we were old enough to say *fuck*. For a time, every other word out of her mouth was that one. Jenn would say it a little, but I couldn't say it at all, so I told them whenever I said *dang* that I was really saying the word I couldn't say. It stuck with me, and what Jackson didn't know was that whenever I said *dang* to him, in my mind I was telling him to eff off. It didn't matter that I was the only one who knew that; it made me happy to dang him to hell.

Jenn laughed. "You so do still do it. But back to the kissing. What did he say after he kissed you?"

"Nothing. He got mad."

"At you?" she said.

"Maybe a little at me, but mostly at himself I think. I don't know why he kissed me."

"Did you want him to kiss you?"

I hated how soft Jenn's voice was, asking that question, as if she felt sorry for me. "No." At both their looks of disbelief, I shrugged. "Yes, but no because now I can't stop thinking about it. Adam was a great kisser when we were together, but now… just wow. He's obviously had a lot of practice since then." And knowing that hurt. It shouldn't. It wasn't like he was cheating on me. I had my life. He had his.

"Funny how both of you are clamming up now. Adam's a hot guy. You're not going to tell me anything I don't know by admitting that he has women in his life." I shook my head. "You know what, you're right. I really don't want to know."

"What about you?" Jenn asked. "Other than Jackson?"

"There hasn't been anyone else, and it wasn't like I ever wanted Jackson in my bed. That was all his and my mother's doing." It wasn't until I looked down at my empty plate that I realized I'd eaten the whole sandwich while we were talking. No supper for me tonight. "Enough about me." I wadded up my sandwich wrapping.

At hearing the rustle of paper, Beau rose from his bed in the corner and came and sat at my feet, his big brown doggy eyes resting hopefully on me. "Sorry, Beau boy, I didn't save you anything."

Autumn went to the counter and reached into a canister, then came back to the table. "Give him these."

I took the doggie treats from her. "Lookie here. I do have something for you." His ears perked up, and his tail swept the floor.

"You'll have to come over to my house and meet Daisy, his mother," Jenn said. "Plus, you need to see the log cabin Adam and Connor built for us. It's awesome."

That led to the story of how Dylan had found Daisy living on the streets and half-starved. Another hour passed before Jenn had to leave to get ready to go to work. She was the manager at Vincennes, the best restaurant in town.

After she left, Autumn and I walked across the bridge to Adam's house so she could show me the alarm code.

"Have fun playing with the monster," she said as she was leaving. "Call me when you're ready to come back."

"I can walk back over by myself."

"Not with Jackson on the loose. I mean it, Savannah. Call me."

Right. Jackson. I kept trying to forget about him.

CHAPTER SIXTEEN

~ Adam ~

THE MEETING WITH LUCAS BLANTON had gone great. He loved the plans for his log cabin, and he'd narrowed down his choice to two properties for his dinner theater. Both were on the main road through town, one at each end. Connor and I had taken him up to the land he'd purchased so he could see where the cabin would be situated. He'd chosen a site at the top of one of our mountains, and the view was spectacular. On a clear day he'd be able to see Asheville.

Now we stood on the possible dinner theater property at the south end of town after spending some time studying the one at the north end. "This one has more drive-by traffic," Connor said.

I built the homes, Connor sold them and the properties, so I kept quiet and let him do his thing. Any questions on the building itself would be mine to answer. While Connor and Lucas talked pros and cons of the two choices, I walked to the street, then turned and studied the space. This would be my first commercial job, and I was looking forward to the challenge but also a little nervous.

As I mentally mapped out where the building would sit, the traffic flow, and the parking, the pulsing wail of a siren sounded behind me. Glancing over my shoulder, I saw a police cruiser pull up behind a car. At seeing who was behind the wheel of the car, I grinned. Tommy Evans, the same cop who had given Jackson Marks a warning for going a few miles over the speed limit, walked up to the driver's side window.

I couldn't hear what Tommy said, but Marks yelled, "This is bullshit," so loud in response that every word was clear. Before Marks saw me and went even more ballistic, I walked back to Connor and Lucas.

"Someone's not happy," I said.

Connor squinted at the car, then laughed when he saw who was in it. "What'd Tommy stop him for?"

"Tommy gave him a warning yesterday for going too fast. Today he gets a ticket for going too slow."

"No joke, that's hilarious," Connor said, a big grin that matched mine on his face.

Lucas eyed the traffic stop happening in front of us. "Who's that?"

"Jackson Marks, the man Savannah told you about this morning." I was curious how Lucas would react.

He snorted. "That's priceless."

"It's about to get even better," I said at seeing Hamburger's ancient pickup truck roll to a stop in front of Marks's car, effectively blocking him in. "Watch."

Hamburger climbed out of his truck, fiddle in hand. He put it up to his chin as he ambled toward where Tommy stood, talking to Marks. By the time he reached them, his bow was dancing across the strings as he lit into a bluegrass song. Next to me, a low laugh began from Lucas, then swelled to full-blown hilarity when Marks screamed like a banshee, "Get that crazy man away from me."

And Tommy? He set his ticket book on top of the car, then began clapping to the beat of the music. Hamburger bounced on shuffling feet as his bow picked up speed. Marks banged his fists on his steering wheel. Even from where we stood, it was obvious the man was about to blow.

"We might want to be ready to step in if things get out of hand," I said.

We took a few steps closer. Hamburger finished his song, Tommy picked up his ticket book and started writing as if nothing strange had happened, and Marks had apparently reached his limit. He pushed his car door open, hitting Tommy in the hip.

"Sir, close the door and remain in the car," Tommy warned.

"Assaulting ah officer of tha law," Hamburger bellowed. "That's jail time. Ya ain't gonna like the pillers."

"What's a piller?" Lucas asked.

"Pillow. Hamburger doesn't like the jailhouse pillows."

"I assume he's had the opportunity to test them first-hand?"

Connor laughed. "Many times."

"Uh-oh," I said at seeing Gloria Davenport's car coming to a stop behind Tommy's cruiser. Gloria was the roving reporter for *The Valley News*, and she could smell a juicy story from the next county.

When Marks ignored Tommy's warning and exited his car, I said, "Senator, the woman with the camera is our local reporter. It might be best if you took yourself off before you find yourself on the front page of our town's newspaper."

"More like gossip rag," Connor said.

Lucas shifted, putting his back to Gloria. "As much as I hate missing the show, that's probably a good idea. I'm leaning toward this property, but let me think about it overnight. I'll call tomorrow and confirm which one."

After Lucas left, I turned my attention back to the scene playing out with Marks.

"Get her out of my face!" Marks screamed when Gloria lifted her camera to her eye.

"This is public property, sir. I have a right to be here." Gloria kept on taking pictures.

"Take my picture, Miz Gloria." Hamburger grinned for the camera as he played his fiddle.

Connor and I looked at each other, then burst out laughing. "We'll have to make sure those photos get leaked to the New York papers."

"Great idea."

"We should probably go back up Tommy." As much as I was enjoying this, it was about to get out of hand. Marks was furious enough to hurt someone. As we headed that way, Dylan arrived, parking his Mustang in front of Hamburger's truck.

"Calvary's here," I said. We came to a stop at the hood of Hamburger's truck, close enough to step in if help was needed, but with Dylan's arrival, hopefully it wouldn't be necessary. I took out my phone and started the video. Savannah was going to love seeing this.

"What's the problem here?" Dylan asked, putting himself between Tommy and Marks.

When Gloria went in for a close-up, Marks slapped the camera out of her hands, knocking her into Hamburger. "Get that goddamn thing out of my face!"

In the blink of an eye Dylan had Marks's arm behind his back and bent over the hood of Tommy's cruiser.

"Wow," Connor said. "Didn't know he had those kind of moves in him."

"Guess you have to learn stuff like that when you're a big city cop." Dylan had been a cop in Chicago before coming to Blue Ridge Valley, and we were damn lucky to have him.

"As a member of the free press, I have a right to be here," Gloria yelled at Marks. She snatched her camera from the road. "You better hope you didn't damage it, sir." Up went her camera again as she clicked away.

"What's his name?" Dylan asked Tommy as if he didn't already know.

"My name? My goddamn name? I met you at your wedding, dumbass."

"Where you there? Don't remember you at all." When Marks struggled to get out of Dylan's hold, Dylan held out his hand. "Give me your handcuffs, Tommy."

Connor snorted. "Oh boy. Look at Hamburger. I think

he's about to crash his fiddle over Marks's head."

It was true, Hamburger was holding his fiddle in the air and dancing on his feet like a boxer. He might not like the jailhouse *pillers*, but he loved Dylan Conrad.

"Ya cain't be calling our chief naughty names," Hamburger said. "He cain't do that, right, Chief?"

"If nothing else, it's not a neighborly thing to do, Hamburger. What'd you stop him for?" Dylan asked Tommy.

"He was going too slow."

Dylan darted a glance at Connor and me, an amused smile playing on his lips. "Mr. Marks," he said, turning his attention back to the man. "Traveling too slow is a safety hazard. It forces cars to try to pass you, and in these mountains that creates a dangerous situation."

I chuckled. The road through town was as flat as an Iowa cornfield, and you could see traffic coming at you from one end of town to the other.

Marks looked pissed enough to chew off the head of a nail. "I don't know what kind of idiotic game you country bumpkins are playing, but you'll be hearing from my lawyer for false arrest."

"Who said you've been arrested?" Dylan looked at Tommy. "Did you put him under arrest?"

"No, Chief. I was just trying to write him a ticket."

"These handcuffs say I've been arrested." Marks turned his back so everyone could see the offending cuffs.

Dylan sighed as if his patience was being tested. "No, sir. I only put them on you because you were threatening the good residents of Blue Ridge Valley. At no time did anyone say you were under arrest. If you think you can behave yourself, I'll remove them."

After Marks had his hands free, he put them on his waist and sneered at Dylan. "You haven't heard the last of this."

"Mr. Marks, you don't seem to much like our town. I'm not sure why since it's such a charming place, but perhaps you'd be happier going back to where you came from."

"You tell me where Savannah is, and believe me, I'll be gone so fast you won't remember I was here."

"If Savannah wants to see you, I'm sure she knows how to get in touch with you. A little warning, though. The next time you threaten one of my officers or one of our residents, you will be under arrest, and that's not an idle threat. Good day, Mr. Marks."

"Since ya ain't under arrest, can we talk 'bout my Hollywood movie now?" Hamburger said as he brought his fiddle up to his chin.

Marks turned red in the face but managed to keep his mouth shut as he slung his body back into his rental car and slammed the door.

"Most fun I've had all week," Connor said.

"It sure was, and I got it all on video. Let's get out of here before Marks sees us. That would probably send him over the edge." The man had been so focused on the group around him that he hadn't noticed us. We slipped away, and I headed home, wondering if Savannah had come over to play with Jinx.

She had come over, and she was still here. I leaned against the wall and studied the woman curled up asleep on my sofa. Jinx was snuggled up to her breast, a place I wouldn't mind being. I shook my head to clear it of that errant thought. She looked peaceful in sleep, the worry and uncertainty that existed now in her eyes hidden by her closed lids. She looked more like the Savannah I had loved.

After pulling off my work boots, I walked on silent feet to her and eased down on the coffee table. Jinx blinked his eyes open, looked at me, yawned, and then tucked his nose under his tail. If Savannah told me today that she still loved me, that she wanted to stay in the valley, what would I do? In the nine years she'd been gone, I had done my best to get over her. And as much as I wanted to, I always knew I never had.

Unable to resist touching her, I brushed her hair away from her face. There had been many times that I had tangled my fingers in those long black strands, marveling at how silky soft they were. My gaze fell to her lips. How many times had I kissed that mouth? However many, it had never been enough. I brushed my thumb over her bottom lip, getting a soft sigh in response.

Did her subconscious remember my touch? She claimed that she didn't like Jackson Marks, that she never had. If true, and I had no reason to doubt her, then she wasn't sighing for him. But what did it matter? Our time had come and gone, and the blame for that was mine.

"I'm sorry, Savannah," I whispered, tracing her lip again.

CHAPTER SEVENTEEN

~ Savannah ~

ADAM WAS KISSING ME. I was dreaming, and I knew I was because it was Adam the boy kissing me, promising that he would always love me. Even though he was the Adam from my past, I was today's Savannah. Older. Wiser.

"You won't always love me," I told my dream Adam.

He brushed his thumb over my lips. "I'm sorry, Savannah," he whispered, then vanished. I wanted to beg him to come back, to keep his promises, to save me from the darkness engulfing me in this dream world. There were monsters at the edges of the dark, their greedy eyes watching me, waiting for me to surrender to their will. Their faces took form, their features materializing into those of my mother and Jackson.

"Please, no," I begged, recoiling from their outstretched hands. "Adam, I need you," I whispered, but he'd abandoned me.

"Savannah, wake up. Sweetheart, you're dreaming."

Adam's voice penetrated the darkness, and I reached for it, wanted the light he would give me if I could only find him. Jackson grabbed me with one hand and held up a fistful of carrots in the other one.

"Eat them," he ordered. The carrots wiggled, coming alive. Orange worms stretching their thin bodies toward me.

"No," I screamed.

"Savvy, wake up!"

My eyes shot open, my heart pounding so hard that I

gasped for breath. "Adam?" He was perched on the edge of the sofa, leaning over me, his eyes full of concern. "You called me Savvy." I'd forgotten he used to call me that. No one but Adam ever had and only when we were making love. He'd always rasp *Savvy* into my ear as he came, filling me with his love.

He smiled as if remembering. "Yeah, I guess I did. You were having a nightmare."

"It was awful."

"Do you want to tell me about it?"

"No." I wanted to forget it. "I guess I should head back over to Autumn's now that you're home." I sat up, dislodging Jinx. He gave me an annoyed meow, then jumped down and headed for the kitchen.

"You don't have to run away just because I'm here. Would you like to sit on the back deck and have a glass of wine with me?"

"Seriously? It's freezing." Anyway, it probably wasn't a good idea to spend any more time with him than was necessary. Being around Adam hurt.

"I have a fire pit and there's no wind today. It'll be warm enough."

Before I could decide, my phone rang. Adam moved off the sofa, picked up my purse from the coffee table, and handed it to me. I fished my phone out.

"I don't recognize the number," I said.

"Why don't I answer just in case Marks is using a different phone?"

"Okay." I handed to him.

After answering, he listened for a moment, then handed it back to me. "It's Jill Thornwood, the attorney that Lucas Blanton recommended."

"This is Savannah."

"Hello, Savannah. This is Jill Thornwood. Lucas Blanton said that you could use my help."

"Did he explain why?"

"He gave me a brief summary. It just so happens that I'll be in Asheville next Monday. Will you be available to meet with me?"

"Yes." I wanted to ask if she was going to require a retainer, but I was embarrassed to admit I had no access to any money. I decided I'd cross that bridge when I came to it.

"Good. In the meantime e-mail me your full name, address, bank balance and account numbers, and anything else you think is relevant. Once I have that, I'm going to begin the process of getting a court order to freeze your accounts so that your manager can't access your money. I'll text you my e-mail address."

That was going to make Jackson angry, but I didn't care. "Okay." We made arrangements on the time and location where I'd meet her.

After I disconnected, Adam said, "Well?"

"And so it begins. I'm meeting with her Monday morning at nine. She's taking a deposition later in the day at the law firm of Reynolds and Beckerman in Asheville, and I'm to meet her there."

"I'll take you," Adam said as he walked to the kitchen.

"No. I've imposed enough on you. This is my problem to take care of." Hadn't I promised myself that I was going to take control of my life? Adam didn't answer, which meant he was going to argue with me on this. He came back with a glass of wine in one hand, a beer in the other, and Jinx riding on his shoulder.

"Do you know how many calories are in a glass of wine?" I asked, taking it from him.

"Nope, and don't want to know." He settled on the sofa, propped his sock-clad feet on the coffee table, and gave me a lazy perusal. "Besides, you can stand to gain a few pounds."

"No, I can't." I took a small sip of the wine, then set the glass on the table. "Adam, I appreciate everything you've done for me. I do. But I can't keep depending on you."

"Why did you call me? When you walked away from your home, from your life, you called me. Why?"

"And your point is?"

He pulled Jinx off his shoulder, dropped the cat onto the floor, and then leaned toward me. "You called me because you knew you could trust me, that no matter what has happened between us, I would be there for you. Well, I'm a part of this now until you're safely ensconced back in your home with Jackson Marks out of your life."

"I can't keep asking my friends to take care of me. It's time for me to learn how to take care of myself." He was too close. I could smell his woodsy scent and feel his heat. *What would it hurt to have one last time with him?* my body asked, remembering how it felt to be held by Adam. He must have seen something in my eyes, something too telling, because his flared and darkened. He let out a breath.

"Savvy," he murmured.

"I-I have to go." Before I made the mistake of throwing myself at him.

He put his hand on my knee, keeping me in place. "No, don't. Stay and have dinner with me. Please."

"Why? What do you want from me?"

"Damn if I know." He sighed. "Maybe we have unfinished business."

He'd finished any business between us when he'd broken up with me, but what good would it do to drag up old history? "The attorney's waiting for me to send her some information. I really need to go do that."

"Use my office and computer." Jinx jumped back onto Adam's lap, and he trailed a finger down the cat's back, getting a drawn-out meow. "Besides, the monster's ready for playtime again, and he just told me he wants you to stay."

"Ah, I was wondering what he said."

"Go on. Get what you need to send her done. I'll make us some dinner."

Against my better judgment, I nodded. "Okay. But I really don't need dinner. If you have some fruit, that'll do."

"That won't be enough for me, though." He stood—dislodging Jinx—and held out his hand. "Come on, I'll show you my office."

I put mine in his and let him pull me up. The information I needed for the attorney was in my wallet, and I grabbed my purse from the coffee table. It wasn't until we reached his office that I realized we were still holding hands. When he was my boyfriend, the first thing he'd do when coming up next to me was take my hand. Adam was a toucher, and for me, a girl starved for affection, I had been a sponge, soaking up his attention.

My hand felt so right in his, as if the nine years separating us had melted away. That was so not good. I'd be leaving in a week or two. Even knowing that, the idea of one night with him refused to leave my head. I had stored up memories of the boy. I wanted a memory of the man to take back with me.

How did one go about seducing a man? I was a famous model. I hobnobbed with the rich and famous. People would be surprised if they knew I was clueless where men were concerned. Partly because I was shy but mostly because my mother and Jackson had isolated me. I was sorely lacking in social skills, but the more time I spent with Adam, the more I felt like I was coming back to the girl he'd once loved. And he had kissed me, so maybe I could entice him to do it again. One kiss could lead to another and that could lead to...

"Take your time," Adam said, interrupting my thoughts. "I'm going to jump in the shower, then whip us up some dinner."

"Ah, okay. This won't take long." I slid onto the chair at his computer, hoping the heat burning my cheeks hadn't turned them pink and he wouldn't ask why I was blushing. "Oh, I should call Autumn and let her know I'm staying here for a little while."

"I'll do it."

"Thanks." I peered up at him and smiled. His gaze fell to my lips and lingered there. Deep in my body was an awakening. An ache between my legs began with one soft throb followed by more insistent ones. The only man who'd ever had that effect on me was Adam, and it had been so long since I'd felt this kind of want.

"Savvy," he murmured, his eyes lifting to mine. Then he blinked, the heat in his eyes fading away. "Shower. Now." As he walked away, I thought I heard him mutter, "A cold one."

Maybe it wouldn't be so hard to seduce him, but did I really want to? A part of me did, wanted that memory. The part that was responsible for protecting my heart said it was a bad idea. But I was coming alive again, and wasn't that a good thing? I wanted to feel Adam's hands on me, his mouth and body on mine. There was no other man I wanted to touch me, and I didn't see that ever changing.

Was he in the shower right now, his body wet and glistening? We'd taken a shower together once when his parents had been at a party and Connor out on a date. Adam had washed my hair and body, and I'd washed him. Then we had made love with the water raining down on us, and it was one of my favorite memories of my time with him.

What would he do if I joined him now? The idea fled as soon as it entered my mind. I didn't have the nerve to do something like that. If he rejected me, I would be humiliated.

Jinx jumped onto my lap and then onto the desk. After a thorough examination of every object, he batted a pen to the floor, watching in fascination as it fell. Apparently liking this new game, he moved on to a wire cup filled with paper clips, knocking it to the floor.

"Your daddy's not going to be happy with you," I told him but didn't try to stop him. He was having too much fun.

After my mother had died and I'd found out that Jackson's name was on my bank account but not mine, I'd written down the account number. At least it was only my name on my apartment, but how hard was it to evict someone? Hopefully Lucas was right and the attorney he'd recommended was a shark. I sent her an e-mail detailing everything I thought she should know, including a summary of how Jackson—thanks to my mother—had ended up in control of my money.

That done, I picked up the things Jinx had knocked to the floor, then scooped him up and headed downstairs. As I passed Adam's bedroom, I heard his voice and glanced in the open doorway. I came to a complete stop.

Lord help me. He was on the phone, his back to me as he stood looking out the window, his hair wet from his shower, and a white towel tucked in at his waist. Although he'd had a nice body, the boy I'd known intimately had been leaner and much less muscled. The man, though, was like something out of a fitness magazine. Broad shoulders, a tapered waist and lean hips leading down to long legs. His was a body honed by honest work, his muscles defined but not those of a gym rat. I swallowed hard.

I spent my days around people considered beautiful, including men, and maybe I was prejudiced but I didn't think I'd ever seen anyone as gorgeous as Adam. Nine years and he could still make my heart pound in my chest.

Jinx let out a growl, not wanting to be held anymore, and I lowered him to the floor. Adam turned at hearing him, and although he still spoke to whoever was on the phone—something about kitchen cabinets—his eyes locked on mine. I couldn't move, almost couldn't breathe. It was as if he held me in some kind of magical beam as he talked while watching me.

Adam ended his call and set his phone on his dresser. Still with eyes on me, he said, "Stop looking at me like that,

Savannah."

"Like what?" I whispered. But I knew what he saw on my face. A woman who wanted him. I always had, and I thought I probably always would. The heat in his eyes was proof that he wanted me, too.

"Like the way you used to." He closed the distance between us, stopping a few feet from me.

"How can you remember that after nine years?"

CHAPTER EIGHTEEN

~ Adam ~

"I REMEMBER EVERYTHING." HOW SOFT AND silky her hair was when I'd rake my fingers through it while I plundered her mouth, how perfectly her breasts fit in my hands, and how she would cry out my name when I made her come. Standing here, looking into those gray eyes, all I wanted to do was strip her naked and lose myself in her body the way I used to. I wanted to make her mine again. Instead I turned my back on her before I did something stupid like kiss her again.

"Adam?"

"Go on downstairs. I'll be there in a minute." That soft voice saying my name with a question mark at the end was going to be my undoing if she didn't leave. The towel I had wrapped around me wasn't doing much to hide the effect she was having on me.

"Adam," she said again as I listened to the sound of her approaching footsteps.

I squeezed my eyes shut when she put her hand on my arm. "If you don't leave my bedroom, Savannah, I'm going to have my mouth on yours in about two seconds."

"What if that's what I want?"

Damn her. I spun and proved that I meant what I'd said. She wrapped her hands around my neck, and I lost myself in her taste, in the feel of her pressed against me. When she tried to crawl up my body, I slipped my arms under her knees, then backed her up against the wall.

"Tell me to stop," I said with my lips still on hers.

She pulled away and looked straight into my eyes. "I

can't. I haven't been touched by someone who truly cares since you, Adam. I need this. I need you."

"Then you have me." Even though it was going to kill me all over again when she left. I buried my face against her neck and put my tongue on her skin where I could feel the rapid beat of her pulse. Knowing her heart pounded for me tore down the last of my resistance. I had never been able to deny this girl anything, and it seemed that still held true.

When I scraped my teeth down her neck, she moaned and tightened her legs around my waist. I turned with her in my arms to take her to my bed. The lights from a car turning into my driveway lit up my window.

"Someone's here." Connor or Autumn would have called before coming over, and people in these parts tended not to drop by unannounced around suppertime. I dropped Savannah's legs, letting her feet slide to the floor. "Stay upstairs until I find out who it is." Grabbing the T-shirt and sweatpants that I'd tossed on my bed to put on after my shower, I headed downstairs, dressing as I went.

A look though my door's peephole confirmed the bad feeling I had as to who was on the other side. It was inevitable that Jackson Marks would find his way to my house. I just wished it had been when Savannah wasn't here. Hopefully she would obey and stay out of sight. Since I wouldn't put it past him to nose around if I didn't make an appearance, I flipped on the porch light as I opened the door.

"You lost?"

"Where is she?"

"Who?"

"Don't fuck with me, Hunter. I want to know where she is."

"If you mean Savannah, she's not here, nor did she choose to tell me where she's staying." She had said she was going to have to face him eventually, and although I wished I'd thought to discuss this with her first, I decided to arrange for when that would happen.

"She did tell me if I saw you to give you a message. She'll meet you at the park on the south side of town Tuesday morning at ten." That would give her a chance to talk to her attorney before seeing him.

"And I'm supposed to hang around this hick town until then?"

I shrugged. "Your itinerary's not my problem." I shut the door in his face. The dude was beginning to look haggard, a fact that pleased me. Every time I'd seen him before tonight, he came across as conceited, a man who prided himself on the price and cut of his clothes and his five-hundred-dollar haircut. Tonight his shirt was wrinkled, his hair was messy, as if he'd constantly combed his fingers through it in frustration, and his eyes had a wild light to them.

As much as I liked seeing him falling apart, that only made him more dangerous. Definitely a concern. He yelled a few choice words before stomping back to his car. After watching out the window to make sure he left, I headed upstairs. Would he stick around until Tuesday? My guess, he'd still look for her. He wouldn't leave until he found her, which gave me an idea that would serve two purposes. Making a detour, I went to my office and made two calls, one to a pilot friend and one to my brother.

"Is he gone?" Savannah asked as soon as I walked into my bedroom after finishing my calls.

"For now." Obviously she'd come far enough down the stairs to hear it was Marks at the door. "Change of plans, though. We're going to New York tonight."

"Huh?" She plopped down on the edge of my bed, the one I'd been within seconds of having her naked on. A shame that had been interrupted, but maybe it was for the best.

"You want him out of your apartment, right?" My gaze slid to the bed. Or I could forget my idea and go with my original plan.

"More than anything."

"So we go to New York. I change the locks on your doors while you tell your doorman… Do you have a doorman?" At her nod, I said, "You tell him and management that Jackson Marks doesn't live there anymore. Then we pack up all his stuff and leave it somewhere for him to pick up." I raised a brow when she stared at me as if I'd lost his mind.

"We can't just take off like that."

"Yes, we can. It's all arranged. A friend is flying us to New York. We'll be there and back before your Monday meeting with the attorney."

Connor had thought I was crazy, too, when I'd told him my plans, but he'd finally agreed to keep an eye on Marks for the next few days. He would also see that Mary, Hamburger, and the rest continued their shenanigans with Marks.

When she stayed silent, I walked to her, stopping in front of her. "You said you wanted to take control of your life. In order to do that, you have to get Jackson Marks out of your life and especially out of your apartment. It will be just that much harder if you wait until he's back and encamped there. When you stepped off the plane, you had the saddest eyes I've ever seen, but being back home and with those who love you, I've seen glimpses of the girl I used to know." I put my hand on her chest, over her heart. "Somewhere Savannah is still in there. You just have to find her again."

"I'm still Savannah," she whispered. "Sometimes I forget, but no more," she said, her voice growing stronger with each word.

"No more," I agreed. "Let's do this." Surprising me, she surged up and into my arms.

"Yes, let's." She buried her face against my neck. "Thank you, Adam. Thank you so much."

Eff me. I had an armful of woman wrapped around me, one I'd once loved enough to set free to follow her dream. Having her back home—much less wrapped around me like my favorite blanket—was messing with my head. And other parts of me. I gently—and reluctantly— pushed her away.

"I need to pack a few things, then take you over to Connor's so you can, too."

Her bottom lip disappeared as she sucked it into her mouth.

"What?" I hoped she wasn't changing her mind.

"I didn't decorate my apartment."

"Okay." Why that mattered, who knew? But I was willing to say whatever necessary to get her on the plane.

"Welcome home, Miss Savannah," her doorman said, his curious gaze on me, then on the overnight bag I carried.

"Thank you, Frank." She headed straight for the elevator. "Can't say it's good to be home, though," she said after we were out of earshot of the doorman.

"Do you not like New York?"

She gave an exaggerated shiver. "Not in the winter. Too dang cold."

As we rode up, she tapped her fingers against her leg and kept her eyes glued to the door. It was more than the cold that had her on edge. I put my hand on her shoulder. "Hey, everything's going to be all right."

"Nothing's right anymore."

I didn't know what to say to that. She'd slept on the plane, and I'd wondered if she had so we didn't have to talk. When we came to the door of her apartment, she paused, stared at it, then let out a breath.

"I didn't decorate it."

"Yeah, you told me that." What in the world was on the other side of that door? Maybe it hadn't been such a good idea to bring her here. She'd shut down the moment we'd headed to the airport.

"It's not so bad," I said when I saw her living room. Actually it was. The floor was glossy black marble, there was a humongous white leather sofa, and two black leather ultra-modern chairs that couldn't possibly be comfortable. Red velvet drapes framed tall windows, and the artworks on the walls looked like something Andy Warhol would have painted. The coffee table and end tables were chrome and glass.

She shuddered. "I hate it. Jackson redecorated after he moved in. You haven't seen the worst of it yet."

I followed her down the hallway and into what I assumed was their bedroom. If I didn't know better, I would have thought we'd just walked into a high-class whorehouse. A round bed sat in the middle of the room. The sheets were black satin, the bedspread bloodred, and the walls were painted a stark white except for an accent wall that matched the color of the spread. Heavy black curtains framed these windows. A large painting of a nude woman covered one wall. I was happy to see that it wasn't one of Savannah.

"Good God," I finally said.

"I know, right?" She giggled, slapped her hand over her mouth, and then peered up at me with tears in her eyes. "How did my life get to this?"

Because I'd let her mother convince me that freeing Savannah to follow her dream was the right thing to do. I thought... No, I didn't think it. I was pretty sure I'd made the worst mistake of my life by listening to Regina Graham. This room, hell, this entire apartment was as far from the Savannah I knew as the earth was from the sun, and I'd condemned her to this? To someone like Jackson Marks?

The way she looked at me with that sadness in her eyes was my undoing. "Come here, Savvy." I held out my arms.

She walked into my embrace without hesitation. "I'm

scared," she whispered against my chest.

"We'll get him out of your life." I squeezed my eyes shut, liking too much how holding her felt right. Her scent, her body, everything about her was familiar yet not. The press of her face on my chest eased, and I opened my eyes to see her looking up at me.

My gaze fell to her lips, ones I must have kissed a thousand times. *Make that a thousand and one times*, I thought as my mouth covered hers. Often during the past years I'd convinced myself—or tried to—that I'd gotten Savannah Graham out of my blood. But with my lips molded to hers, I knew I'd only been lying to myself.

CHAPTER NINETEEN

~ Savannah ~

"NOT IN HERE." EVEN THOUGH I wanted Adam to kiss me more than anything, I didn't want it to happen in this room. I might sleep in here, but this was Jackson's space, and it was just plain ridiculous.

Adam pulled away and rested his forehead against mine. "I've never been able to think straight around you." He took my hand and pulled me out of the room. "We have a busy day tomorrow and should get some rest."

"Yeah, it's late. You can sleep in the guest room."

He glanced into the bedroom, and his nose wrinkled in distaste. "Are you sleeping in there?"

"No." Other than to get some clothes, I didn't plan to spend any time in there until I could toss out the bed and get a new one. "I'm good on the sofa."

We argued over who was going to take the couch for a few minutes, but I held my ground. After making a bed for myself, I settled in, thinking that as tired as I was, I'd fall right to sleep. Wrong. Adam was the blame for that… or more directly, that he'd kissed me again. Why, though? Did he still have feelings for me or was it simply a matter of lingering chemistry between us? Did he still love me the way I still loved him?

Probably not, but that didn't stop me from slipping into bed with him in the early hours of the morning when I couldn't fall asleep. I decided I was justified in doing that since it was his fault I was still awake. I inched my way across the bed until I was touching his arm. Within minutes my eyelids grew heavy.

"Savvy?"

"Mmm?" I opened my eyes to see Adam peering at me.

"Why are you in bed with me?"

"I couldn't sleep." There wasn't a window in this room, but from the light coming in through the open door, I could tell it was morning. "What time is it?"

"It's early. Come here." He pulled me to him, spooning me. "Go back to sleep."

"'Kay." But I couldn't, not with his body wrapped around mine and his face buried in my hair. I wanted to stay cocooned by him, though, so I pretended to sleep while soaking up everything about this moment—his body heat, his scent, his skin on mine. His breaths evened out, and when I was sure he was asleep again, I pulled his hand against my chest, linked our fingers, and pushed back so that every part of me was touching him. He gave a sigh of what sounded like contentment that brought tears to my eyes.

Our chance had passed. I knew that, but I would selfishly horde these special moments until it was time to leave him again. Apparently I did go to sleep because when I woke up, Adam was on his back and I was sprawled over him with one of my legs captured by his. Because we'd been in high school when we were together, I'd never woken up with him in the morning. He looked so peaceful asleep, more like the boy I'd loved.

Unable to resist, I touched his bottom lip with a finger, smiling when his lips twitched. Before he opened his eyes and found me covering him like a blanket, I started to ease away.

The arm he had around my back tightened. "Going somewhere?"

"I guess we should get up."

"Is that what you really want to do? I'm asking because you were molesting my mouth a few seconds ago. Thought maybe you had something else on your mind."

"No," I whispered. "It's not what I want." I'd almost denied it, but this was supposed to be the new me, and that included going after what I wanted.

He flipped me over, and with his chest over mine, he looked down at me. "Tell me what you want, Savannah."

"This off." I tugged at the T-shirt he'd worn to bed.

I'd only been with two men, Adam and Jackson. With Adam, intimacy had been a beautiful thing. The boy who had loved me had made love to me as if I were his treasure. Jackson in bed had been all about power and control. It had been ugly and humiliating. I wanted Adam to wipe those memories away. I wanted to be treasured again.

"This won't mean anything. Are you sure you're good with that?"

No, I wasn't. I wanted it to mean everything, and his words sent an ache to my heart. But he was right. We weren't Adam and Savannah anymore. We were only two consenting adults who would share some time together before we each went back to our lives.

I put my finger on his lips. "Shhh. Make love to me, Adam. That's all I'm asking for."

His eyes turned soft as he lowered his mouth to mine. His lips brushed over mine, teasing at first, then growing hungrier. The kiss grew deeper, more passionate, the soft caresses firmer and more demanding. It felt as if sparks flew around us, electrifying the air. He slid his hands to my back, slipping under the camisole I'd worn to bed. His fingers trailed up and down my spine, causing me to shiver as pleasure followed the path of his hands. When his tongue probed the seam of my lips, I opened for him. I would always open for this man.

While his tongue explored my mouth, I was busy exploring his body. The new muscles he'd acquired since we were together—the ones I'd been dying to touch—were firm and rock-hard against my fingertips. Heat poured from him, warming me. I had the stray thought that if Adam was always next to me, I'd never be cold again.

"Are you sure you want this?" he said again.

I liked that he asked, and I knew if I said no, that he would stop. "I'm sure. Are you?"

"God, yes."

There was so much emotion in those two words, as if this meant more to him than just sex with a random woman. He rolled away, pushed off the bed, and stood.

"Adam?" Had he changed his mind? If so, I might die.

"Condom," he murmured as he headed for the dresser where he'd left his wallet.

I watched him, appreciating the view of his back, of the shoulders that had grown in width since high school. When he turned, condom in hand, his beautiful eyes held mine prisoner as he prowled back to me. My heart, already thumping in my chest, beat even harder.

He stopped at the edge of the bed, his gaze still on me, and dropped the condom on the night table. When he put his hands on the waist of the sweatpants he wore and raised a brow, giving me one last chance to say no, I sat up and pulled my camisole over my head. A thrill shot up me when he exhaled a long breath as the blue of his eyes darkened.

"So beautiful," he whispered and then pushed his sweats down his hips. He stepped out of them before sitting on the edge of the bed.

No, he was the beautiful one. Being here with him, the way he was looking at me with heat burning in his eyes, made me feel intoxicated, as if I'd consumed an entire bottle of wine. He leaned over me and kissed me again. This kiss was different. It was gentle and tender, and if I didn't know better, I would have thought he had feelings for me. *Don't start thinking like that, Savannah*, I warned myself. He'd broken my heart once, and I wouldn't let him do that to me again.

He pulled away, stared hard at me for a moment, then

smiled as his gaze lowered to my boy boxers. "These are sexy as hell, but it's time for them to come off."

"Okay." I lifted my hips, and he removed them, tossing them to the foot of the bed. He put his hand on my shoulder and then trailed his fingertips down the valley of my breasts. With my weight loss they were smaller than they used to be, and I wondered if he was disappointed. If so, he didn't let it show.

"I'm going to feast on you," he said, stretching out next to me. He cupped a breast. "I'm going to taste you here." He danced his fingers down my stomach to my sex. "And here."

"Are you asking permission?"

"No, Savannah. I'm taking what I want." He pinched my nipple as if emphasizing his intentions.

"Ah," I breathed as a bolt of pure pleasure shot through me, and I realized I'd forgotten what desire felt like. This Adam was new, and excitement burned in my blood. Although I wanted to take control of my life, here, in this room with Adam, I needed him to take charge.

For the next half hour his mouth and hands were all over me. I don't think there was a place left on my body that he hadn't touched, that his tongue hadn't tasted, before he seemed satisfied. Well, he should be since he'd twice made me climax. His mouth and fingers were magical things. While I tried to catch my breath, he rolled on the condom, then sat back against the headboard.

"On my lap, Savannah."

"Yes, sir," I said and smirked as I straddled him. He smirked back. I lowered myself onto him, moaning as he filled me.

"Good girl," he murmured as I began to move. "This morning is all for you, Savvy. I'm yours however you want me."

Did he even grasp what those words did to me? They slayed me. I would have walked away from everything for him. The chance to be a famous model, my mother, the big bank account. Arching into him, I buried my face in his neck. He put his hands on my hips and scraped his teeth along my shoulder, then moved to my earlobe and sucked it into his mouth. Hot, raw need burned through me when he rocked his hips, matching my movements.

I lifted my head so I could see his face, and I had the passing thought that I could drown in those eyes looking back at me with so much desire for me in them. He wrapped a hand in my hair and pulled my mouth to his. It wasn't a gentle kiss. It was fierce and demanding. A kiss that consumed me. He let go of my hair and cupped a breast, flicking his thumb over the nipple. Dropping his hand back down to my hip, he latched his mouth onto the nipple.

He stroked deep into me as he sucked on my breast. Spiraling toward the edge, I clenched my core muscles around his hard length. "Adam."

"Let go, baby. I've got you."

I believed him. As convulsions took possession of my body, I felt Adam stiffen and then shudder. With a low growl he pulled me to him and claimed my mouth again. *I love you.* Those were words I'd once been free to say to him, but now I could only think them in a secret part of my mind. My eyes burned, and I closed them to hide my tears from Adam.

CHAPTER TWENTY

~ Adam ~

I'D TOLD SAVANNAH THAT BEING with her wouldn't mean anything. The words had been meant for me, a reminder that nothing would change. But I'd been lying to myself. Being with her had meant everything. I glanced down at the woman curled against me. She had fallen asleep again with her head on my chest.

What just happened had been a mistake. In the heat of the moment my brain had gone on vacation, forgetting how deeply my heart had hurt when I'd lost her. Now I was going to relive that pain when we parted again. So stupid. I eased out from under her and slipped from the bed. Grabbing my overnight bag, I headed for the shower.

The water rained down on me, and I lifted my face to it, wishing it would wash away the thought that kept circling around in my brain. Being inside Savannah, I'd felt like I'd come home again after a long absence. When we were together, she'd been my everything, and now the hunger for her I'd managed to taper over the years had returned in force. It was all back now, the sounds she made, how she tasted, and how she smelled when I buried my nose in her hair. I couldn't do this again.

After I dried off and dressed, I called Connor to tell him we'd be returning tonight. Then I called my pilot friend to let him know the change of plans. I'd thought to stay over until Sunday, take advantage of doing some sightseeing with Savannah while we were in the city. But for my own peace of mind I needed to put distance between us. The sooner we got her problems solved, the better.

Savannah was still asleep, so I left her a note and then went in search of a hardware shop where I could buy new locks for her door. Forty-five minutes later I was back. Savannah was up and in the kitchen when I returned.

She smiled at seeing me. "Good morning."

"Morning." I'd brought the necessary tools with me, and I headed straight to the guest room where I'd left my overnight bag. That soft smile she'd given me as I walked by was the last thing I wanted to see. It made me want to go to her, wrap my arms around her, and beg her to promise to still be smiling at me like that fifty years from now. That I was having thoughts like that made me angry.

"Why don't you start piling up everything of his you want out of here before we leave," I said when I came back. I set my tools on the foyer table, next to the new locks I'd bought, then looked over my shoulder at her. She stood in the middle of her living room, her smile gone, her wounded eyes searching mine. What did she hope to see? That I still had feelings for her? So what if I did? It wasn't going to make any difference in her leaving when all was said and done.

My brain was a tangled mess where this woman was concerned. The part of me that still wanted her thought I should take what I could get while I could. Then there was the sane part that called me ten times a fool for even considering opening myself up to the hurt that would come when she left.

I raised a brow when she didn't move. "We're going back to the valley this evening, so you need to get a start on getting his stuff ready to go."

"You said we were staying over tonight."

"Changed my mind. I need to get home." Where I could turn her back over to Connor and Autumn.

"I'm sorry." Her gaze shifted to the floor. "You're busy, and I'm taking you away from work."

My anger was at myself, and I was being an ass. I closed

the distance between us, put my fingers under her chin, and lifted her face. "You have nothing to be sorry for, okay? I'm just..." What did I even want to say to her?

"Just what?"

Damn those gray eyes that had always held her every emotion in them. I couldn't lie to them. "The truth game?"

It was something we'd started when we were first dancing around each other in high school. My teenage hormones had raged out of control anytime I was near her or thought about her. She had been so shy that she'd get tongue-tied if I tried to talk to her. One day when I'd caught up with her in the hallway and asked how she was, her cheeks had blushed a pretty pink, and she'd stammered some incoherent words. Her awkwardness around me all of a sudden had been puzzling. We'd known each other since first grade, our group—her, me, Connor, Autumn, Jenn, and Natalie—had been tight, so I didn't get why overnight she couldn't talk to me.

"It's an easy question, Savannah," I said. "'I'm fine, thanks,' or 'I'm not so fine today.'" I smiled to soften my words.

"The truth?" she whispered.

"By all means."

"I-I feel funny when you're around."

"Yeah?" I leaned over and put my mouth near her ear. "Funny good?" She nodded, her cheeks turning pink again. I think my chest expended to double its size. "Because you like me?" When she nodded again, I said, "I like this truth game. Want one from me?"

"Yes."

"I feel funny good when I'm around you, too." Her smile and the way her eyes had gone soft at my answer sent an arrow straight to my heart, and she owned me from that moment on.

From then on we'd been inseparable, and if one of us was hesitant to express our feelings or what was on our mind, all we had to do was say, "The truth game," and we'd be honest with each other. Everything between us had been perfect until I'd screwed up and listened to her mother.

"Yes, the truth game," she said in answer to my question.

I shoved my hands into the pockets of my jeans. This was not a conversation I wanted to have, yet I'd led us right to it. "Okay, here it is. This morning should never have happened. Being around you messes with my head. When all is said and done, are you coming back here?"

"I don't have a choice." She glanced around her horrid living room. "This is my life. I don't know how to do anything else."

"You don't much like your life, do you?" The truth of that was in her eyes, and it sucker punched me. I'd set her free to live her dream, and even though I'd seen hints from her in her few visits home for her friends' weddings that she wasn't happy, I'd wanted to believe I'd done the right thing.

She shrugged. "What's to like?"

"You don't have to come back here, you know." As soon as the words were out of my mouth, my heart rate kicked up as I waited for her to agree. If she stayed in the valley, could we find our way back to each other?

"I just told you I don't have a choice. I have obligations, and I need the money."

Well, that answered that. "Right. Let's get the things done so we can head back." I turned away from her, not wanting her to see the hurt in my eyes that I knew was there.

"Adam?"

"Yeah?" I picked up the screwdriver.

"The truth game."

As much as I wanted to pretend I didn't hear her, that was *our thing,* one I couldn't ignore. I faced her. "Okay."

"Why did you break up with me? One day you said you loved me, and the next you said you didn't."

That was a question I'd hoped she would never ask.

"Does it matter anymore?"

"It's never stopped mattering." Her eyes filled with tears, and her lips trembled. "Never mind. You're right. It's no longer important."

She headed down the hall, leaving me torn. Go after her and give her the truth, or keep my mouth shut, knowing if I did it would truly be the end of us. But wasn't that what I wanted, what would be the best for both of us? How many times when thinking of her had I told myself that our time had come and gone? Thousands? Yet…

"Damn it." Despite my brain screaming to let it go, my feet followed her down the hall. I found her in the godawful master bedroom. She had a drawer open and was throwing white T-shirts in a pile on the bed.

"Savannah." She ignored me as she slammed the empty drawer shut before opening another one. Socks went flying, some landing on the bed, some on the floor. "I lied. About not loving you."

She stilled, bent over the drawer. Her chin dropped to her chest, and a visible shudder passed through her. "Why?" she said so softly that I barely made out the word.

I scrubbed a hand through my hair, then leaned against the doorframe and rammed my fingers into my pockets. What the hell was I doing? I'd never told her about her mother's visit, hadn't tried to explain anything to her back then, only telling her that I was too young to be tied down. And she was right. The night before, when we'd made plans for me to go to New York with her, I had promised to love her to eternity.

"I was just a mountain boy with no idea how to act around the kind of people who would come into your life. You know, the beautiful people, the rich and famous, and all that. I didn't want to be a hindrance or an embarrassment to you. You had a dream, and I didn't want to be the reason you didn't make that happen. The day would come when you would resent me for standing in your way, and

I couldn't live with that. I let you go because I loved you, not because I didn't."

Wasn't doing that for the person you loved a grand gesture, a sacrifice of your own happiness for the other person's? Honestly I thought my confession would, I don't know, soften her heart, make her appreciate what I'd given up for her. The understanding smile I was waiting for didn't happen. Her eyes narrowed, and she yanked out the drawer and threw it at me. I was too far away for it to come near me, but her intention was clear. She wanted to take my head off.

"Hey," I said, throwing up my hands. "You're the one who wanted to play this particular truth game. I did it for you, Savannah."

"You bastard." She scooped up balls of socks and hurled them.

I batted them away as they came at me. "You shouldn't have asked if you can't handle the truth." Christ, that sounded like something right out of a movie. "Savannah—"

"No, you shut up right now. Every word you just said was right out of my mother's mouth, the exact same things she told me. She got to you, didn't she?"

There was no use denying it at this point, so I nodded.

"Do you know what I told her when she tried to convince me that you were too much of a"—she made air quotes—"hillbilly to fit in, in a big city? That you'd be miserable?"

Deciding it was best I kept my mouth shut, I just shook my head.

"I told her that you were the smartest man I knew and that you'd figure out how to make a life there that you'd be happy with. What I didn't tell her was our agreement that we'd give it two years and if either one of us was unhappy, we'd come home."

She picked up more socks, started to throw one, then

stared at her hand before letting them drop to the floor. "I can't believe you've reduced me to throwing stupid socks. I'm not finished," she said when I opened my mouth.

I snapped it closed.

"You would have never allowed yourself to become a hindrance to me. I knew that down to my toes, and I told her so. And as for being an embarrassment to me… Have you ever looked into a mirror, Adam? I would have been the envy of every woman who saw me on your arm. I told her that, too. As for the dream of me becoming a famous model, that was always my mother's dream, not mine. You damn well knew that. Not that the idea didn't have its appeal, but if we'd decided to stay in the valley, get married, and have a houseful of kids like we talked about, I would have been happy. In hindsight I can honestly say I would have been happier considering the way my life turned out. I would have never, not in a million years, resented you for anything."

I felt like all the air had been sucked out of my lungs. I'd been a stupid, stupid boy.

"But did you even consider talking to me about those things after she spewed her poison? Didn't you think you and I were important enough to be honest with each other about any doubts we might have had? I didn't have any, but obviously you did. And just as obviously, you didn't believe in us."

"Savannah…" My throat closed, the lump in it bigger than a damn boulder. I couldn't get any other words past it. She'd believed in us, had trusted me to do the same, and I'd crumbled the minute the Wicked Witch had, as Savannah just said, spewed her poison.

"Don't Savannah me." She waved her hand, shooing me away. "Go fix the locks. The sooner we can leave, the faster I don't have to look at you."

"What about how fast you replaced me?" Yes, all the things she'd accused me of were true, but I'd gone almost a year before dating after she'd left. She sure as hell couldn't say the same, and I realized now that I'd never quite forgiven her for that.

She scrunched her eyebrows together. "What are you talking about?"

"That baseball player, Declan Bauman. I saw the pictures of you with him. There were even engagement rumors. You sure weren't missing me."

"For God's sake, Adam, that was nothing but a publicity stunt, arranged by my mother and Jackson right after I signed with him. If you thought I could replace you that easily, that fast, then you didn't know me at all. I don't want to talk to you anymore." She marched to me and pushed me out the door.

"I'm sorry," I said but not to her face.

Those words I owed her came after the door slammed behind me. I stood on the other side of that closed door, my chin lowered to my chest, my hands fisted at my sides, my eyes closed, and my lungs sucking in air as any hope that we might have a second chance died as fast as it had birthed. All these years I'd justified my anger at her on something that was false, and she was right. I should have known better.

If I lived the rest of my life miserable without her, it was what I deserved.

CHAPTER TWENTY-ONE

~ Savannah ~

BACK AT AUTUMN AND CONNOR'S house I claimed exhaustion and went straight to my room. The flight back to the valley had been silent, only necessary words spoken between Adam and me. I hadn't thought it was possible for him to hurt me again. I'd been wrong. How had he believed I could love anyone but him? He really hadn't known me, and even after all these years, that hurt.

As for my mother, I couldn't bring myself to think about her yet and what she'd done. She'd always steamrolled right over anyone in the way of what she wanted, including me, so I wasn't surprised by Adam's confession. It was easier to put all the blame on him for not trusting in me and in the power of us.

My mother had trained me from birth to hide my emotions, presenting only a calm and composed exterior, and today was the first time I'd ever slammed the door in anyone's face. It had felt so good that I wanted to do it again. In fact, I might do it to whoever was knocking on the door right now.

"Savannah, can I come in?"

"Yeah, sure." I should have known Autumn would be too impatient to wait until tomorrow to hear how my trip home went.

"Hey, are you okay?" She scooted onto the foot of the bed, curling her legs under her.

"Why wouldn't I be? Just because my life sucks lemons right now isn't a reason to…" I sighed. "Sorry. I'm being bitchy."

"Considering what you're dealing with, you're entitled." She grinned. "Besides, it's not like you haven't been on the receiving end of a few of my bitchy days. How did it go? Did you get all Jackson's stuff out of your apartment?"

"Yes, even the stupid round bed thanks to Adam. He got my doorman to call a few of his friends and paid them to haul everything, including all the furniture except in the guest bedroom, to one of those storage units. I'll have the attorney I'm meeting with tomorrow send Jackson a letter telling him where it all is."

"Wow! Yay, Adam."

"If you say so." Dang, why did I say that? A hungry dog eyeing a juicy bone had nothing on Autumn when it came determination. When she raised a brow, I sighed, loudly this time. "Can't we talk about this tomorrow?"

"The answer is no." She lowered her body to her side and propped her head on her hand. "Spill."

"You're annoying, you know that?" But I loved her, and over the past nine years I'd missed her and Jenn desperately.

She smirked. "Connor says the same thing, but you both adore me anyway. Now tell me why you're saying Adam's name like he's the devil after all he did for you this weekend."

So I told her, and by the end stupid tears were rolling down my eyes. "After I slammed the door in his face, I locked myself up in my bathroom and cried my eyes out. Even after all these years, it hurt like crazy to learn that Adam hadn't trusted in my love for him. How could he believe I was about to marry some baseball player I'd just met? I don't know which one I'm more furious with. Adam or my mother."

"Your mother, of course." She reached over and squeezed my ankle. "Give Adam some leeway, Savannah. He was just a boy, and back then none of us was a match for your mother. She scared the bejesus out of me, and of us all I was the least scareable. And then he reads that you're almost engaged not long after you leave? Honestly, when I saw that, I didn't know what to make of it either, and you weren't sharing."

"But he should have believed in me." That was what I was stuck on, that he hadn't trusted in my love for him.

"Sure he should have, but what eighteen-year-old boy has the necessary tools to face a fire-spitting dragon."

"My mother wasn't that bad, just difficult."

She snorted. "Okay, keep telling yourself that, but she was definitely a dragon." She sat up and scooted over to my raised knees, putting her hands on them. "Look, I get where you're coming from, but I see Adam's side, too. She played on his love for you, convincing him there was a real possibility that you'd come to resent him someday. If anything, he proved how much he loved you by freeing you to make your dream come true."

"Being a famous model was never my dream."

"Are you sure about that, or is that twenty-twenty hindsight talking?" She swung her legs off the bed, stood, then stared down at me. "The answer doesn't matter to me, but I think it does to you. Just be honest with yourself."

She left, quietly closing the door behind her. "Bull's-eye," I murmured. If nothing else, Autumn knew right where to shoot her arrow. Yes, as far back as I could remember, my goal had been to grace the covers of *Cosmo, Vogue, Elle,* and all the other glamour magazines. But the motivation had always been to make my mother proud of me, to see her look at me with approval in her eyes for once.

Even after I'd made my mother's dream happen, she hadn't been satisfied. But that wasn't what I needed to come to terms with tonight. It was me and Adam, and if I could forgive him. I didn't know.

In the past few days I'd had the chance to see him in his element. It was obvious that he loved building his log homes. What if he had gone to New York with me? Would he really have found a way to be happy? As a naive teen, I'd believed so, but now I wasn't so sure. Now I could admit that he probably would have been miserable, but he would have tried to hide it from me.

Adam was a mountain boy through and through. The city would have crushed his spirit. It would have killed me to see resentment in his eyes when he looked at me. He should have talked to me after my mother paid him a visit, but my anger at him was cooling. Autumn was right. He'd done what he'd believed at the time was best for me, sacrificing his own happiness.

I thought about it for a moment, then texted him.

R U free to take me to Ashville to meet with the attorney?

It didn't take long for him to answer.

Yes

That was it, one word. But I couldn't blame him after the way I'd jumped on him. We had too much history between us, too many years of knowing each other, not to be friends.

Jill Thornwood looked like a sexy librarian with her dark hair in a low bun on the back of her neck, her black glasses, navy pencil skirt and jacket, and crisp white blouse. After introductions, Adam and I sat in the chairs in front of her desk. I'd included him in this meeting because he was my friend and I wanted his input. That was how I was trying to think of him now, nothing more than a good friend. So far that wasn't working so well, especially when Sexy Librarian's gaze had roamed over him in appreciation. Not that I blamed her, but I wanted to scratch her eyes out so she couldn't ogle him like that.

He looked great in dark blue pants and a light blue button-down, but I liked him better in his worn jeans, flannel shirt, and work boots. Once we got down to business, she kept her attention on me, so she got to keep her eyes.

She picked up a pen and wrote my name and the date on a legal pad. "Although we covered some of this on the phone, Savannah, take me through your relationship with both your mother and Jackson Marks."

It was hard to explain the control my mother had had over me from as far back as I could remember, but I did my best to help Jill understand. I told her about how she'd gotten sick, how that was when she'd brought Jackson fully into my life. Then I told her about the night he'd threatened me with a knife and how I'd left without planning to.

"A mother should have her child's best interest at heart, but it doesn't sound like yours did," she said when I finished.

"Well, what's done is done. The question is, where do I go from here? I need to get this mess over with so I can try to salvage my career."

Jill nodded. "Since you took care of getting him out of your apartment—and by the way, it's a good thing that it's your name only on the mortgage—"

"And the only reason for that, it was my name and income that got the loan."

"Right, so he can't fight you on throwing him out. The next step is to petition the courts that you can handle your affairs, including your bank account, which I did last week. As of today, your account is frozen, along with all your credit cards. He can no longer get to your money."

"That was fast."

She grinned. "You can thank your senator friend for helping to make that happen already. A little word in the right ear does wonders."

"Wow, I'll have to buy him a dinner." Next to me, Adam grunted. Was he jealous? I glanced at him, but he was busy studying the floor. I wished I knew what was going on in his mind.

"The problem," Jill said, "is that your mother originally set the bank account up as a custodial account for her child, with her as the primary, and then later assigned that role to Jackson Marks. Now we have to prove that all the monies belong to you and no one else, and that you're of age and perfectly capable of handling your affairs."

"Will you be able to do that?" Adam asked.

Jill gave him a firm nod. "Absolutely." She picked up a piece of paper, handing it across her desk to me. "This is a letter terminating his position as your agent and manager. Read it over. If you approve, it will go out registered mail today."

"It's good." I handed it back after reading it.

"What do you think Jackson's reaction will be when he gets this and finds out you've removed him from your home?" Jill asked.

A shiver snaked down my back at her question. "Not good."

"My advice would be to consider taking out a restraining order."

I hated that it came down to that, but it was probably going to be necessary.

Adam waved his hand toward me. "She's supposed to meet him tomorrow."

"Don't," Jill said. "It won't achieve anything and will likely turn ugly."

"You have any problem with me meeting him to tell him she won't be showing up and to give him the key to the storage unit where his stuff is?"

Jill sat back in her chair and gave Adam a long appraisal. "I'd advise against that, too. But it's your decision. Can you keep your cool no matter what he says?"

"Debatable," Adam muttered. He glanced at me. "I think I should let him know he needs to find a new place to live and give him the storage unit key. See what kind of reaction I get. Might be a good idea to have Dylan go with me."

"Definitely." Maybe Jackson would be the one to lose his

cool and end up in Dylan's jail. A girl could hope.

"Keep me updated." Jill stood. "I'll be back in Raleigh tomorrow. You have my cell number, Savannah. Don't hesitate to use it. And we'll get all this taken care of, I promise." She smiled as she shook both our hands.

"She seems to know her stuff," Adam said as he drove the car onto I-40.

"I feel a lot better after talking to her." Her confidence in the outcome was something I'd needed to hear. "I hope she gets my bank account freed up soon. I hate having to mooch off my friends."

"That what friends are for, to mooch from. Besides, we know you're good for it, so it's a temporary loan, not a handout."

"Thanks," I whispered. I didn't want to think where I'd be right now without my friends, but especially Adam.

He smiled, and I smiled back, doing my best to ignore the flutter in my heart. The tension that had been between us on the drive over this morning had eased, and it seemed we were finding our way back to being friends. If I wished for more, that would stay my secret.

"Have you at all considered staying in the valley?"

CHAPTER TWENTY-TWO

~ Adam ~

I HADN'T MEANT TO ASK THAT question again, and when Savannah's smile faded, I wished I could take it back.

"I have to go back," she finally said, turning her gaze to the passing scenery.

"You don't sound too excited about that." I seemed to be doing everything in my power to see her out of my life and back in New York, yet her answer wasn't the one I wanted.

"Because I'm not, but I have obligations. And I need the money."

"I thought you said you had plenty." Not my business, was it? "Sorry, that's none—"

She glanced at me with a frown on her face. "I can pay you back as soon as I have access to my bank account."

"That wasn't why I said that. It just seems like if you're not happy and you can afford not to do it, why do something you don't enjoy? What would make you happy?"

"I want enough money to be able to buy several acres of land here in the valley." She stared down at her hands resting in her lap. "I've never told anyone this before, but my dream is to open an animal rescue foundation. A home for abused and unwanted animals. Dogs, cats, horses, pigs, whatever. And I want to train some of them to be therapy animals." She shrugged as she peeked up at me.

"I think that's great." And there was that shy smile I knew so well, the one I'd lived for when we were together.

"Really?"

"Yes, really." I exited the highway onto the road that would take us into the valley. "What made you want to do that?" It wasn't something she'd ever talked about before.

"I spent a few days at a farm where they took in rescue animals. It was a photo shoot to help raise money for them. I loved it, Adam."

As she told me about the different animals and the work the couple did, her eyes lit up with excitement. In the back of my mind I was processing the fact that she wanted to come home and make her dream come true here. I didn't want to be excited about that, but I was.

"Have you worked up a business plan?"

The light in her eyes faded. "No. I don't really know where to start."

"Okay, why don't we work on that a little while you're here? Between me, Connor, and Autumn, we should be able to help you put some numbers on paper. We could also scout out some land, see what's available to give you an idea of the cost."

"Oh, yes, can we?"

"Absolutely." I grinned at seeing her eyes sparkle again. Making this girl happy had always been my favorite thing to do.

Later that night, after a dinner of stew and cornbread, we sat around the table with Connor and Autumn. At my encouragement, Savannah told them her dream.

"Beau can be your mascot, you know, his picture on all your brochures and stuff," Autumn exclaimed. "He's famous around here."

At hearing his name, Beau jumped up from where he was napping at Autumn's feet and barked his agreement.

Autumn scratched his head. "See, he thinks that's a great idea."

"Okaaay," Savannah said, and I was pretty sure she barely

refrained from rolling her eyes. "Exactly why is he famous?"

Autumn related how she, Connor, and Beau had saved Lucas Blanton's sister from a bear. "There was even a parade in Beau's honor."

"Seriously?" Savannah said, laughing.

"Yeah, organized by Mary." Autumn grinned. "So you can imagine how that went."

While the girls were talking, Connor had been scrolling through property listings. "Look at this one." He turned his laptop screen toward Savannah. "Thirty acres, fairly flat land with a good-sized creek running through it. Already has a barn on it. Owner motivated."

"Yes, something like that is exactly what I envision," she said, her gaze meeting mine. "Come look."

I leaned toward her to see the pictures of the land and caught her scent. I'd noticed before that she still used the same fragrance as in high school—something vanilla with a hint of caramel—that had always made me want to lick her. That urge hadn't gone away, and before I did just that, I settled back into my seat.

Connor scowled at me, and I read his message loud and clear. *You're falling for her again. Not good, brother.* As if I didn't know that, but I didn't know how to stop these growing feelings that were both old and new. The funny thing, now that I'd been around her for a few days, I didn't see the model who graced the covers of fashion magazines. Unless I reminded myself who she was, I forgot she was *the* Savannah. She was simply a girl that I'd grown up with, had fallen in love with, and had lost.

"Can you take me to see it?" Savannah asked, glancing at me.

"I'll take—"

"Yes," I said, cutting Connor off. I appreciated that he wanted to protect me, but it was my life, my choice to decide what I was willing to risk where Savannah was concerned. "I have to meet Marks in the morning to give him the keys to the storage unit. After that's done, I'll pick you up. We can have lunch, then ride out to see the property."

If Connor scowled any harder, his lips were going to be permanently broken. "Why don't we all go? Make an afternoon of it."

Autumn glanced at Savannah, a silent inquiry in her eyes. *Is that what you want?*

"Perfect," Savannah said, her gaze on me.

Was that disappointment I saw on her face? Had she hoped to spend the afternoon alone with me? I'd convinced myself that because she would return to her life in New York, nothing would come of our time together. But she wanted to come home, and now one question burned hot in my mind. Was there even the slightest chance for us? Make that two questions. Did she wish for a second chance?

"I'll go with you in the morning to meet with Marks," Connor said, dragging my thoughts back to the here and now.

"Not necessary. I called Dylan this afternoon. He's going with me. Thought it would be a good idea to have our police chief there."

Connor nodded. "Even better."

I pushed away from the table. "I'm going to call it a night. I need to be at the jobsite early before I have to go meet Marks."

"Good night," Savannah softly said, and there was something in her voice that sounded like longing.

Or I was hearing what I wanted to hear. I really didn't know anything anymore.

I was sprawled on my couch with a cold one, trying to work through the mess going on in my mind, when I got the urge to go down to the river. "Damn it, Connor," I muttered. It was freezing out. Why wasn't he snuggled up next to Autumn instead of waiting to give me his brotherly advice? Which—just to be clear—I did not want.

A river divided mine and Connor's properties, and when either one of us needed to talk, we'd meet at the water's edge. I couldn't explain it if I tried, but somehow we both felt a compulsion to go to the river when one of us was there waiting.

Did my brother even realize that at this time of night it would take at least nine layers of clothes to stay warm? I knew what he wanted to talk about, and I was sorely tempted to climb into my warm bed instead. Letting out a long sigh, I bundled up.

"Keep my seat warm," I told Jinx, deciding to leave him free. How much trouble could a cat get into in twenty or so minutes? Although I was talking about Jinx. After a detour to put him in his playpen, I made my way down to the river.

"This couldn't wait until tomorrow?" I grumbled. My brother stood on the other side, his hands stuffed into the thick jacket he wore. "It's damn cold."

"How many times did we meet like this, me here, you over there, after Savannah left?"

"Is that a rhetorical question?" We'd each placed a bench on our own sides, and I eyed mine, knowing this could take a while. There had been times, especially when I was going through Savannah withdrawal, that we'd sat for hours talking. He'd been there for me through it all, and I loved him for it. I wasn't loving him so much right now, though. It was freezing, and definitely too cold to park my butt on an ice-covered bench.

"It's a question that I hope will remind you of how broken you were and for how long. You're falling for her again, brother."

"Well, you did say she was my kryptonite, although it really won't matter because we're both going to die from hypothermia." I paced and rubbed my cold hands together that my gloves were *not* keeping warm.

"This isn't funny, Adam. You're already thinking she's going to come back because of this animal thing she's talking about doing. And that's all it is. Just talk. She'll go back to New York, back to her glitzy life, and forget about you again. You need to stay away from her while she's here."

"No can do." He was probably right, though, which meant that I should listen to him. I got that his concern was for me, but what if this really was a second chance for Savannah and me and I turned my back on it? In the time she'd been gone, not one woman had come close to replacing her. And I'd sure as hell looked.

"She walked away from you once without looking back, and she'll do it again."

I sighed. "No, she didn't." It was time for my brother to hear the story. "I broke up with her, Connor. I'm the one who broke her heart."

He'd been pacing, too. Trying to keep warm, I assumed. He stopped and faced me across the river. "You're just saying that to cover for her. You as much as had your bags packed, ready to go with her."

"And I planned to until her mother paid me a visit." I told him what Regina Graham had said and how she'd convinced me that Savannah would end up resenting me. "I couldn't bear the thought of that, so I set her free."

At the time I'd believed—or maybe hoped was more accurate—that after a few months in New York City Savannah would realize that life wasn't what she wanted. That she'd come home. When she didn't, I decided that Mrs. Graham had been right, and I'd done the smart thing. Now I knew I'd been wrong, and Savannah had paid the price.

"And you never told me this because…?"

I winced at the hurt in his voice. We'd never had secrets from each other, except for this. "Because you would have told me I was an idiot for listening to Mrs. Graham and would have convinced me to go after Savannah. Tell me I'm wrong."

"You're not wrong, but what's done is done. She's not the Savannah you were in love with back then. You still need to back off."

"Look, I know you're worried I'll go off the deep end again, but it's my decision to make where she's concerned." I waved my hands at him. "Right now, though, I can't feel my fingers or toes anymore, and I really prefer the girls don't find our frozen bodies out here in the morning. Good night, bro."

As I jogged back to my warm house, I couldn't help thinking about Connor saying Savannah wasn't the same girl I'd been in love with. I couldn't deny the truth of that. It was entirely possible that if I spent enough time around her, I'd find that I wasn't attracted to this Savannah. If so, wouldn't that be a good thing to know? I'd finally be able to let her go.

"And here he comes," Dylan said.

I watched Marks swagger our way. "Fun times ahead." The sun was shining and there wasn't any wind, so it was considerably warmer than it had been last night down by the river. The public park was deserted, though, since it was too cold for picnics. I was glad there was no one else around in case this conversation got nasty.

"Where's Savannah?" Marks said, stopping a few feet away from us and crossing his arms over his chest. He narrowed his eyes at Dylan.

"Not here." I tossed the key to him. He didn't try to catch it, and it landed on the ground in front of him. "You might want to pick that up. It's the key to a storage unit where all your belongings reside since you no longer live in Savannah's apartment."

He stared hard at me for a long moment as if unable to

process my words. "The hell you saying?"

Although I wanted to either roll my eyes or punch him in the face, Dylan had lectured me to keep my cool. If a fight started, it was going to be Marks hauled off to jail, not me. "That is a key to where you can find all your stuff. The storage unit's address is on the tag," I said slowly and clearly.

The idiot laughed. "Nice try. Now where's Savannah?"

"She doesn't want to see you, talk to you, or live with you. The locks on her apartment have been changed, and management has been informed that you are no longer welcome in the building."

"You can't do this."

I glanced at Dylan. "I've said all he needs to know. Want to stop by Mary's for coffee and doughnuts?"

He patted his flat stomach. "Always ready for that. Hope she has some hot ones."

Ignoring Marks, we turned to leave. I shook my head on a laugh when I saw Hamburger get out of his rusted-out truck and head our way, fiddle in hand.

"You think you can just walk away?" Marks snarled, getting my attention back on him. He lowered his shoulder and came at me.

Good. I was ready for a fight. I fisted my hands, waiting for the man who'd put a knife to Savannah's face to get within striking distance.

Dylan stepped between us. "Mr. Marks, stop right where you are."

Marks ground to a halt, his rage-filled eyes looking at me over Dylan's shoulder. "You better be watching your back because I'm not done with you, you son of a bitch."

And this was what Savannah had been dealing with? Between her mother and this man, it was amazing that she wasn't curled up in a corner somewhere, babbling nonsense.

"Bring it on, douchebag." I hadn't wanted to put a man on his ass before as much as I wanted to on this one.

He came at me again, and when Dylan stepped in front of him, he plowed right into our chief of police's chest before bouncing back. I was impressed that Dylan hadn't given an inch.

"Assaulting a lawman," Hamburger bellowed. "I seen it with my own eyeballs." He danced on his feet while waving his fiddle in the air. "You ain't gonna like them jailhouse pillers, Mr. Agent Man."

As much as I longed to step around Dylan and finish what Marks had tried to start, I figured I'd better keep my cool if I didn't want to end up with my head on one of those pillows in the cell next to Marks.

"Mr. Marks," Dylan said. "You have one chance to walk away. Get in your car, collect your things from your hotel room, then take yourself to the airport. If I see your face in our town one hour from now, I'm going to arrest you for…" He grinned at Hamburger. "Assaulting a lawman."

Hamburger's head bobbed. "I seen it, I did."

A low growl sounded from Marks's throat, but he snatched the key from the ground and then headed to his car.

"Can we talk 'bout my Hollywood movie afor ya go, Mr. Agent Man? The sheriff said ya got an hour." Hamburger shot us a big grin as he scrambled after Marks.

"God, I love this town," Dylan said as we watched Marks slam his car door in Hamburger's face.

"You say that a lot." Dylan had come to us from the Chicago police department, where I'm sure he saw stuff that would give me nightmares. He'd given up trying to explain to Hamburger that he wasn't a sheriff.

"What in the world is that?" I asked at seeing someone riding up on a pink moped, the person all bundled up like Ralphie's brother from *A Christmas Story*.

Dylan sighed. "That would be Mary on her new toy."

"You have got to be kidding me."

"I wish."

At his sour expression, I laughed.

"Not funny," he muttered. "She came too damn close for comfort to riding it through the door of the police department. If Tommy hadn't just walked out and was able to stop her, I'd be replacing a glass door today. She was coming by to ask if she needed a moped driver's license. Unfortunately, one's not required in North Carolina, but I was sorely tempted to lie and tell her yes." He narrowed his eyes. "And get that smirk off your face."

"Can't help it. It's too funny. I do hope she doesn't kill herself on that thing, though."

Instead of parking it next to our cars, she rode it right up to us, and when it didn't look like she was going to stop, we both jumped out of the way. She did manage to stop the thing, but if we hadn't moved, her front tire would have been resting on our shoes.

"Mary, I'll give you five hundred cash if you'll park that thing and never get on it again," Dylan said.

She made a pfffing noise. "Keep your money, Chief. This girl's having too much fun."

It was hard to keep a straight face at the sight of her dressed in a shocking pink snowsuit and a pink helmet on her head as she sat on the pale pink scooter. Even her boots were pink, and because she was so short only her toes touched the ground.

"Miss Mary!" Hamburger scurried back to us, his gaze shining bright on the moped. "That's some purty motorsickle ya got there. I'd sure like me one of them."

"No!" Dylan roared.

Hamburger jumped at his outburst, Mary almost fell over, scooter and all—would have if Dylan hadn't caught the handlebar—and I lost it, laughing so hard that my stomach hurt.

"Do I need to remind you how much you love this

town, Chief?" At Dylan's glare I walked away, leaving him to deal with our town's favorite cartoon characters.

I had a lunch date with the lead in my own story.

CHAPTER TWENTY-THREE

~ Savannah ~

"ALL PINK?" I GASPED THROUGH my laughter, wishing I could see Mary dashing down the street on her scooter.

Adam grinned. "From head to toe."

We were at Vincennes, Adam devouring a loaded pizza and me moving my Greek salad around on my plate. Connor had a last-minute house showing, so he and Autumn hadn't come with us. Jenn had scooted into the booth next to me, taking a short break.

"My poor husband," she said. "I think those two characters make him wonder what he was thinking when he took the police chief job."

"They do keep things interesting." Adam frowned as he eyed the lettuce on the end of my fork that I was nibbling on. "As long as Hamburger keeps giving him moonshine and Mary keeps loading him up with hot doughnuts, he'll stick around."

He bit into a slice of cheesy pizza that smelled so good my mouth watered. When that piece was devoured, he cut the next one in half lengthwise, putting one of the halves on the side of my salad plate. He kept on eating as if he hadn't just done that.

Jenn reached over and snatched a pepperoni from his pizza. "You left sticking around for me out of that."

"I'm really sorry, Jenn, but you got nothing on Hamburger and Mary in the way of keeping our chief entertained." Adam smirked at her.

She patted her still flat stomach. "I beg to differ. I'm

definitely number one on his entertainment list. Although, maybe I should be worried. He did once say he was going to marry Mary for her doughnuts."

"Can't say I blame him," Adam said.

While they bantered, I broke off little pieces of the pizza Adam had given me, savoring each bite. Lord, Vincennes made the best pies, better than any I'd had in New York when I could sneak a slice past my mother.

"You're looking great," I told Jenn. And she did. She had a beautiful glow on her face that I tried not to envy. "Have you had any morning sickness?"

"Not so far." She rapped her knuckles on the table. "Knock on wood it stays that way."

"Jenn, got a sec?"

I looked up to see a black-haired man poking his head around the kitchen door.

Jenn stole one more pepperoni from Adam's pizza. "Coming. That's Angelo, the owner. Time for me to go play restaurant manager." She slid out of the booth. "Lunch is on the house today."

"Thanks," Adam said.

"She's glowing." I pushed the last half of my salad aside. Sometimes the way Adam would look at me—like he was doing now—I felt that he could see into my soul. It had always been that way, and I used to love thinking he saw me, the real me. Now, though, it was an effort not to close my eyes, shielding my thoughts from him.

"Do you want children?"

"My life is such a mess that I haven't really thought about a future, especially one with kids in it." Long ago I'd pushed any yearning to have children out of my mind. It was just something I never allowed myself to think about. Although seeing how happy Jenn was made me wish things were different. "All I ever heard from my mother on the subject was that having babies ruins your figure."

His lips curled in distaste. "You need to get your mother

out of your head once and for all."

"You think I'm not trying?" I didn't want to think about her or the children I would never have. "Can we go see the land now?" He must have heard the tension in my voice because he reached across the table and put his hand over mine. I stared at our joined hands and wanted to cry. I wanted to crawl across the table and curl up in his lap and make the past nine years go away. Go back to before, when we were each other's world.

"I'm sorry, Savannah. I didn't mean to upset you." He stood, dropped a five-dollar bill on the table for a tip, then pulled me up, and without a word walked me outside. "I have some things to say to you, but not here," he said after we were in his car.

We rode to the property in silence. I was a messy jumble of thoughts. I was free now to live my life the way I wanted. But what was that way? My determination to return to the life I knew faded a little with each day I spent in the valley. This place was home, it was the land I loved, it was where I had real friends. But what would I do here? If I didn't go back and earn more money, I wouldn't be able to make my rescue animal foundation come true.

And what things did Adam have to say to me? I peeked over at him. He seemed lost in thought. If only I could read his mind. There had been a time when I could, but he wasn't that boy anymore. And that boy? He'd grown into a man I admired and respected, and still loved. He caught me looking at him, and his soft smile went straight to my heart.

Maybe I should get the hell out of Dodge, go back to New York today before I humiliated myself and begged him to love me again. Hopefully I had a little pride left, enough that I'd be able to stop myself from doing that.

"This is it." Adam pulled onto a dirt road and stopped.

We got out, meeting at the front of his car. "It's beautiful." Even more so than the pictures showed. The land had a gentle roll to it, sloping down to the fast-moving creek. A red barn sat on the flattest part, the area around it cleared of trees. Everything was brown now, but I could imagine the grass and trees all green, and my animals having plenty of room to play. I scanned the surrounding mountains rising in the distance. It also wasn't way out in the middle of nowhere. I think it only took us about fifteen minutes to get here. I loved it.

Adam glanced at me. "Well?"

"It's perfect."

"It does look good, but you should check out a few other properties before you decide." He moved in front of me. "Are you sure this is something you want to do? It will be a lot of responsibility. Not something you can manage from a distance."

"I know." Maybe it was a pipe dream. If I couldn't take control of my own life, how was I supposed to take on the responsibility for a bunch of damaged animals? "When I was at that farm, it was the first time I felt something in here"—I put my hand over my heart—"since losing you. I thought I could have a real purpose in life, something besides looking pretty enough to sell magazines to people I don't know and never will. What I do is meaningless, and I want to mean something to someone, even if it's animals."

If I was being too honest with him, it was because he was doing that thing again, looking into my soul. My secrets weren't safe from him, so there was no reason to try to hide them.

"You mean something to me."

My heart skipped a beat, then another one. *Easy, Savannah. He just means you're his friend, is all.* "Thank you for being my friend when I needed one the most. I didn't want to dump my problems on you, but I didn't know where else to go." I forced a smile. "Poor me, huh?"

It was ironic, actually. Women looking at my picture on the magazine covers would think I had it all—looks, money, a glamorous life, and a hot boyfriend—and wish they were me. Well, they were welcome to that life. I didn't want it.

"I'm glad you did call me." He reached up and tucked my hair behind my ear. "The truth, though—I wasn't at first. I wished you'd called anyone but me. But you did, and I couldn't say no to you."

"You should have. I swear that all I wanted from you was a small loan. I never expected to find myself back in the valley." I looked around me. "Back home." And with him.

"Is this still home for you, Savvy?"

I closed my eyes for a moment at hearing his voice softly say my name, as if it carried memories for him, too.

"Is it?" His eyes searched mine for an answer.

"Yes, it always will be." Not just because it was my hometown, but because this was where he was, and he was home to me.

"Then stay. If you really hate your life in New York, don't go back."

"And do what? I have no skills. I'm not even sure how much money I have. Maybe I'll find out that Jackson wiped out my bank account."

"We'll figure all that out." He stepped closer. "Together."

"What are you saying?" Hope was fighting for a foothold, but I crushed it. I refused to be a charity case.

He slipped his hand under my hair, curving his fingers around the back of my neck, pulling me to him as he lowered his mouth to mine. Everything in me reached for him, wanting to crawl under his skin and live there where it was warm and safe. Where there was love.

I tried to resist. I swear I did, but Adam's lips on mine demolished any thought of why this wasn't a good idea. When I opened my mouth, inviting him in, he wasted no time tangling our tongues, tasting me, letting me taste him. Even though we'd made love this past weekend, that had seemed like putting the past to bed, getting that done and out of the way so we could forge a friendship.

This, though… This had nothing to do with the past. It was new, full of possibilities. I wished it wasn't cold and we didn't have thick jackets on. I wanted to feel my breasts pressed against his chest, wanted to feel the fast beat of our hearts, skin to skin.

He pulled away and touched his forehead to mine, our harsh breaths mingling in the chilled air. "This is what I'm saying. Whatever was between us still is, Savannah. We have a second chance and a choice. We can let it slip through our hands, and if it does this time, that's it. There will never be an us. Or we can find out if this is real."

What he was offering, a second chance, was all I'd thought about since we'd made love. I wanted that so badly, but panic was squeezing my heart. I no longer trusted happy endings. If I let Adam back into my life and he walked away from me again in the end, I wasn't sure I'd survive it.

"I'm not the girl you used to love, Adam." I stepped away from him. As soon as he learned that, he would leave me again.

"You are. You're still Savannah. Maybe you think you've lost her, but she's still there." He tapped my chest. "She's in here. You just have to find her."

I looked around me, at the mountains, the land I'd fallen in love with the minute I'd seen it, the red barn, and then the creek. It was a pipe dream. I wasn't clever enough to turn this place into a refuge. I wouldn't even know where to start.

And Adam? What did I have to offer him? Enough to hold his interest for the rest of our lives? I didn't think so, and I'd always be waiting for the day he gave up on me and left. He must have seen something in my eyes that clued him in to my thoughts. A muscle ticked in his jaw, and he stuffed his hands into his coat pockets.

"I can't." Even to my own ears I sounded pathetic.

"When did you turn into a coward?"

Tears burned in my eyes. "The day you said you didn't love me." I turned my back on him and the property I wished I didn't love.

We rode back without a word exchanged between us. I kept my gaze on the window, but my vision was too blurry to see anything. At least I didn't outright cry. The anger at learning how he'd let my mother convince him to break up with me was still there, but I didn't blame him for being disappointed in me. He'd offered me a second chance, but I wasn't brave enough to take it.

CHAPTER TWENTY-FOUR

~ *Adam* ~

I WANTED TO KISS SAVANNAH INTO next week or however long it took to make her admit that we were meant to be together. Instead I let her get out of the car without saying a word to her, watched her until she was safely inside Connor's house, and then drove home to lick my wounds. I'd fought wanting her back in my life from the moment she'd stepped off the plane until listening to her laugh when I'd told her about Mary's pink scooter. I'd always loved her laugh, and as the sound settled over me and inside me, I knew I was fighting a hopeless battle.

A part of me had hoped that making love to her would finally get her out of my system, but she was embedded in me, like some kind of computer code. I let Jinx out, filled his food bowl, then grabbed a beer and crashed on the couch. For a brief moment I considered driving to Asheville tonight and hooking up. But I'd tried getting Savannah out of my system that way in the past and it hadn't worked. Discarding that idea, I played with Jinx for a bit before putting him back in his playpen and heading to the jobsite.

When I got there, I found Connor giving a client a tour of the almost finished model home. Ignoring his greeting, I spied my crew loafing out back. It was their bad timing to be taking a break when I was ready to chew someone's head off.

"Early break, boys?" I pointedly looked at my watch. Lunch and break times were set, the only way I could keep them from trying to con me. Most of my crew were good, responsible men, but there was always one or two who would try to push the limits, sneaking in extra breaks or extending their lunch hour when they could get away with it. I learned early on that if they had set times for both, it made my life and theirs less stressful, since I wasn't yelling at them.

"Connor told us to clear out while he had his client here," my foreman said.

Okay, my bad. But I wasn't in a forgiving mood. "Then make yourselves useful. Pick up the trash lying around and put it in the dumpster until you can get back inside." My foreman, who'd been with me from the beginning and knew me well, raised a brow at the snarky tone of my voice. To his credit, though, he kept his mouth shut and got the guys to work.

Still in a pissy mood, I decided I should clear out for the day, leave my crew in peace. When I reached the front of the house, Connor's client was driving away, and my brother was leaning against my car door, arms crossed over his chest.

"Don't want to hear it, so move your ass." He was going to call me out on my attitude. Then he was going to want to start digging, find out what my problem was.

"Tough shit." He crossed his ankles, letting me know he'd stand here all day if he had to. "Talk."

"It's too cold for true confessions in the middle of a parking lot." I sighed when he just shrugged. "Fine. I'm going home and brew a pot of hot coffee. You can follow me... or not."

He snorted. "Nice try, brother."

"It was worth a shot," I muttered.

Back at my house I let Jinx out, then started the coffee while Connor rummaged in my pantry. "You need to go shopping, dude. There's nothing good to eat in here."

"Intentional. Keeps unwanted guests from overstaying their welcome." I looked meaningfully at him.

"You're funny." He moved from the pantry to the refrigerator, his head disappearing inside. "Ah, here we go."

Damn, he found the box of chocolate chip cookies from Mary's that I'd hidden in the produce drawer. And yes, I hid goodies from my brother because whenever he was over, he ate the good stuff, especially since Autumn had gotten on her only-healthy-food-allowed-in-their-house kick.

"Those are mine."

"Not anymore."

"Bastard."

"If I am, you are. Same mother and all that," he said around a mouthful of cookie.

He had me there. I poured us each a cup, added the same amount of cream and sugar to each, then took them to the kitchen island. After pulling a stool to the other side to face him, I took a seat. He pushed the box of cookies to the middle after grabbing a handful.

"What'd she do?"

"Why is that the first thing you assume, that Savannah did something?" I picked up a cookie and dipped it into my coffee.

"Am I wrong?"

"Do I have to talk about this?" I wanted to be irritated at him for sticking his nose in my business, but if the roles were reversed, I'd be doing the same thing for him. Had, in fact, gotten in his face about Autumn when they'd briefly split.

"Yep. At least until the cookies run out."

"Then I'll talk reeeeeal slow." He threw half of a cookie at me, making me chuckle. Since he wasn't going anywhere, even if the cookies ran out, until I told him what had happened, I said, "I asked Savannah to stay."

That got his attention. "And?"

"She said no. There, you can go home now."

"I knew it."

"What, Connor? What did you know? She could have just as easily said yes."

"But she didn't, and that's exactly what I would have expected from her."

Now I was getting pissed. He didn't know her, not like I did, and I didn't like him cutting her down like that. I decided I might as well go all in so he'd understand. "The thing is, she loves me."

"Has she told you that?"

I could see the skepticism in his eyes. "Not in so many words, but she does. She's afraid. Doesn't trust or believe in herself. This is just a guess, but I know her, Connor. I understand how she thinks, and she doesn't believe I can love the woman she is today."

"Are you sure you're not just trying to hold on to the past?"

It wasn't like I hadn't asked myself that same question, but I resented Connor asking it. It sent a protective streak for Savannah through me. I got his doubts and why he was worried, but I didn't have to like it.

"Doesn't matter, does it? She's going back to her life in New York, and I'll carry on with mine here."

"I know it doesn't feel like it, but it's for the best."

I pulled the box to me, peered inside, then closed the lid. "No more cookies for you. Go home." Conner sure hadn't thought it was for the best when Autumn walked away from him, and he needed to leave before I punched him in the face.

"Why don't you come over later for dinn—" Connor frowned. "Not a good idea. Savannah will be there." He stood. "Want me to come back later? We can watch a game or something."

"No. I'm going to make it an early night." He held up his hand, and we fist bumped. After he left, I crashed on the couch. A few minutes later Jinx slinked by, a scrap of blue material clutched in his mouth.

"Jinx, that better not be what I think it is." He ran under the couch. It took five minutes to catch him, and sure enough, it was Savannah's panties that he was clinging to for dear life. After prying his jaws open, I got them away from him and stuffed them in my pocket.

I held him up in front of my face. "You're a very bad cat. What'd you do? Sneak back into her bag after I got them away from you the first time?"

He growled at me.

"No one else is happy with me right now, so you might as well join the party."

"Mawwua," he said, voicing his displeasure.

For the rest of the night he followed me around, chattering like a magpie. If I had to guess, he was demanding I return the panties.

"Not happening, bud."

If anyone was going to be in possession of her panties, it was going to be me.

Voices penetrated my subconscious. It took me a few seconds to realize it was the police scanner on my night table. Connor and I both were emergency rescue and firemen volunteers. I listened, waiting to hear if it was a call I'd need to get up for. Within moments of learning it was a fire, my phone buzzed, Dylan's name coming up on the screen. At the same time I answered his call, the dispatcher gave the address of the fire.

"The hell?" It was our model home. "I just heard it on the scanner," I said without preamble.

"Figured you would but wanted to make sure. You want to call Connor?"

"Yeah. We'll be there soon." I disconnected, but before I could call my brother, my phone buzzed again, his name coming up.

"I'll pick you up in five," he said when I answered.

In four minutes I was dressed and standing at the end of my driveway. The lights of Connor's car appeared as he crossed the bridge. As soon as I was seated and belted in, he hit the gas. We both had emergency lights in our vehicles, and when we reached the highway, he flipped the switch, turning his on. I hadn't paid attention to the time in the rush to get dressed, and I glanced at the car's clock to see it was after three. I scrubbed my hands over my face, wishing I had a cup of coffee.

"You think one of your crew left something on, a power tool or whatever?" Connor asked.

"I doubt it. They know better. Besides, I can't think of anything they would've been using today that would start a fire." Connor barely knew the difference between a screwdriver and a wrench, which had always amused me. But then the sight of an Excel spreadsheet—one of his favorite things in the world—gave me hives, so I guessed we were even.

He glanced over at me. "What are we going to do if it's a bad one—you know, if the model is completely destroyed?"

"Let's hope that's not the case, but if so, we file an insurance claim and rebuild." We did not need this. We could afford the deductible, but it would hurt. Not to mention, Autumn had a grand opening scheduled in a few weeks, and she'd gone all out. Total headache if we had to start over.

When the property came into view, I let out a relieved breath. Although there were fire trucks and police cars parked in the lot, I didn't see a fire. And most important, both our model homes were still standing.

"Where's the fire?" Connor asked, stopping the car as close as we could get.

"Just be happy you don't see one."

"True that." We stepped out and went looking for the fire chief. We found Dylan instead.

"What happened?" I said, walking up to him.

"Come with me. Ray will tell you."

Ray was our fire chief. Connor and I followed Dylan around the second model home, the one we'd started on last month. Ray was in the back, on the phone.

"Appreciate it, Dave." He stuck his phone back on his fireman's coat pocket. "That was the county's arson investigator. He'll be out in the morning, so until he finishes his investigation, your property's off-limits, boys."

"Arson?" I scanned both model homes, the one almost finished, and the one we'd recently started on.

Ray clicked on an industrial flashlight, shining it at the corner of the new one, showing us a pile of water-soaked trash. "He—maybe a she, but probably a he—built a little pyramid of flammable shit—"

Dylan snorted. "Love it when you get all technical, Ray."

Ray chortled. "That turn you on, Chief?"

"As amusing as you two are, you're telling me this was intentional, Ray?" There was only one person who came to mind who might do something like this, but he'd left town yesterday. Hadn't he?

"Yep. Most people don't realize that log homes are naturally fire resistant."

"More so than stick-built homes," I said. And that was true. It was one of the fears Connor and I constantly battled with people who wanted a log home but didn't want to burn to a crisp in one.

"You know anyone not happy with one of you?" Ray said, his gaze bouncing between me and my brother.

I saw the same answer I'd arrived at in Conner's eyes. "Yeah. I do know someone like that." I looked at Dylan. "We thought he left town yesterday… It is tomorrow now, right?" Between this and my last conversation with Savannah, three days could have passed. That was how out of it I was at the moment.

"I know he checked out of his room, so I assumed he left," Dylan said. "There haven't been any sightings reported. I'll work on finding out if he turned his car in. And yes, it is tomorrow. On that note, I'm outta here."

"Who is he?" Ray asked, his gaze again traveling from me to Conner and back to me.

"The biggest asshole who ever lived. Fill him in," I said to Connor. I walked to the corner of the model to investigate the damage. We'd gotten lucky. The ends of the logs were slightly singed, but that was about it.

There wasn't proof that Marks had done this, but who else would have? If Dylan found out he hadn't turned in his rental car and gotten on a plane, then there wouldn't be any doubt in my mind that he'd been going for a little revenge. How could Savannah want to return to a world with the kind of people like Jackson Marks in it? Why wouldn't she rather be home with the people who loved her?

CHAPTER TWENTY-FIVE

~ Savannah ~

"I NEED TO GO HOME." ALTHOUGH it didn't sound right calling New York home. It never had been.

Autumn gave me a disgruntled stare. "What you need to do is move back to the valley where there are actually people who care about you, tell Adam you love him, and then live happily ever after."

I set down my coffee cup, the little I'd drunk already churning in my stomach. "It's not that easy."

"Only because you won't let it be."

She didn't understand. As much as I'd sworn I'd take control of my life, I'd accomplished very little other than mooching off my friends, missing contract obligations, and getting Adam and Connor's model home almost burned down. Yeah, my stomach hadn't been right since Connor had come home and told Autumn they suspected Jackson of trying to set the fire. When Autumn had passed that on to me this morning, I knew I had to leave. I didn't trust Jackson and didn't even want to think what he might do next to my friends, their only crime being their desire to help me.

As for Adam and me, I'd spent most of the night staring at the ceiling, trying to see us together in the future, and I just couldn't. Maybe it was nothing more than a lack of confidence in myself that put doubts in my mind that I could make him happy long-term. And maybe it was because my mind was a mess right now and I wasn't thinking straight. I didn't know.

The decision I came to was to return to New York, get

my life straightened out there. Until I did that, I had nothing to offer Adam other than a broken shell. He'd said that somewhere inside me I was still Savannah. I needed to find that girl, and I needed to do it on my own. It was the only way I'd ever believe I could make him happy... if I was happy first.

Of course, I risked him moving on before I could offer him a *whole me*, but if that happened, then his love for me wasn't bone-deep and lasting. And if I told Autumn that and she accused me of testing him, I wouldn't be able to deny it. I think I probably was.

"You're a million miles away. What's going through that head of yours?" Autumn said.

"Nothing and everything." I stood and took my coffee cup to the sink. "I'm going to book a flight. Would you be able to take me to the airport sometime today?" I kept my back to her as I rinsed the cup out, not wanting her to see the tears in my eyes.

"I should say no, but then you'll probably steal my car and drive yourself there." She came up behind me, wrapped her arms around my waist, and rested her cheek on my back. "Please give yourself a few more days here. Give Adam a chance... No, give yourself a chance to be happy."

"I can't," I whispered, squeezing my eyes shut against the burn in them.

Autumn, bless her, put my plane ticket on her credit card. On the way to the airport she stopped at a pharmacy.

"Wait here. I'll be right back." A few minutes later she returned and handed me a stack of gift cards.

"What's this?"

"A meatloaf sandwich." She rolled her eyes. "They're exactly what they look like, dummy. There are five thousand dollars' worth, so don't lose them."

I pushed her hand away. "I'm not taking those."

"Stop being so stubborn, Savannah. You think I'm going to let you leave without a penny in your pocket? I love you, but right now I'm not liking you so much." She pulled my blouse away from my chest and crammed them into my bra. "Take the damn things."

So I did, but dang her, she was going to make me cry. "I'll pay you back, I promise."

"In person, when you come home for good. Until then, screw you."

I laughed. That was just so Autumn. "I love you, too, you know," I said when she'd pulled to a stop at the airport.

"Yeah, yeah."

With tears in my eyes and a smile on my face, I walked into the terminal. How had I gotten so lucky to have friends who still loved me after I'd as good as cut them out of my life for years?

The airline agent held out her hand for my boarding pass, but my fingers wouldn't let go of it. "I can't do this," I told her.

She gave me a sympathetic smile. "Are you afraid of flying, hon? Flying is safer than driving a car."

"No, it's not that. I can't walk out on him like this." Why was I telling her that?

"You getting on the plane or not, lady?" the man behind me griped.

"Sorry," I mumbled, stepping out of line.

"It is her, Savannah, the model," a young woman said to another woman next to her as I walked past.

I made the mistake of glancing at her just as she held her phone up to take a picture. *Dang it.* I knew better than to make eye contact with strangers. Dropping my chin to my chest, I hurried past. In an effort not to be noticed, I'd tucked my hair up in a ball cap, had forgone makeup, and had dressed down, wearing jeans and a sweatshirt under my coat. Sometimes that worked and sometimes it didn't, like now.

I hated my life.

The happiest I'd been since moving to New York was the past few days in the valley... the home of my heart. Since that was the honest to God's truth, I asked myself why I was even thinking I had to go back to the city. I didn't have an answer. Nor did I know what I was going to do now. What I needed was time alone to think.

Refusing to call one of my friends to come to my aid again, I went to the rental car agency, and using some of the gift cards Autumn had given me, I signed for an economy car. It was actually amazing that I'd kept my driver's license current since I never drove myself anywhere. Because I hadn't been behind the wheel of a car in nine years, it took me twice as long as normal to get back to the valley. Astonishingly I arrived without wrecking the car.

When I reached the middle of town, I pulled over in a gift shop parking lot. *Now what, Savannah?* I had no idea what to do other than I really did need time alone to think and plan. If I went back to Autumn's—and she'd be thrilled to see me—I wouldn't be left alone. And then there was Adam. He'd know I was back.

I wanted Adam in my life. Like crazy wanted. But I needed to be a woman who had something to offer him, who wasn't afraid of her own shadow. He deserved my best, and that was what I'd give him. When I had my life in order, I would tell him I loved him. If by then he didn't want me anymore, I wouldn't want to die, not like I wanted to the first time I'd lost him. But to love Adam and have him love me back, I had to love myself.

That was my truth, and I meant to get there.

The sun had set, and I couldn't sit here all night. About the time I decided it would be best to drive to Asheville and get a room, I noticed the lights were on across the street in Mary's Bread Company. I chewed on my bottom lip, debating the wisdom of involving Mary. The thought of driving all the way back to Asheville in the dark decided me.

The closed sign was on the door, so Mary had probably locked up, but I could see her moving around inside. Jackson may or may not have returned to New York, but I wasn't taking any chances of getting caught by him in the middle of a parking lot at night. After scanning the area around me and seeing no cars nearby, I ran to the door and knocked. Mary's eyes widened when she saw me, and she hurried to the door and let me in.

"Hi, Mary," I said, watching to make sure she locked up behind me.

She put her hands on her hips. "Savannah Graham, what in the world are you doing running around by yourself at this time of night?"

"Let's go in the back, out of sight of your display windows."

I followed her into the kitchen. "Wow, it smells so good in here. Are you baking?"

"Birthday cake for a customer picking it up first thing in the morning. Now answer my question."

It was hard not to smile at the tiny woman dressed in lime green from head to toe, and by head I mean her hair was as green as a lime along with her clothes, shoes, and eye shadow.

"I wanted to talk to you. Ahem…" I didn't even know what I wanted from her.

"Just spit it out, girl."

"Okay. I was supposed to get on a plane this afternoon, so everyone thinks I'm heading back to New York."

"Well, obviously you're not on an airplane. What's going on, Savannah?" She pointed to a small table and two chairs pushed against the wall. "Sit. You talk, I'll bake."

The story spilled out in a tumble of words, probably not making a lot of sense as my thoughts were all mixed up. The strange thing was how easy it was to talk to her. I think maybe because it didn't seem as if she was paying attention.

It was more like I was just working things out in my mind. For over an hour I talked about my mother, Jackson, how much I hated modeling but didn't know anything else, and how much I missed the valley, my friends, and Adam.

"I love him, Mary," I admitted. "I think he still cares for me, but I have to be happy with myself before there can be a chance for us, and I'm not."

While I was talking, she'd slid a saucer with a slice of red velvet cake—my weakness—in front of me, along with a cup of hot chocolate. I tried to ignore them, but that lasted about three minutes before I gave in. It was impossible to resist a slice of Mary's red velvet cake, and there was nothing better than hot chocolate on a cold winter's night. And besides, I was having a pity party with Mary, something strange enough to make me think maybe I was dreaming being here in her kitchen. And if I was, I wasn't really eating cake, right?

After taking a sheet cake out of the oven and setting it on a rack to cool, Mary poured herself a cup of coffee, then sat across from me. "I wish your mother was here so I could slap her silly. She's got you messed up nineteen ways to Sunday, girl."

"I can't blame it all on her. There were plenty of times when I should have stood up to her."

"Maybe, but looking backward gets you nowhere fast. What do you need to be happy, dear?"

That was one of the few questions I knew the answer to. "I need to find me."

Mary snorted. "You kids today. You make things so much harder than they have to be. Stop feeling sorry for yourself and allow yourself that happiness you crave."

Was that all my problem was? I'd never thought about it before, but I honestly couldn't remember a time when I didn't feel sorry for myself except for the year I was with Adam. Every time my mother had dragged me off to film a commercial, I felt sorry for myself. When she wouldn't allow me cakes for my birthdays, I felt sorry for myself. When she'd hauled me off to New York, away from my friends, from Adam, I'd felt sorry for myself. Thinking about it, I realized I was drowning in sorrys.

I buried my face into my hands. "I'm pitiful."

"Maybe you're the one I should slap silly," Mary muttered. "Lift your damn chin, Savannah Graham." As if she had sole control of my chin, it lifted at her command. "Much better. Now, exactly what do you need, right now, this minute?"

"Time. A few days to get my head straight and take care of some things. I don't suppose you have a bed here I can borrow?" When I went to Adam, I wanted to have my life straightened out. For my own sake I needed to prove to myself that I was capable of fixing my own problems.

"I can do you one better. I have a rental cabin not far from here. It's empty now, so you're welcome to stay there."

That was almost too easy. Suspicious, I narrowed my eyes. "You have to promise not to tell anyone I'm there. Not Autumn, not Jenn, not Adam, not—"

"Got it. I can't tell anyone you're there. The pantry's empty, so I'll send enough food with you to get you through a few days." She tilted her head and studied me. "That's all the time you need to figure out what you already know, right?"

"Yeah, just a few days." Reason number three hundred and fifty-two why I loved the valley. There was always someone you could turn to when in trouble. I stood and, bending my knees, hugged her. "Thank you, Mary."

She patted my back. "Personally I don't get you kids 'needing to get your heads straight' thing. You just need to decide what you want and go get it."

Was it really that easy?

Even though I protested that I didn't need that much, she filled a bag with lunch meats, bread, cheeses, another slice of red velvet cake, and a box of hot chocolate. Once she was satisfied that I wouldn't starve, we got in our cars and I followed her to her cabin.

"Need to turn on the water for you." She disappeared around the side of the house. "There, you're good to go. The fireplace is gas, and I'll show you where the switch for that is."

"Love the hot tub," I said once inside and seeing the red, heart-shaped tub tucked into the corner of the room. It was a one-room cabin with a king bed, a sofa, the hot tub, and a small kitchen. It was simply adorable.

"Honeymooners love the hot tub." She smiled as she looked at it. "I've had a few fun times in it myself."

I laughed. "TMI."

"That's another thing about you kids today. You're just too sensitive. Us old people do have sex, you know."

"Right. Glad you cleared that up. I've always wondered." I opened the only door in the cabin to see it was the bathroom. "This is perfect, Mary. Thank you."

"You're very welcome. Adam built this place for me. Seems right that you're here." She showed me where everything was, then said, "Lock up behind me."

"Thanks again, Mary." She waved her fingers at me as she left. Knowing that Adam had built Mary's cabin, I walked around, trailing my fingers over the walls, the kitchen counter, any place he would have touched with his hands. He was a true artist. "You're amazing," I told him even though he couldn't hear.

I put the food away, then went to the sliding glass door. Opening it, I saw a balcony and walked out. Dang, it was cold. Shoving my hands in my pockets, I walked to the railing and looked down on the lights of Blue Ridge Valley. The view would be amazing in the daytime, but I liked it now. It was a clear night, and it looked like there were a million stars in the sky. I lowered my gaze back to the valley.

That was my home down there and where Adam was. I wanted so badly to find a way to stay, but first I had to fix my problems. Adam couldn't do that for me.

CHAPTER TWENTY-SIX

~ Adam ~

IF I NEVER HAD ANOTHER day like this one, I'd be elated. Between Marks trying to burn down our model home—and there was no doubt in my mind that it was him—and Savannah walking away from me without a backward glance, I was ready to get a good drunk on. I was furious at the world, and my heart felt like it had been stomped on by a gorilla wearing cement shoes.

I'd hunkered down and buried myself in work until my crew had grown tired of my snarly attitude, begging me to go home or a bar if that worked better for me. I'd seriously considered the bar suggestion but decided if I was going to get a drunk on, I'd rather do it at home. Hopefully if I pickled my brain enough, I wouldn't spend the night thinking about Savannah.

Beer was my usual preference, and then only one or two, but something stronger was called for tonight. "It's a whiskey kind of night," I told Jinx as I opened a can of cat food. He turned his back on me, apparently still angry over losing Savannah's panties.

I'd just poured a glass of whiskey to the brim when I got the urge to go down to the river. "Damn it, Connor." Letting out a frustrated sigh, I set the glass on the counter, put on my heavy coat, and headed out to see what my brother had to say.

"New rule," I said when I reached him. "In the winter, if one of us has something to say, we do it like normal people. Inside, preferably with a roaring fire going."

"This is where we talk about the heavy shit. We can't do

that all cozy in front of a fire."

"We could certainly give it a try." I jammed my hands into my pockets. "Say what you came to say so I can get back to the night's agenda."

"What, getting drunk?"

"That's what you summoned me here to talk about?" It was annoying to have someone who could read your mind when you wanted to get drunk without getting a lecture.

"Savannah left."

"What?"

"Thought that would get your attention. Autumn took her to the airport this afternoon."

"Back to New York?"

"Yep."

"She couldn't even tell me she was leaving? If nothing else, a voice mail or e-mail wishing me a good life?" What little was left of that heart the gorilla had stomped on decided it had had enough. "See you around. I have a date with a bottle."

"Adam—"

"Don't want to hear it." I strode away, refusing to listen to my brother say he'd told me so. As much as I didn't want to, I worried about Savannah's safety without me there to protect her.

Back in my house, I shed my coat and then headed straight for the glass of whiskey. Before I could start on my drinking binge, my phone buzzed. Seeing Dylan's name on the screen, I gave the whiskey a look of longing as I answered.

"Yeah?"

"Marks hasn't turned his rental car in," Dylan said, getting right to the reason for his call. "I haven't been able to verify yet that he was on a plane back to New York, but I'd say not."

"I want to prove he was the one who tried to burn my model house down, and then I want him charged."

"Working on it, believe me. Nothing would make me happier than to see him in one of my jail cells. Too bad you don't have security cameras."

"They'll be installed in three days." Not that that helped on this.

"Good." Dylan hesitated for a moment, then said, "Autumn told Jenny that Savannah went back to New York."

"So I understand."

"Well, I'll let you know if I find out exactly where Marks is."

"Appreciate it, Chief."

I disconnected, set my phone on the counter, and reached for the whiskey. My doorbell rang… repeatedly. If that was Connor, I was going to kill him. Jinx had learned that the doorbell meant people to play with had arrived, and he raced into the living room. I put my eye to the peephole.

"It's your most favorite person in the world," I told him as I opened the door to Autumn. "Why are you here, and where's your ugly half?" I asked, looking behind her and not seeing Connor. She rarely showed up at my house without him.

"Someone's in a pissy mood." She marched past me even though I hadn't invited her in.

"Someone's plan to get the mother of all drunks on keeps getting interrupted."

"Well, I have a few things to say to you while you're still sober and able to follow a conversation." She said that with her hands on her hips while glaring at me. Then she picked up Jinx and brought him to her face.

"Hard to take you serious when your nose is buried in fur and you're giggling." Leaving her to it, I headed for the kitchen. Maybe Jinx would be useful for once in his life and keep her entertained long enough for me to pour that whiskey down my throat.

"Put that drink down, Adam Hunter."

Or not. I set the glass on the counter, turned, and raised a brow, waiting to hear what I'd done to get her riled up. And believe me, an annoyed Autumn was never a fun thing.

Hands on hips again and fire in her eyes, she said, "What are you going to do about Savannah?"

"Nothing. Good-bye."

"Men!" She stomped her foot for emphasis.

I expelled a frustrated breath. "What do you expect me to do? I asked her to stay. She said no. And then she left. Something I wish you'd do so I could proceed with my plan for the night."

"Getting drunk never solves anything."

There she was wrong. Get your mind pickled enough and you didn't think about stupid things like gorillas stomping on your heart. Get drunk enough and you forgot you even had a heart.

"Do you love her?"

"Never stopped." And on that true confession I picked up the glass. If Autumn wouldn't leave, then by damn she could witness my journey into oblivion. She snatched it out of my hand and poured the whiskey into the sink. "Hey, that was supposed to end up in my stomach."

"Tough titties."

"You sounded like Granny just then." Granny was Hamburger's mother and older than dirt. You never knew what was going to come out of her mouth.

"Did not. But back to Savannah."

"Must we?"

"Just listen, okay? No one has ever fought for Savannah for the right reasons. All her life she was beaten down by the one person who should have taught her how to be a confident woman. And if what her mother did to her wasn't enough, Jackson came along and finished the job. She's been programmed to believe that the only thing she's good for is to look pretty, that she has nothing to offer."

Her eyes softened. "Especially to you."

"I don't disagree with you, and the way her mother treated her makes me angry to this day. But I tried. She—"

"Not hard enough. Not the first time and not this time. She loves you, Adam. Always has. You let her go the first time, and now you're doing it again."

"I know I didn't fight for her when I should have." I rubbed the back of my neck in a useless effort to soothe the building tension.

"No, you didn't, but you were young and thought you were doing the right thing. You don't have either one of those excuses now. So I ask you again. What are you going to do about it?"

I straightened and looked my hopefully future sister-in-law in the eyes. "I'm going after her."

Autumn pumped her fist. "Yes! Now you're talking."

"Miss Savannah hasn't returned home, Mr. Hunter," Savannah's doorman said. His eyes narrowed. "Not since she left with you."

"She left North Carolina yesterday to come home. Maybe you weren't on duty when she arrived?" She had to be here. "Could you ring her apartment?"

"Whoever's on duty notes when residents return after a trip, sir. She's not here."

"At least call her apartment and make sure there hasn't been a mix-up."

"We don't mix things up, but I'll check to make you happy."

When he disappeared into what I assumed was the office, I called Savannah's number. "Where the hell are you, Savannah?" I said when I got her voice mail. After disconnecting, I realized how curt my message sounded. I called her back. "Sorry if I sounded like a jerk. I'm in New York because we need to talk. Please call me."

The doorman returned. "Miss Savannah hasn't come back."

Where the hell was she?

CHAPTER TWENTY-SEVEN

~ Savannah ~

THE NEXT MORNING I BUNDLED up, grabbed a blanket, and took my cup of hot chocolate out on the deck to watch the sun come up. It was freezing, but I wrapped the blanket around me and let out a happy sigh as I breathed in the fresh mountain air. I'd slept better last night than I had in a long time. Just knowing that I'd made the decision to stay in the valley had lifted a weight that had sat on my chest since the day my mother hauled me away.

Something cold fell on my nose, and I looked up to see that it was snowing. I laughed and stuck out my tongue to catch the flakes. Snow in New York was ugly, but here, it was beautiful when the mountains and the trees were covered in white.

The cold finally drove me back inside. It was too early to start making calls, so I spent a few minutes walking around the cabin, admiring the beauty of the log walls, the stone fireplace, the mantel, and the pine floors. Adam was an artist as much as someone who put paint to canvas or words on paper that made your heart sing when you read them. I trailed my hand over the mantel. I didn't know wood, so didn't know what it was, but I was in awe. The edge was ragged yet smooth to the touch. No splinters. It was polished to a high sheen but still rustic looking.

"It's beautiful, Adam." I wished he were here so I could tell him that.

It was the perfect honeymoon cabin, and thinking of that and Adam, an idea took seed in my mind. A way to hopefully earn a lot of money while going out on a high with my modeling career. The more I thought about it, the more excited I got.

As soon as it was a reasonable hour to start making calls, I turned on my phone, frowning at seeing a handful of text messages pop up on the screen.

Where R U

That one was from Autumn, as were the next three telling me to call her.

Call me

There were two voice messages from Adam, but I didn't listen to them. I didn't want to talk to anyone yet, and if I called Autumn, she wouldn't give up until she got me to tell her where I was and why. I texted her.

What's up

It didn't surprise me when my phone rang a minute later, her name coming up on the screen. I let it go to voice mail, then waited for her text. It only took a few seconds to show up.

Damn it!!! Call me!

No. I'm fine. Just need a few days to think. Will call you when I'm ready 2 talk. Promise.

You R killing me here, S.

I replied with a heart and a smiley face. I glanced at my watch, predicting that my phone would ring in five minutes. It only took three. This call I'd take, knowing Jenn would back off if I asked her to. I also knew my friends needed to be assured that I was safe, something I wanted to give them.

"I know you just talked to Autumn." I'd taken my phone to the sofa, curling up and watching the snow fall while I waited for Jenn to call.

"Yeah, I did. Are you okay?"

"Better than I've been for a while." I almost relented and told her where I was and why, but having these few days to myself, for myself, was important. My friends would be there for me if I needed them, something I didn't doubt for a minute. It was tempting to lean on them, but that wasn't the way to learn how to stand on my own two feet. Adam had said that Savannah was still inside me, that I only had to find her. I meant to do just that.

"I need a few days to take care of some things and to do some thinking, Jenn. Please don't ask me any questions, okay? I'm not ready to talk yet."

"Been there and understand. As long as you're safe, we'll wait. But you go more than three days without getting in touch and I'm sending out the bloodhounds."

"Thank you. I love you, especially if you can get Autumn to calm down. Tell her I love her, too, and that I really am fine."

"I can actually hear in your voice that you are, and it's about time."

It really was. "Adam left a message, too, and I'm not ready to talk to him yet either. Would you tell him I'll call him in a few days?"

"Yes. You should know that he went… You know what, never mind. You do what you need to do, and everything will work out the way it's supposed to. Love you, girl."

"Ditto."

I wondered what she'd started to say about Adam, but if it had been important, she would have finished telling me. Next I called my attorney. Her assistant said she was in court this morning and would return my call after lunch. My next call was to an agent I'd met several times and had liked.

When I told the woman who answered the phone my name, she said, "The Savannah?"

I smiled at hearing the surprise in her voice. "That would be me."

"Marla will be right with you."

"Savannah, this is a pleasant surprise," Marla Armstrong said seconds later.

"I need an agent." Blurting it out like that wasn't how I'd wanted to approach her, but I'd never handled the business end of my career. Between that and my shyness, my nerves had taken over. I took a deep breath. "I was hoping you'd be interested in talking to me about representation."

"You're kidding, right?"

My heart fell. She wasn't interested.

"I mean, hell yeah I want you, but if this is a joke, it's not a funny one. Please tell me you're serious, Savannah."

Oh. Okay. I could breathe again. "I'm serious."

"What about Jackson?"

"I'm ending my contract with him. My attorney sent him a termination letter last week, but I'll have to finish out my obligations with him. You should also know I'm only going to model for one more year. After that I'm retiring."

"I can't tell you how sorry I am to hear that, and honestly I'd need to think about investing my time and efforts in you if it's only for a year."

"Understandable, but maybe what I have planned will change your mind." I wanted Marla, but I got where she was coming from. I almost apologized for bothering her. Then I listened to the voice in my head. *Sell her on your idea, Savannah. You can do it.* "If you have a few minutes, I'd like to tell you how you and I can create a big splash and make some big money doing it."

"Okay, big splash and big money has my attention. I'm all ears."

"I'm not sure how many obligations Jackson has committed me to, but he never books me out more than two months in advance unless it's for something like the Paris Show."

"That's odd."

"Yeah, but he wants me to be available if something huge comes along at the last minute." Like the nude shoot for the French magazine, but I didn't tell her about that. "It does happen often enough to reinforce his way of doing business. I'm thankful for that now because I'm not contractually tied down for the next year or more. The next two months will be finishing out my obligations with him. But that gives us time to plan."

"For?"

"For Savannah's Farewell Tour. We double my fee and limit the opportunities to sign me for a photo shoot to two a month. Something along the lines of here's your last chance to have Savannah on your cover or in your show." I bounced my foot as I waited for her reaction. When all I could hear was her breathing, my heart beat so hard that I thought I might hyperventilate. Maybe my idea was a stupid one. I sucked my bottom lip in, clamping my teeth down on it to keep from saying something stupid like, *Yeah, that's dumb. Sorry I bothered you.*

"Hell, Savannah, I just drooled all over myself," Marla finally said. "Wow! I mean, I'm sorry you're retiring. I'd love to have a lot of years with you, but if you're gonna go out, this is the way to rock it. Just brilliant. And double your fee? Meh. We can do way better than that."

Okay then. I think my grin reached both ears. "Thank you," I whispered, unable to say more than that.

She snorted. "No, I'm the one thanking you. When can we meet?"

"I'm not in New York right now, so in a week or two. I have to take care of some things, but I'll keep in touch. Oh, my last photo shoot has to be for *Bride's Magazine*."

"Interesting. Is there a reason for that?"

"Yes." At least I hoped so. "I'll explain when I see you. In the meantime, would you happen to have a recommendation for a bodyguard while I'm in New York? I don't want to get caught alone by Jackson."

"Actually I do. I use Farrant Security when I need a bodyguard for one of my models. If you'll send me your schedule, I'll make the arrangements."

"Thanks. I really appreciate it."

After we disconnected, I stared out the window at the falling snow as a sense of satisfaction settled inside me. I was taking control of my life finally, and it felt dang good. If I'd gotten on that plane and returned to New York, I would have fallen right back into my old life, maybe even letting Jackson back in. I believed that down to my bones. It would have been easier to go with what I knew versus taking the plunge to create a new life, one where I would be happy.

If I'd stayed at Connor and Autumn's, I would have spent my time feeling sorry for myself, and as much as I loved her, she would have aided me in that by trying to take care of me. And in the end I probably would have returned to my old life. But an angel in the form of a tiny, slightly crazy woman, fond of outlandish clothes and putting her nose in other people's business, had appeared when I needed her the most. She'd given me a magical place to hide for a few days and an adorable little cabin the man I loved had built, where ideas seemed to fill the air and one could believe that dreams did come true.

Thank you, Mary.

It was snowing harder, and I must have drifted off watching it because I jerked awake when my phone rang. It was Jill Thornwood calling back with good news. My bank account had been unfrozen and was now solely in my name.

"That was fast," I said.

"It was, but you have friends in high places."

Lucas Blanton? Had to be. "I'll be sure to thank him."

She chuckled. "I never said it was a him."

"But you're not saying it wasn't." It could only be Lucas, and I did want to thank him. "Do you know how I can log in to my bank account?"

"Yes. I'll e-mail you the log-in and instructions for setting up a new password. In other news, Jackson Marks is back in New York and has received notice that you're terminating your contract with his agency. He's demanding to talk to you."

"You spoke with him?"

"Earlier today. He's threatening to sue you for breach of contract if you don't get in touch with him. He has no grounds to do so as you're following the terms of your contract with him, and I told him that. I also told him that if he wanted to go down that road, we would countersue for mismanagement of your financial affairs."

"I have no proof that he did."

"Not yet, anyway. I threw it out there to see if he would bite, and he did by immediately backtracking. That tells me he has something to hide, so if you want to investigate—"

"No, I just want him out of my life." It wouldn't at all surprise me if Jackson had diverted money to his own bank account, but pursuing it would only prolong my contact with him. Whatever he might have taken from me, I'd consider as severance pay. And I really wasn't sure I could win against him, as my mother had given him full control of my career and money.

"As for talking to him, I told him that I'd pass his request on to you. You don't have to, and I don't see any reason to, but it's up to you."

"I'd rather not." He'd show up at the photo shoots he had scheduled for me for sure, and I was glad I'd thought to have Marla arrange security for me.

"He's furious that he's been evicted from your apartment and that his name has been removed from your bank account."

"I'm sure he is, but I honestly don't care."

"And you shouldn't. If he contacts you directly, let me know immediately."

"I will. And thank you. You've made this easier than I thought it would be. If you get a bill in the mail to me soon, the first check I write in my life will be to you."

She laughed. "Love it. I'll be tempted to frame it for that reason, but I won't. It will definitely get deposited. Might take a picture of it, though, for my personal pleasure."

"I might take a picture of it myself."

"You should. Take care, Savannah, and call me if you ever need legal help again."

"Definitely. Thanks again."

Jill's e-mail landed a few minutes later, and after changing the password, I saw my bank balance for the first time in my life. "Ten million," I murmured in shock. I'd thought it was around two or three million. If it was that now, but Jackson had considered my money his candy jar, what would it have been?

Out of curiosity I searched for the net worth of Candice Chandler, a top model like me. According to Google she was worth fifteen million. I should have a net worth of at least that, if not more. I spent very little money on myself, other than the mortgage on my New York apartment, monthly utilities, and necessities. Could he really have diverted that much of my money into his own pocket?

When I'd thought it was probably a few thousand here and a few there, I was willing to let it go. But in the millions? If he'd do that to me, he'd do it to the next girl given a chance, and I couldn't let that happen. I e-mailed Jill and told her that I'd changed my mind, giving her the go-ahead to audit my bank records from the day Jackson's name was put on my account. Once that was done, I put him out of my mind.

The one thing I refused to let him do was to steal this new happiness living in my heart. I'd taken steps today to create the life I wanted, and feeling proud of myself was powerful and heady, a new emotion for me. Everything was falling into place, but there was one very big item on my list.

What was the best way to ask a man to marry you?

CHAPTER TWENTY-EIGHT

~ Adam ~

NO ONE KNEW WHERE SAVANNAH was. At least she'd talked to Jenn, so we assumed she was safely tucked up somewhere. Dylan had learned that Jackson Marks was back in New York, and both Mary and Hamburger took credit for running him off. If Dylan could prove that Marks had started the fire, he'd be back soon enough, charged with arson and standing trial. One could hope.

But where was Savannah? That was the question I wanted answered. I hadn't been able to stop thinking about what Autumn had said, that no one had ever fought for her, and I wanted to be the one to finally do it. I wanted to be her hero. First I had to find her. She'd asked Jenn to tell us to leave her alone for a few days, and I was respecting that… only because I didn't have a clue where she was.

A big storm was coming, one of those once-every-ten-years blizzards we get in the Blue Ridge Mountains. Since it made sense that Savannah was holed up in a hotel, maybe in Asheville or even Charlotte, I wasn't worried about her being stranded somewhere. While I waited for her to surface, my crew and I prepared for the coming weather by making sure everything was locked up tight.

We were finishing up and I'd already sent half of the guys home when my phone rang, Mary's name appearing on the screen.

"Hi, Mary. What's up?"

"I need you to come by the store."

"Because?" I was anxious to head home before the storm

hit, which according to the weather app on my phone was about twenty minutes away.

"There's something I need you to check. Now, Adam," she said, then disconnected.

It was already snowing hard as I drove to Mary's. The only things on the road were the snowplows and me. I congratulated myself on choosing the four-wheel drive Jeep this morning when I hit a patch of ice. Mary had better have a good reason for keeping me out in this mess.

"I need you to go to my cabin and turn off the water," she said when I walked into her shop.

Was she kidding? "Mary, I shut down the cabin two weeks ago."

"That was before I took George up there for the weekend."

"Who's George... Never mind, I don't want to know." He would have been her flavor of the month, what she called her boyfriends. She had a rule. Thirty days and then she moved on because she said any longer than that and they would fall in love with her. I had no idea where she kept finding them, but find them she did.

"We had a lovely weekend. He really enjoyed the hot tub."

"Mary," I growled, "I said I didn't want to know." Giving her my best glare, I said, "You do know there's a blizzard coming, right?"

"Of course I do. I don't live in a cave, Adam. That's why you need to go to the cabin. Imagine the mess if the pipes burst. You'll be the one who'll have to repair the damage, and if you refuse to turn off the water before that happens, you'll be responsible for the costs."

"Your logic is flawed, woman, but fine, I'll go turn the damn water off."

"Language, young man." She picked up a large box. "Here, take this home with you. It's food that will spoil if I lose power."

"And if I lose power?"

"You're a big boy. Eat everything." She pushed the box across the counter. "Off with you. Time's a'wasting."

The next time I saw Mary's name come up on my phone's screen, I was going to ignore it. The drive up the mountain to her cabin normally took about twenty minutes. That was doubled today. It was going to be real tricky going back down. If I slid over the side and died, I swore I was going to come back and haunt that little woman for the rest of her life.

About a mile from the cabin I passed a compact car in the ditch. I stopped and checked to make sure there wasn't anyone in it. Whoever the driver was had been lucky they'd run off the road on the mountain side and not the drop-off side. It was a steep drop, and no one would have ever known they'd gone over. A tree branch had gone through the passenger-side window, breaking it. Hopefully whoever was driving hadn't been hurt, and they must not have had a passenger since I didn't see any blood. I guessed they'd called someone to pick them up.

When I came to a stop in the driveway, it was snowing so heavily that I could barely see the cabin. I was going to hold a grudge on this one for Mary sending me up here in this weather when all she had to do was turn off the damn water before she left after her party weekend. The wind was blowing like a son of a bitch now, and I leaned into it as I made my way to the cabin.

I squinted against the snow blowing in my eyes. Someone was huddled at the door. It had to be the person from the car. Considering the slim build, I guessed it was a woman. She had a coat on over a hoodie, so I couldn't see if it was someone I knew. This was the closest building to where she'd wrecked, and she was no doubt trying to break in to get out of the weather. Couldn't say I blamed her.

"Hello," I called, not wanting to sneak up on her and scare her. "Is that your car in the ditch?" It was possible that Mary had saved a life by sending me up here, so I was going to have to let go of my grudge. That kind of pissed me off. I wanted to stay mad at her.

The woman glanced over her shoulder. "Adam?"

Savannah? What was she doing here? I jogged to her. She was trying to get the key in the lock, but her hands were shaking so badly that she couldn't get it in the slot.

"So c-cold."

"Let's get you inside, baby." Her lips were blue, her breathing was shallow, and her eyelashes were coated in ice. I was a trained rescue volunteer, and just looking at her I could tell she was going into hypothermia. To protect her from the wind, I wrapped my body around her back, took the key from her shaking hands, and unlocked the door. She stumbled, and I scooped her up in my arms, kicking the door closed behind me.

She wasn't dressed for this weather. "We have to get you out of these wet clothes."

"O-k-k-kay."

When her eyes slid closed, I patted her cheek. "Don't go to sleep on me, Savannah."

"'Kay." She opened her eyes, then closed them again.

Leaving her for a moment, I turned on the gas to the fireplace, then went to the thermostat and set it as high as it would go. Thank God we still had power, but how long would that last? I pulled the quilt from the bed, then made fast work of getting her out of her clothes. She was still shivering and that worried me, as did her wanting to go to sleep. After I had her wrapped in the quilt, I went in the bathroom and turned the shower on as hot as I thought she could stand it.

Next I stripped down to my boxers, and then I went and got my girl. Dropping the quilt on the floor, I stepped into the shower with her in my arms.

"Hot." She tried to turn away from the water, burying her face against my neck.

"We have to warm you up, Savvy."

I had a thousand questions, the first being what the hell was she doing up here in Mary's cabin? Obviously Mary knew she was here, the reason for the ruse in sending me up the mountain. Thank God she had. When Savannah stopped shivering, I stepped out of the shower. I set her on the counter, grabbed a towel, and dried her off.

"You're looking a lot better." I smiled at her as I traced her lips with my finger. "They're not blue anymore."

"Didn't you know, blue's the latest hot color for lips."

I rested my forehead against hers. "Don't ever scare me like that again."

"Sorry. When the snow started falling harder, I checked the weather and saw it was going to be bad. It seemed a good idea to go back down to the valley. Didn't get very far, did I?" She frowned. "Mary promised not to tell you I was here."

"She didn't. She said I had to come up and turn off the water so the pipes wouldn't burst. I'm going to have to have a little talk with her about fibbing." I put my fingers under her chin, forcing her to look at me. "You better be glad she did."

Instead of kissing her the way I wanted, I picked up the quilt and handed it to her. "Wrap yourself up and come sit by the fire. I'm going to put your clothes on the hearth to dry."

"Adam?"

"Yeah?" I stopped at the door, glancing back at her.

"I am glad you're here."

Me too, I thought, but I only nodded. Out of sight of her, I walked to the fireplace and put my hands on the mantel. Up until now, the priority had been to get her warm, and my EMT training had kicked in, leaving no room to think about what might have happened if I hadn't come up here. I bowed my head as the fear that I might have lost her finally hit. She might not be mine anymore, but I didn't think I could bear a world without her in it.

"Hey."

I hadn't heard her step next to me, and I glanced over my shoulder. She opened the quilt she'd wrapped around her, an invitation I couldn't refuse. When I moved to her, she draped the quilt over my shoulders, cocooning us.

"I'm still wet," I said, burying my face against her neck.

She leaned her head next to mine. "I don't care."

"What's happening here, Savannah?" I had no idea what the rules were, what she wanted from me.

"We need to talk, but first…" She pulled away and stared at me, and I waited for what was first. "First, make love to me. Please, Adam."

Calling myself every kind of fool, but unable to refuse her, I pushed the blanket away, letting it drop to the floor. "In front of the fireplace where you'll stay warm." She dropped to her knees, and while she was spreading out the quilt, I grabbed the two pillows from the bed. As I stood over her, my gaze roamed across her body. All I had to do was look at her and I was aroused. She lifted her eyes, catching me staring at her. When she gave me that shy smile, the one I remembered so well from high school, I let go of the pillows and dropped to my knees in front of her.

"If I had any sense at all, I'd get us off this mountain before the storm gets worse. But I'm a selfish man, Savannah. If this is my last chance to be with you, I'm taking it."

"I—"

"No, don't talk."

"But I want to tell you—"

"Shhh. Don't talk. Just feel." I covered her mouth with mine. Whatever she had to say, I didn't want to hear. I knew my heart was ready to spill out of my chest, landing at her feet, not caring if it got stomped on. Because that was going to happen when she left. If she left. Because I was going to do everything in my power to convince her she belonged with me. I was going to fight for her, something I should have done a long time ago.

I kissed a path across her cheek to her ear, getting a moan when I swirled my tongue around the shell. I slid my hands down her arms, and when I reached her hands, I threaded my fingers around hers. I hoped I never had to let her go.

We were still on our knees, and her head dropped onto my shoulder. She pulled her hands out of mine and tugged on my boxers. Rolling her down to the quilt with me, I pushed my boxers off. "I don't have a condom with me, so we're going to get creative in other ways."

She giggled.

"You think that's funny?"

"No, not that. I discovered a box of them in the night table by the bed. I guess Mary keeps them stocked for her guests."

"Of course she does." We both laughed, not at all surprised considering we were talking about Mary. "Stand by." The night table was only a few feet away, and I was back to her in seconds.

"Now, where were we?"

CHAPTER TWENTY-NINE

~ *Savannah* ~

"YOU SAID SOMETHING ABOUT GETTING creative." He was on his knees, raw hunger in his eyes as his gaze roamed over me, sending a fire racing through me. I'd lived through a nine-year drought without seeing a man look at me like that.

A beautiful smile curved his lips. "Right." He tossed the box aside, then crawled over me. "And I think I'll start my creative journey right here." He trailed his tongue down the valley of my breasts, working his way to a nipple, twirling the tip of his tongue around it and sending shivers traveling under my skin.

"Mmm, delicious," he murmured as he moved to the other one.

"Please."

"Patience, Savvy, patience."

"Easy for you to say."

He chuckled. "Not really. Now hush and just feel."

I hadn't thought I'd ever get warm again, but heat filled the last of the cold places as Adam made love to every inch of my body. We'd been each other's first, losing our virginity together, sometimes fumbling as we learned what pleased us. He was no longer that boy but a man who had learned much in the time we'd been apart.

He spent long minutes exploring my body with his mouth and tongue, so tender and intensely focused on me that it brought tears to my eyes and hope to my heart. When he sent me soaring, following me over the cliff, I almost told him that I loved him. But it wasn't time yet.

Adam fell asleep, spooned behind me with his arms wrapped around me. As I watched the snow fall outside the window, I couldn't help wishing that we could shut the world away and live here forever.

"What are you thinking?" Adam murmured, his breath tickling my neck.

I turned around to face him. "I thought you were asleep."

"Just dozing." He trailed his palm down my hip. "How are you feeling?"

"Extremely satisfied." I smiled. "You have some new, very sexy moves since we did this as kids." That got me a pleased-with-himself grin.

"Glad you approve, but I meant are you warm inside."

"Like you wouldn't believe."

He laughed at that. "From the cold, silly girl." He put his hand on my cheek and kissed me. "You scared me. I don't even want to think about what might have happened if I hadn't come up here."

"I couldn't stay in the car with a broken window and knew I had to get back to the cabin. Toward the end I just wanted to curl up in the snow and go to sleep, but if I did, I knew I'd die and never see you again."

"Christ, Savannah."

He made love to me again, and there was a desperation to it, as if the thought of losing me was unbearable. I let the happiness invade my heart, no longer afraid to embrace it. For the first time since high school, I believed I was worthy of being loved.

Afterward we both slept for a little while, with him curled around me, holding on to me as if he were afraid I might slip away from him. The ringing of his phone woke us, and I could see that the sun was beginning to set. Adam mumbled something incoherent, then went in search of his phone, finding it in the coat he'd dropped on the end of the bed.

"You're a devious little thing," he said.

I assumed Mary's name had come up on his screen.

After a moment he said, "She's fine now, but I don't even want to think about what might have happened if you hadn't sent me up here."

He went to the window and stared out at the storm. What was it with men being comfortable walking around in all their glory? And what glory Adam was, I thought as I admired his backside while listening to him tell Mary that I'd wrecked my car. The rental company wasn't going to be happy, but right now I didn't care. Nothing could steal the joy taking root in my heart… Unless Adam stole it. He had the power to do that if he didn't want me in his life.

"We're stuck here until the weather clears," he said to Mary.

That was definitely okay as far as I was concerned, and he didn't sound at all unhappy to be stuck here with me. As he listened to something she said, he glanced at me, catching me staring at him. One eyebrow went up, and his lips curved in a smirk. I could see the question in his eyes clear as day. *Like what you see?*

The answer would be a resounding yes. Wanting to see his reaction, I let my gaze roam over him and licked my lips.

"Gotta go, Mary." He listened for a moment before saying, "Already found them." Not taking his eyes off me, he tossed the phone onto the bed and then prowled toward me, reminding me of Jinx, single-minded and about to pounce on his favorite toy.

I giggled, which was weird because I'm not a giggler. But the anticipation of being devoured by my naughty cat was delicious and exciting. Adam dropped down over me, catching himself on his elbows.

"And why are you laughing when you look at me? A man is sensitive about his manly parts being ridiculed, you know."

"Yeah? Maybe you should see what you can do to make

me stop thinking."

"There's a challenge I'm definitely up for." He smiled down at me, and I could swear there was affection—maybe even love—for me in his blue eyes.

I trailed my hand down his stomach to his erection and wrapped my hand around it. "Yep, you're definitely up."

"You're playing with fire, woman," he growled before his mouth crashed down on mine.

I stopped thinking.

CHAPTER THIRTY

~ Adam ~

"NOT LAUGHING SO MUCH NOW, are we?" I brushed the hair away from Savannah's face. Her cheeks were flushed pink and her eyes had that sleepy, satisfied look of a woman just thoroughly loved. It was going to kill me all over again if I couldn't convince her to stay.

She snuggled into me. "Mm, you pounded my giggles right out of me."

"Apparently not," I said when she giggled again. "And I hope you got more out of that than just a pounding."

The laughter in her eyes faded, and her expression turned serious. "If I tell you something, you promise not to freak out?"

Not a question any man wanted to be asked. "I can't answer that without knowing what you're about to say, but I promise I'll try not to."

She placed her palm on my cheek, stared into my eyes, and said, "I love you."

My heart stumbled over itself. They were words I'd ached to hear from her again for nine years, but what good were they if she left me again? The cycle would begin anew. Hours of long talks with my brother down by the river, the life bleeding out of my heart. He was going to be pissed that I'd let myself fall for her again. The thing of it was, I'd never unfallen. I rolled away, scanning the room for my clothes.

"You don't have to panic, Adam. I just wanted you to know, but I don't expect to hear them back."

"I can't do this again, Savannah." I glanced at her, hating

that she was wrapping the quilt around her, pulling it up to her neck as if needing to hide. I hated the hurt in her voice. But what the hell did she want from me?

"Again?" She slapped her hand down on the floor. "Again?"

"You're repeating yourself." I snatched up my jeans, not sure why I was so mad. I'd been the one to break up with her, but it had been for her own good. Or so I thought. She hadn't blinked when I'd told her it was over, had just trotted herself off to New York and made herself famous. She was the girl I'd loved and lost but had to see her face on magazine covers in every grocery store and pharmacy I went in.

"You left me, Adam. Said you didn't love me anymore."

"I lied."

"So you said." Her lips trembled. "I don't understand why you blame me, why you say you can't do this again when you were the one who broke up with me."

Yeah, I was being an ass. "Look, I'm sorry." I sat on the edge of the bed. "I've thought about us a lot the last few days, what happened, why I found reasons to be angry at you. When I look back on it, I realize it was stupid thinking, but my naive young brain thought that you should have known I was lying when I said I didn't love you. Your mother convinced me letting you go was the right thing to do, but I wanted you to convince me she was wrong. You didn't. You just turned your back on me and walked away."

"How was I supposed to do that when I didn't know at the time she was the reason you broke up with me?"

"I just said it was stupid thinking." The slight twitch of her lips said she agreed with me, but that little twitch also told me that she was trying to understand. This was a long overdue conversation, and I needed to get the rest of it out.

"The next thing I hear about you is that you're almost engaged to that baseball player. After you left, I was a broken man, but you seemed unaffected, dating a celebrity, your smiling face everywhere. I used those things to put some of the blame for what happened back on you, maybe as a way to try and get over you." I shrugged. "I don't know, except at the time, when I said I didn't love you, you walked away without a word when I wanted you to call me out for lying to you."

"You made me believe you, that you didn't really love me, so there didn't seem to be anything left to say. Do you think I wasn't broken, too? You crushed my heart, Adam. After that I didn't care what happened to me. I'd been taught to smile on command, and those smiles you saw were fake. I was nothing more than a robot, going where I was told to, smiling when I was told to because nothing mattered anymore. I was dead inside without you. As for the night you broke up with me, I turned away from you because I refused to let you see me cry."

The thought of her crying over me made me want to slap the boy I'd been. I'd somehow believed that I was the only one hurting. "When you said you loved me a few minutes ago, they were the words I've longed to hear since the day I lost you. I want to beg you to stay, and I would if I thought there was any chance—"

"Do you love me, Adam?"

I took her hand and pressed her palm on my chest. "You've owned my heart since the day you admitted that you felt funny around me. Yes, Savvy, I love you. Always have. Always will."

"If I stayed, didn't go back to New York, would that make a difference to you?"

"What are you saying?" My heart thumped hard against my ribs, wanting to but afraid to believe she really meant it.

"That I want to stay here. With you."

"Do you mean that?"

"I've never been more sure of anything in my life… if you want me."

If I wanted her! A laugh escaped. "Come here, Savannah." She came, quilt and all. I pulled her onto my lap, then rolled us over on the bed. Lifting onto an elbow and locking eyes with her. "I love you, Savvy."

"I never stopped loving you, Adam. I wanted to, I tried to, but you never gave me my heart back."

"And I never will." She was mine. I'd just not realized until now that we had always belonged to each other, even when we were miles apart. I pressed a soft kiss to her lips. As much as I didn't want to ruin this moment, I had to know. "How is this going to work? Are you going to still model? Won't you have to be in New York to do that?"

Her eyes lit up. "I have it all worked out."

I lowered my head to the pillow, and as we lay on the bed, facing each other, I took her hand and tangled my fingers around hers. "Tell me about it."

"The reason I came up here to the cabin was because I had to get away from everyone so I could think."

"Even me?"

"Especially you."

Well, that hurt.

"I've never made my own decisions, you know that. It was past time that I started. If I was going to have any respect for myself, I had to figure things out on my own."

Okay, I got that. "I wish you'd at least told us you were coming up here. What if Mary hadn't sent me on a false pretense?"

She rolled her eyes. "Do you really think Mary wouldn't have made sure I was safe knowing I was here?"

"True, but you almost weren't."

"And then you saved me." She tightened her fingers around mine. "To answer your question, yes, I'll have to return to New York. I have contracts to fulfill. But I'll travel there from here."

As she told me about the exclusive farewell year she had planned, I could see the pride she had in herself. It was something I'd never seen in her before, not even when we'd first been together. We'd been in love and happy, but she'd still been under her mother's thumb. She hadn't had a sense of self-worth, and as much as the male in me wanted her to let me take care of her, I could see that this was something she had needed to work out for herself.

"What?" she said at seeing me smile.

"I wish you could see your face, see how bright your eyes are. You're not the same woman who came back with her tail tucked between your legs."

Laughing, she punched my arm. "I don't have a tail. But seriously, thank you, God, I'm not the same. I didn't plan to walk out that night, but once I did, I made a promise to myself that I would take control of my life."

"And you are. I'm so proud of you, Savannah."

"There's one more thing."

"What's that?" I said when she hesitated, sucking her bottom lip into her mouth.

"Ahem... It's about the last job, my finale." She took a deep breath. "I love you, Adam, but I need to know. Do you see a future for us?'

Didn't she already know the answer to that? "I see it as clear as day."

"Good. Seriously good, but we need time to get to know each other again. I'm hoping that we'll be ready around this time next year. The last shoot I'm arranging is for *Bride's Magazine*. If we're not together then, I'll still do it, but it won't be real. If we are ready for that next step, I want to let them photograph our wedding."

I kissed her hard. "What if I don't want to wait a year?" It seemed to me that going on ten years was long enough to wait.

"It will go by fast, I promise."

"Not fast enough for me." I kissed her again, which led to a little bit of lovin'... okay, a lot of lovin'. Later, with her tucked up next to me and me tracing circles on her stomach, I said, "About our wedding, won't that end up being a media circus?"

"Not if I handle it right. It won't be announced ahead of time, and I'll only do it if the magazine agrees to keep it a secret until after the wedding. It's not that I want the publicity, but they'll pay a small fortune, more than enough to keep my animal rescue sanctuary going for a long time."

I still wasn't crazy about the idea, but she was right. It would be big money, and if she wanted to do it just for the money, I'd have a problem with it. But her dream of rescuing animals was important to her and a part of her taking control of her life. It was something she needed to do herself.

"As long as we can maintain control of our wedding, I'm on board." I winked at her. "If I decide to ask you to marry me someday."

She grinned. "Maybe I'll ask you."

"Even better, but I want a romantic proposal. You have to go all out if you want me to consider it."

"Oh, Adam, trust me. It will be the proposal of all proposals."

That deserved another kiss, which led to loving her again. She might be a new and improved Savannah, but she was still my Savannah.

CHAPTER THIRTY-ONE

~ Savannah ~

"I HEARD THAT," ADAM SAID, PULLING me against him and nestling his face into my neck.

It was morning, still snowing and dark and gray outside. We'd made love half the night, almost as if we couldn't get enough of each other. Since we had nine years to make up for, it wasn't surprising. We hadn't even gotten out of bed to eat dinner, and my stomach was growling with a vengeance.

I snuggled into him for one last time before I got up. "I'll make us some breakfast. We have lunch meat, bread, assorted cheeses, and cake. What's your preference?"

"The food," he exclaimed.

"Well, yes, it's all food." I didn't want to get out of the warm bed, didn't want to leave the warmth of his body, but we needed sustenance.

"No, I mean Mary sent food with me. It's still in the car. Not sure what all's in the box, but it's probably frozen solid." He kissed my neck, then rolled out of bed. "I better go get it." He dressed, headed for the door, and then pivoted, walking back to me. Bending over, he gave me a lingering kiss.

"Now I'm fortified enough to face the elements." He winked before walking away.

Wow, just wow! I put my fingers on my tingling lips. The man could kiss. I scrambled out of bed, and by the time he came back in, covered in snow and carrying a large box, I was dressed in yoga pants, a sweatshirt, and socks, my hair up in a messy ponytail.

Adam dropped the box on the counter as his gaze roamed over me. "You look like a mountain girl." He smiled. "My mountain girl."

"Sorry. I'll find something nicer to put on." That was the kind of thing Jackson would've said, seeing me not looking my best, and it hurt that it was coming from Adam.

His smile disappeared. "I'm not criticizing you, Savannah." He held out his hand. "Come here."

When I reached him, he put his hands on my waist, lifted me, set me on the kitchen counter, and then pushed his body between my legs, settling his hands on my thighs.

"You're beautiful in your glamour shots, but that's not the girl I love. When you look like this"—he leaned away and eyed me—"you're my Savannah, not that woman I can't touch on the cover of magazines."

Tears burned my eyes. I was so used to being censured for the least little offense. It was hard to believe him, but I wanted to. "Jackson calls me a hick when—"

"To hell with Jackson Marks." Adam's eyes blazed with fury. "Get him and everything that man ever said or did to you out of your brain."

"I'll try."

"You're going to do more than try, and every time you even hint that you doubt yourself because of him, I'm going to kiss those thoughts right out of your head. Like this."

He claimed my mouth in a kiss so consuming that he left no room for Jackson. The only man in my mind was Adam. I couldn't stop my tears.

"I love you," I whispered when he finally pulled away.

He wrapped his arms around me and put his mouth next to my ear. "After I give you a punishing kiss for letting him slip into your head, I'm going to spank you."

I giggled even as tears ran down my cheeks. "You wouldn't dare."

"Try me." He put his fingers under my chin, lifting my

face, his eyes capturing mine. "I love you back, Savvy. Have since I was seventeen." He let go of me and stared at the box he'd brought in. "Whatever's in there is a block of ice." His gaze shifted to me. "Your man is hungry. What's for breakfast, woman?"

"Me?" I said, forgetting about food.

Adam's lips curved up. "Food and then you." He smirked. "You don't have a clue how to feed your man, do you?"

"Busted," I said, knowing Adam would make sure I ate.

"Savvy, Savvy, Savvy," he muttered. "How did you ever survive without me?"

"I pretty much didn't," I admitted.

His gaze shot to mine. "That changes today."

I got up from the bed and went to the window. The snowstorm had passed, and between the moon and the white of what I guessed was a foot of snow, it was almost like the sun was shining in the middle of the night. It was a magical winter wonderland, and as I marveled at the beauty I was seeing, I was pretty sure that magic lived in my heart… Magic that Adam had put there. I glanced over to where he was sleeping and said a little prayer that this was real and I wasn't dreaming.

We'd—Adam actually—made a breakfast of Black Forest ham wrapped around cheddar cheese slices. For lunch we'd piled rye bread high with pastrami, provolone cheese, and mustard. By the time dinner rolled around, the box of food Mary had sent up with Adam had thawed, and we'd feasted on quiche, fruit, and slices of red velvet cake. Deciding I would worry about taking the extra pounds off after we returned to civilization, I hadn't picked at my food.

In between our meals we'd made love and talked and planned. I was almost on overload, so many thoughts crowding my head that it was impossible to sleep. Adam had called his brother after we'd finished breakfast to tell him we were snowbound and to feed Jinx, and then he had called Dylan to see if there was any news on Jackson. Unfortunately there was no evidence that Jackson had been the one to set the fire, no fingerprints on the gas can and no witnesses. I'd so been hoping there would be and he would be arrested. Since that wasn't going to happen, I was going to have to deal with him when I traveled to New York. But I'd worry about that tomorrow. Tonight I was too happy to think of him.

"Can't sleep?" Adam said, coming up behind me and slipping his arms around me.

I tilted my head back, looking up at him. "There's so much happiness in my heart that I think it might explode." I turned my gaze back to the window. "It's beautiful out there, like a magical land."

He rested his chin on my shoulder. "Yeah, it is. Are you really happy, Savannah?"

"More than I thought possible. Just promise I'm not dreaming."

"I'm real. You're real. Come back to bed and I'll prove it."

"You're insatiable," I said, laughing.

"Don't mock me. I have nine years of missing you to make up for."

"There is that."

He took my hand and led me back to the bed. A little later we bundled up and went out on the balcony to watch the sunrise. As it peeked over the mountains, Adam stood behind me, his body wrapped around mine.

"I missed the mountains so much," I said, leaning my head back until my cheek was next to his.

"Do you think you'll miss New York, at least all the things there are to do? It can get pretty boring here."

Would I? It was nice having world-class restaurants, the theater, and shopping at my fingertips. "Maybe a few things, but I was never happy there. And I am here. This is the home of my heart. I wish I was done with modeling and never had to return to New York."

"When do you have to go back?"

"Next week, but only for two days this time." I didn't doubt that Jackson would be at the shoot, even after Jill had warned him away. I shuddered at knowing I'd have to deal with him.

"I'm coming with you."

As much as I'd love to have him there to keep Jackson away from me—because I knew he would—I had to do this myself. If I let Adam take over, I'd be right back where I'd started, letting others dictate my life. Not that Adam was anything like my mother or Jackson, but I was determined to hold on to the new me, the one who made the decisions where my professional life was concerned.

I turned in his arms to face him. "Thank you for offering, but no. This is something I need to take care of myself."

"Savannah—"

I put my fingers over his lips. "You can give me a thousand reasons why you should be there to protect me, and you'll probably be right on every one of them. But please understand, the night Jackson put a knife to my cheek and threatened to cut me was the moment I woke up to what I'd allowed my life to come to. Even then, I packed for a trip to Paris that I wanted no part of because he told me to. I didn't plan to walk out that night, but I did, and I made myself one promise. No one would ever control me again."

"I don't want to control you," Adam said past the fingers I had pressed to his mouth.

"If I thought you did, I wouldn't be here with you right now. Someday I want to take you to New York and show you all the good parts. But for this trip, you're not invited."

"Okay, I don't like it, but I get it. I won't follow you there as much as I want to, if you promise to call me every day… No, make that at least twice. When you wake up and before you go to sleep."

"That I can promise." And how could I not love this man who had always got me?

"It's going to be a long two days without you."

"For me, too, and I hope it's only for two. It's always possible there could be problems with the shoot, which might add a day or two more." I could see in his eyes that he wasn't crazy about me taking off without him, even though he understood my reasons.

"And if Jackson messes with you, promise you'll call the cops."

"Absolutely, but I'm hiring a bodyguard, so I shouldn't have a problem with him."

He slid his arms around my waist. "You could hire me."

"Nice try, lover boy." He chuckled as if he had been kidding, but I knew he wished I'd do just that. If there was trouble with Jackson, though, I didn't want Adam in the middle of it.

Adam glanced over at the snow-covered road. "It looks like we'll be stuck here at least another day. What shall we do?"

"Oh, I don't know. Read a book?"

He snorted. "Wrong. Let's play in the snow and then fire up the hot tub."

"You're so clever."

"That's why you love me." He kissed my nose.

"Ah, I've been wondering why." I grabbed a handful of snow and threw it at him.

"Now you've done it," Adam said, his hands busy making a snowball.

Thus began an all-out war. Mary's cabin had a wrap-around porch, giving us plenty of room to chase each other. "Where are you?" I sang, peeking around the corner.

"Right here," he said from behind me, dumping a bucketful of snow on my head.

"Oh, you're gonna pay for that." I shook my head, sending snow droplets flying. The wind had died down to nothing, and the sun was out. After yesterday's ridiculous winds and freezing temperatures, it was surprisingly comfortable out.

When Adam laughed, I tackled him, sending us both down to the deck. He rolled us over until he was on top of me. My laughter died as he stared down at me, his eyes turning soft.

"Tell me again."

I didn't have to ask what he meant. "I love you."

"So I didn't dream you said that."

He lowered his mouth to mine and softly kissed me. His lips were cold, sending a shiver through me, but when he slid his tongue into my mouth, his heat warmed me. Suddenly he lifted his head, his gaze on something beyond me.

"What's that noise?"

Hearing a loud engine noise, I glanced over at the road to see a snowplow come around the curve, its large blade pushing snow to the side. "Make it go away," I said. "I don't want to be rescued."

"Strange. This isn't a main road. There shouldn't be a snowplow up here." Adam pushed up, then held out his hand to help me to my feet.

We went to the railing. Expecting it to continue on, I was surprised to see it turning onto the cabin's driveway.

Adam huffed a laugh. "Is that Mary in there with Leonard?"

"Who's Leonard?" I squinted at seeing a head of purple hair that could only be Mary.

"The driver. He works for the town."

When the snowplow stopped, Leonard exited, went around to the other side, and lifted Mary out. She was dressed from head to toe in a purple snowsuit that perfectly matched her hair.

"If nothing else, she won't get lost in the snow," Adam murmured, making me giggle.

"Oh good, you're both alive," she said, stopping on the

other side of the deck. She put her hands on her hips, her eyes narrowing on Adam. "You were supposed to call me this morning, let me know you still had power. Since you didn't, I brought Leonard to help me haul off your frozen bodies."

Leonard snickered.

Adam glanced at me and rolled his eyes. "I think she's just being nosy," he murmured for my ears only. "The sun's only been up for an hour, Mary. Couldn't wait to find out if your little scheme to reunite Savannah and me worked?"

"Well, did it?" She turned her gaze on me. "Savannah, you gonna love this man till your dying day?"

I almost said, "I do." That struck me as funny, and I laughed. I honestly hadn't realized how much I missed the valley and the crazy people here until now. Not once during the years I'd been gone had I laughed in pure happiness. I felt like I was waking up after a long sleep.

Adam put his arm around my shoulders and pulled me next to him. "Everything's great, Mary. Now go away."

She looked from me to Adam before giving a satisfied nod. "My work here is done, Leonard. You can take me back down the mountain." She waved her fingers at us over her shoulder, saying, "Ta ta," as she headed back to the snowplow.

"I love her," I said, grinning at seeing Leonard lift her into the machine's cab.

Adam trailed his hand down my arm, and reaching my hand, he linked our fingers. "And I love you. I think there's a hot tub calling our names."

"Lead the way." I'd follow this man anywhere.

"I'm Dax Stockton from Farrant Security," the man waiting in the lobby of my New York apartment said, holding out his hand.

Good heavens, he was huge, and my hand disappeared

inside his when we shook. "Um, nice to meet you." I'd like to see Jackson try to mess with this guy. "I have a car waiting."

"Yes, ma'am. I've already talked to your driver. Marla Armstrong filled me in on your situation. You'll be safe with me, ma'am."

I didn't doubt it. "You can call me Savannah."

"Yes, ma'am," he said, not cracking a smile.

Dax Stockton was all business, I realized as he herded me to the car. I glanced up at him to see his gaze scanning our surroundings. The driver had the back door open, and after I was inside, Dax slid into the front passenger seat. I liked that he hadn't seemed fazed by who I was, nor had he made me uncomfortable by showing any male appreciation in his eyes when he looked at me.

The shoot was in a studio on Park Avenue, a glamour shot for a magazine cover, and as expected, Jackson was waiting just inside the door.

"That's Jackson—"

"Marks. Yes, I know." Dax stepped in front of me. "Mr. Marks, I'm going to ask you politely not to approach Miss Savannah. If you have something to say to her, you can do it from where you stand."

"Who the hell is this, Savannah?"

I peeked around Dax's massive body. "This would be Dax, my bodyguard. I don't think he's someone you want to mess with. Consider this your only chance to talk to me. After today you can communicate through my attorney."

My soon-to-be ex-agent looked like he wished he'd cut me when he had the chance. Although it wasn't planned, walking out that night had been the smartest thing I'd ever done... well, except for falling in love with Adam. I wanted to get this inevitable confrontation with Jackson over with, get this shoot done, and go home to Adam.

"You can't do this." Jackson pointed a finger at me. "I own you."

Dax glanced down at me—and yes, as tall as I was, he towered over me—and raised a brow. The coward in me wanted to nod, giving him permission to handle Jackson while I walked away. But the new me that was emerging decided it was time to stand my ground.

"I own me, Jackson. Not you. I'm honoring my obligations to you, and you should feel lucky about that because honestly, I'm half-tempted to say, 'Screw you,' and disappear from sight. That still might happen, so if I were you, I'd be dang nice to me." Maybe petty, but I couldn't resist throwing at least one *dang* his way.

"I love you, Savannah. All I've ever wanted was what was best for you."

Seriously? In all the years we'd been together, he'd never said those words to me. I stared at him, and as I did, I saw the desperation in his eyes, and yes, maybe something like love. But it was a warped kind of love, a sick obsession.

"You sure could've fooled me," I said.

"You're my masterpiece, my creation." Jackson reached out a hand toward me. "You belong to me."

I'd always seen Jackson as controlling and selfish, but I finally saw the truth. Jackson Marks was a very sick man who'd been able to hide that fact through intimidation and yes, his intelligence. I also realized that there was nothing I could say to him that would make a difference.

"Come on, Dax. Reb's waiting to take my picture." I slipped my arm around my bodyguard's elbow. The funny thing was, before the night Jackson had held a knife to my face, I would have been stuttering all over the place and worse, mumbling an apology in an effort to placate Jackson. Liberation was an amazing feeling.

"I'll ruin you," Jackson yelled at our backs as we walked away.

"Yeah?" I said, glancing over my shoulder. "You try and I'll sue you for every penny you stole from me, so make my attorney happy and go for it." Dang, that felt good. I thought it best not to warn him that my attorney was actually looking into my finances and how much he'd stolen.

We hadn't taken four steps when Dax's arm tensed. He spun and did some kind of karate kick. I turned in time to see Dax's foot land on Jackson's stomach, sending Jackson flying backward. His back hit the wall, and he slid down, legs sprawled out in front of him.

"What happened?" I glanced from Jackson to Dax.

"Your agent was about to attack you, Savannah."

I turned to the new voice. "Oh, hi, Reb. Didn't see you there." Reb Garlander was a much in demand photographer and the owner of Studio on Park. "Jackson was coming at me?"

"Yeah." Reb walked over to Jackson and stared down at him. "That was bad business, dude. I've never much liked you, so it doesn't pain me at all to ban you from my studio for life."

It took all my willpower to keep from clapping. As Reb walked past me, he winked. "I'm ready for you."

"Be right there." But first I had one more thing to say to my soon-to-be ex-agent. He was struggling to get up, and I put my foot on his knee.

"You're going to be sorry, asshole," Jackson said, glaring at Dax.

"You listen to me, Jackson Marks." I pushed my foot down with all my strength. "Fuck you." I'd never said that word in my life, but this first time using it, I seriously meant it.

"You're done playing your stupid games. You don't show your face at any of my shoots from this day forward. You don't call me or try to see me. You need to tell me anything, you do it through my attorney. You don't bad-mouth me to anyone. You break any of those rules and it's game on."

Who would be the next woman Jackson would obsess over? At what point would he lose it and actually hurt someone? I couldn't let that stand, and when I met my new agent for dinner tonight, I would tell her she needed to spread the word that he was dangerous. I was also pretty sure that Reb would put out his own warning about Jackson. Between the two of them and the mess of trouble I would bring down on his head once Jill finished her investigation, Jackson was done in this town.

"Bravo," Dax said when I stepped away from Jackson.

"That felt dang good. Now I need to go to work." Since I'd been to Reb's studio before, I said, "Down the hall to the left."

Dax chuckled. "I know, ma'am. I scouted out your destination yesterday."

"Savannah," I said, already knowing I was now and forever *ma'am* to my bodyguard.

"Yes, ma'am." He gave me the first real smile since I'd walked into the lobby of my apartment building earlier this morning. "Dude's an ass. You're well rid of him."

Didn't I know it.

CHAPTER THIRTY-TWO

~ Adam and Savannah ~

Valentine's Day…

"SOMEONE BOUGHT MY PROPERTY." I glanced over at Adam.

"We'll find you another one just as good."

"But I wanted that one."

"Only because it was the first one you saw, so you set your heart on it." He reached over and took my hand, pressing it down on his leg. "Where are we going?"

"I'll tell you when to turn." I shook off my disappointment over losing the land. Tonight was special, and I was excited to see Adam's reaction when he saw his Valentine's Day gift. He was going to love it, at least part one, his present. I was nervous, though, about part two, not at all sure what his reaction would be.

"I missed you." He glanced at me and smiled.

"Missed you, too." That soft smile of his sent my heart to fluttering every single time.

It was cold, but it hadn't snowed recently, so the roads were clear. Nervous about my plans, I drummed my fingers on Adam's leg. He covered my hand with his, and I settled back in my seat. Adam loved me, he'd often said so, and by the time tonight ended, I would be the happiest girl in the world. I was sure of it… mostly.

I'd finished my last job for Jackson—thank you, God—and flown home yesterday. Since the day I had threatened him, he had made himself scarce. Or maybe it was my bodyguard, with me at all times when I had a photo shoot, that had scared him off. It didn't matter, only that he was out of my life.

Jill and I had discussed breaking my contract with him, but that would have opened me up to him suing me for breach of contract. And I hadn't liked the thought of terminating my commitments to those who'd contracted for me. It wasn't their fault Jackson was a bad man.

Lucas had said Jill was a shark, and was she ever. She'd been able to prove that Jackson had stolen close to six million dollars from me, and two days ago he'd been arrested, his bank accounts frozen, and an article about him appeared in *The New York Times* this morning. I hated that my name was in the article as *the victim*, but I did have the satisfaction of knowing that no other woman would go through what I had because of him. I considered that a win. In the end Jackson would to go prison for a long time.

As of today I had one year to go with my new agent and then I'd be done with modeling forever. But tonight my nerves were buzzing. I was both excited and a basket case over what I had planned.

"Turn on Broken Creek Road." I was expecting Adam's grin at that. He knew right where we were going now.

"I have very fond memories of that overlook," he said, squeezing my hand.

"And I have very fond memories of the back seat of your Mustang."

"Do you now?" He glanced over at me, his eyes filled with heat. "Wish I still had that car. We could recreate a few memorable scenes from our past."

"Do you remember our first time?"

"Like it was yesterday. And I'm still embarrassed."

I laughed. "Well, two virgins in the cramped back seat of a Mustang doesn't make for finesse."

"True, but it was shooting bullets about three seconds after I was inside you that mortified me."

Even now his cheeks pinked at his admission. He was

just too adorable. "What did I know? I thought that was normal. But I will admit that I wondered what the big deal was."

He snorted, and then his expression turned serious. "We were good together, Savannah. We *are* good together."

"I know."

We came to the turnoff for the overlook, a place local kids all knew about. I hoped since it was cold that we'd have the place to ourselves tonight.

"Is that Connor's Jeep?" Adam said.

"Don't know." It was. He and Autumn were keeping an eye on Adam's gift until we arrived. It wasn't the kind of thing one left unprotected for a few hours. They'd no doubt done their share of making out while they waited, so I didn't feel guilty asking them for the favor. And Connor had wanted to see his brother's face when he laid eyes on the present.

"It is him, and Autumn's with him. Weird."

When he pulled up next to the Jeep, I took the blindfold from my coat pocket, handing it to him after he shut down the engine. "Here, put this on."

He stared at the blindfold a moment, then lifted amused eyes to mine. "You going kinky on me, Savvy?"

"Guess you'll have to put it on and find out."

"Just so you know, if you are, I'm good with it." He gave me a classic Adam smirk before slipping the blindfold over his eyes. "Now what?"

"I'll come around and get you."

Connor and Autumn got out of their car, and Connor pointed at the far corner of the lot where Adam's present sat, somewhat hidden behind some brush. Since Connor and Autumn had taken on the task of picking it up and getting it to the overlook, it was the first time I'd seen it. I grinned at the two of them. Adam was going to be so surprised.

I slipped a hand around Adam's arm. "You're going to

have to walk a little. I'll guide you."

"You're not planning to walk me off the side of the mountain, are you?"

Connor gripped Adam's other arm. "Dude, how'd you guess?"

Connor leaned his head behind Adam's back and winked at me. We'd had a long talk a few months ago.

"Would you help me track down the Mustang you and Adam owned in high school?" I asked him one day.

"Why?"

I'd gone over to Connor's house when Adam was at one of his jobsites and Autumn was at an appointment with a client. Connor and I had needed to sort out our differences. We both loved Adam, and it was time he understood I was the best thing to happen to his twin.

"Because I'm going to ask him to marry me," I answered. "I want to give him the Mustang for an engagement present." When Connor looked at me without his usual distrust in his eyes, but with something like acceptance, I knew I'd done the right thing by confronting him.

"I told him you were his kryptonite, and I didn't mean that in a good way. I wanted you to go away because I thought you'd hurt him again."

"I didn't hurt—"

"I know. He finally told me it was all on him." Connor pulled me into a hug, surprising me. "But I was wrong. You're the only woman he'll ever love, and you make him happy. That's all that counts. Welcome to the family, Savannah. If he ever pulls a stupid stunt like that again, you come straight to me. I'll knock some sense back into his stubborn head."

I'd embarrassed myself by bawling, that happy that I had his approval. From that day on, I'd been welcomed back into Connor's world, and I felt honored to be there.

Smiling at each other, we led Adam to the 1970 red Mustang Boss, stopping him in front of the hood. My heart felt like it was going explode, that was how excited I was. I reached up and pulled the blindfold from Adam's head. My gaze was glued to him, waiting to see his reaction.

I blinked, the vision in front of me impossible to comprehend. I looked at Savannah. "It's a car just like the one Connor and I had in high school."

Next to me, Connor chuckled for some reason.

"No," Savannah said. "It is the one."

"*The* one?"

She nodded.

"How?" I walked to the car and reverently ran my hand over the hood, still not sure my eyes weren't deceiving me.

"Connor helped me track it down."

"Her," I said, glancing over at Savannah. "Not an it."

She grinned. "Sorry. I didn't mean to insult her."

Connor was a muscle car nut like me, but I'd always been a tad more of an enthusiast. I'd loved this car, but when Savannah had left, I couldn't bear to look at it. There were too many memories of us that came with this car, and I'd sold it to a collector in Asheville.

"Do you like it?" she asked.

I strode to her, picked her up, and kissed her senseless. "Does that answer your question?" I said when I set her back on her feet.

She laughed, her eyes filled with love and happiness. "I guess it does."

Autumn walked around to the passenger window and peered inside. "I remember us cramming inside this to go to football games."

When Savannah joined her, I bumped shoulders with my brother. "How long have you known about this?"

"She bought it a month ago. Same guy still had it, so it was easy to find. I picked it up this morning." My brother bumped his shoulder against mine. "She's a keeper."

"Yeah, I'll never sell it again."

He glared at me. "Dumbass, I mean Savannah."

"Like I didn't know that, look-alike dumbass."

"How did we get so lucky?" he said, his gaze on Savannah and Autumn as they both stuck their heads inside the car.

"Don't know. Only care that we did. Can you drive my car home so I can hang out up here for a while with Savannah?"

"That's the plan."

My brother kicked at the dirt, which caught my attention. "What?"

"We haven't had a chance to talk much lately." He glanced at the girls, who now had the top half of their bodies inside the Mustang. "I'm taking Autumn to Ashville tonight. I have a room reserved at the Inn on Biltmore Estate. I'm going to ask her to marry me."

"Yeah?" I gave him a hug. "Funny that. I'm going to ask Savannah the same question tonight, and I have a big surprise for her, too." I hadn't told him what I'd done before now because he'd tell Autumn and that woman couldn't keep a secret. She'd let something slip without meaning to.

"What's that?"

When I told him, he grinned. "You two are a trip with your surprises. Let's have dinner tomorrow night to celebrate our engagements. Maybe Dylan and Jenn can join us."

"I'll call them in the morning. Good luck. Not that you need it. Autumn's going to say yes."

"If I doubted that, I wouldn't be asking her." We shared one more hug, and then he walked over to the girls, scooped Autumn up in his arms, causing her to shriek, and carried his laughing future wife to his car. After depositing her into the driver's seat, he went to mine. With a last wave he drove away, Autumn following him.

I watched them go, my heart filled with happiness for him… for me. A little over a year ago, both of us had believed love wasn't for us, couldn't have imagined this day happening. When they were gone from sight, I turned my attention to Savannah. She gave me a sultry smile as she crooked her finger. I willingly went to her.

She took my hand and pulled me into the back seat. I'd forgotten how cramped it was, and we ended up in a tangle of arms and legs. I didn't care. We finally got settled with her straddling me, and we got busy reliving memories.

"I love you," I told her as she shattered in my arms, her breath hot and heavy on my neck. I felt her smile against my skin.

"You've improved on your endurance since our first time," she said.

"Hush, woman. Don't be reminding me of my most embarrassing moment. And since I'm not finished yet, you should be impressed." I closed my eyes, loving the slick heat of her.

"Oh, I am." She leaned back, pushing herself between the seats, and turned the key. "Now we have heat and music."

"Clever girl." I pulled her to me. "I'm still having trouble believing we're sitting in my old Mustang. Thank you for this, Savvy."

"You're welcome. Now show me your appreciation."

So I did.

"I love you, Adam," she said a while later.

"Love you back, Savannah." When she looked at me, worry in her eyes and biting on her bottom lip as if she were about to be standing in front of a firing squad, I said, "Is something wrong?"

"Will you marry me?"

I blinked, wondering if I'd heard her right. And then once I was sure I had, I laughed, happier than I'd ever been in my life. "Oh, Savvy, you're just full of surprises tonight, aren't you?"

"At the cabin you said you wanted a romantic proposal, that I'd have to go all out before you'd consider it. I mean, if it's too soon, if—"

"Savannah."

"—you need more time, I understand. I just thought—"

"Savannah."

"—that we've waited so long, and we're finally—"

Apparently the only way to shut her up was to kiss her.

"Oh," she murmured against my lips.

"Yes," I said against hers.

She pulled away, her eyes searching mine. "Yes?"

I nodded. "I'll marry you. Today, tomorrow, every day of our life if you want."

The most beautiful smile in the world lit up her face. "Once will do it as long as it's forever."

"Once it is then." I put my hand behind her neck to tug her back to me for a kiss.

"Wait." She reached down to the floor and picked up an ice bucket with a bottle of champagne in it that I hadn't noticed. Next came two flutes.

After getting the champagne opened, I poured the bubbly into the glasses. "To us, forever and always."

"Forever and always," she echoed, clicking her flute against mine.

"I have one more surprise for you." She reached for her coat, stuck her hand in a pocket, and pulled out a small blue velvet box.

"What's this?"

"Open it and see."

Inside was a silver band with a vertical row of three blue sapphires on both sides of the diamond.

"It's a man's engagement ring." Her shoulders lifted in a little shrug, and I knew she was trying to pretend it didn't matter what I thought. "It's the latest thing. You don't have to wear it if—"

"Savannah."

"—you don't want to. I just like the idea of—"

"Savannah."

"—other women knowing you're—"

I sighed and kissed her again.

"Savannah, I want every woman in the world to know that I belong to you."

"Really?"

"Yes, really." Even if I hadn't ever heard of male engagement rings, I would proudly wear hers. While I was kissing her, I slipped my hand into my own coat pocket and palmed the small box in there.

When she quieted, I let go of her mouth and pressed the ring box into her hand. "I want to wear your ring. And I want you to wear mine."

"You got me a ring?" She opened the box, letting out a gasp. "It's beautiful, Adam."

I took it from her and put it on her finger. "I was going to ask you to marry me tonight, but since I've already said yes, I'll skip the asking part, and just go straight—"

This time she shut me up with a kiss.

"Where are we going?"

I glanced over at Savannah, now wearing the blindfold. "Patience, Savvy. You're not the only one with a few surprises tonight." She was rubbing her finger over her engagement ring, caressing it. Sometimes it amazed me how in tune we were, even in choosing rings for each other. As soon as I saw the platinum band with a sapphire on each side of the diamond, I knew it was the one for her.

Another fifteen minutes and I pulled onto the graveled road, stopped in the spot I'd scouted out this morning, and shut off the engine. I left the headlights on. "You can take off the blindfold."

There wasn't any doubt she would love her Valentine's present, but I watched her face anyway, wanting to see the moment she understood. She stared at the FOR SALE sign that had a SOLD banner and a big red bow on it, lit up by the headlights.

Finally, "You didn't."

I snorted a laugh. "Yeah, I totally did."

She exhaled a long breath. "You let me think I'd lost it."

"I would never let you lose something you wanted as badly as this."

"You're going to make a great husband. You know that?"

"I plan to try. Now tell me you love me."

She fell into my arms, giving me another beautiful smile. "Always and forever."

CHAPTER THIRTY-THREE

~ Adam ~

Valentine's Day ~ One Year Later…

"How do I look?" Connor ran a critical eye over me. "Damn good-looking, if I do say so myself."

I snorted. "You just complimented yourself."

"And your point is?" He reached up and straightened my bow tie. "I still haven't figured out how the girls talked us into this."

"What? The pink bow ties and cummerbunds or the double wedding?"

"Both, and you left out the part about our wedding being photographed for that bride magazine."

Yeah, I wasn't real happy about that part. At Savannah's request, the magazine had sent a guy named Reb something or other, and so far he and his helper had kept a low profile. He'd been here all week, taking pictures of the area and our rehearsal dinner. The four of us—me, Savannah, Connor, and Autumn—had decided to hold a joint bachelor/bachelorette party at Vincennes, Angelo agreeing to close his restaurant to the public for the event, and Reb had even been there for that.

"Mom would have loved us having a double wedding." I swallowed past the lump in my throat. I'd give anything for our parents to be here to see their boys getting married.

"Yeah, she would've." Connor blinked away the tears in his eyes, and I did the same. "I think if she'd been able to pick our brides, she would've chosen Savannah for you and Autumn for me."

I smiled, remembering how much Mom had loved those girls. "Yeah, she would've been all over having them for daughters-in-law."

Dylan stuck his head in the room. "Your chariot has arrived."

"Have our brides left yet?" We were at my house with our best man, Dylan, and our groomsman, Hamburger. The girls had kicked Connor out this morning, commandeering his and Autumn's house for the day.

"Their limo passed by about ten minutes ago." Dylan grinned. "Hamburger can't decide whether he's more excited about his first limo ride or getting to wear his first tux. He's been admiring himself in the bathroom mirror for the last twenty minutes. He was all over the tux but got stubborn on the shoes. Said his feet didn't like them *fancy* shoes, so he's got on his old lace-up boots."

I laughed. "Gotta love our moonshiner. Think Mary will have pink hair today?" Mary had insisted on being included as a bridesmaid since, according to her, there wouldn't be a wedding for either of us without her assistance. Meddling, more like, but she did have a point. The minute Hamburger heard Mary was a bridesmaid, he had declared he was a groomsman because he'd helped, too. Especially with Savannah and me. True, and all four of us knew there was no use fighting either one of them.

Dylan gave me a *well, duh* look. "Is rain wet?" He glanced down at his cummerbund. "Whose idea was the pink anyway?"

"You can blame Savannah and Autumn, but I think your wife encouraged them," I said.

"Then I'll be having a talk with Jenny later."

I laughed. "Like that's gonna scare her." Jenn had the man wrapped around her pinkie.

"Point taken." He glanced at his watch. "I'm responsible for getting the grooms to the wedding on time. Let's roll."

We collected Hamburger from the bathroom, where he was still admiring his reflection in the mirror. Once seated in the limo, I glanced at my brother, seeing the same happiness in his eyes that I knew was in mine.

"Wow," Connor said when we stood at the entrance to Savannah's barn.

Wow was a good word. The place had been transformed into a winter wonderland. Tiny white lights dangled from the ceiling, looking like thousands of icicles. To our right, at the back end of the barn, was a large white arbor filled with pink and white roses. In front of the arbor were rows of white upholstered chairs for our guests, and beside each aisle chair was a plain white pedestal with pink and white flower arrangements.

The opposite side of the huge barn was set up for the reception. Round tables with pink and lavender flower arrangements on them were placed in front of the long table intended for the wedding party. Off to the side was a stage, and below it was a dance floor.

"Lordy, Lordy," Hamburger said, stopping next to me. I glanced over to see his eyes wide and his mouth hanging open. "It's like ah fairy forest."

Actually that was a good description. "The girls outdid themselves."

"Hey, I helped," Dylan said. "Spent a whole day hanging those lights."

I'd expected the barn to be transformed, but my imagination was lacking. It was also nice and warm because of the outdoor heaters scattered around.

At the sound of a car arriving, Dylan said, "You two are to wait in the tack room. Hamburger and I need to play usher. After everyone's seated, I'll come get you."

Since I'd been here a few times with Savannah, I knew where that was. "This way," I told Connor.

The tack room had been cleaned up, and there were a couple of chairs and a table with bottled water in an ice bucket. Also on the table were two pink roses. "I think we're supposed to wear these."

"With all this pink, it's a good thing I'm a secure man," Connor grumbled.

"Are you nervous?"

"Not at all. I would have done this months ago if our brides hadn't come up with this double wedding in a barn on Valentine's gig. You?"

"Same, and our wedding is not a gig."

The door opened, and Reb poked his head in. "There you two are. I need some photos of you guys hanging out together."

I hated this, but I'd grin and bear it for Savannah.

"If I got it right, Adam, you wear a sapphire earring and Connor, you wear an emerald?"

"Yep," we both said in unison.

"The magazine better do extra print runs for this one. I've never seen such a cool wedding before, and that's not even considering that this is Savannah's last photo shoot," he said as he clicked away on his camera.

That I did like, especially since I knew that never having to model again made Savannah happy. Dylan and Hamburger came in, and Reb took some more photos of us with the two of them. Hamburger was loving every minute of the attention.

"Are you really a moonshiner?" Reb asked, aiming his camera lens at Hamburger's scuffed high-top boots.

Hamburger put his hands over Dylan's ears. "Sure am, but dontcha be telling the sheriff here that."

Dylan huffed a laugh. "The *sheriff* can hear you." He pulled Hamburger's hands away from his ears. "All the guests are seated. Time for the grooms to take their places."

"The sooner we get this done, the sooner we can start the honeymoon," Connor said, sounding as eager to get married as I felt.

Autumn had refused to ask her father to give her away, saying that since he didn't know the meaning of fidelity, he had no business being in her wedding. Because Savannah had no one to give her away, she and Autumn had decided during rehearsal that they would walk down the aisle together.

Connor and I stood side by side, hands clasped in front of us, waiting for the first sight of our brides.

"Which one of y'all boys is which?" Granny, Hamburger's mother, hollered from her seat in the second row.

I pointed at myself. "Adam."

Connor poked a finger at his chest. "Connor."

"Them boys needs name tags," she muttered. Autumn's parents sat in front of her, and she tapped Mrs. Archer on the shoulder. "Look there at my Sonny Boy all gussied up. Ain't he purty?"

I glanced over at Hamburger, who had a wide grin on his face, looking as proud as a peacock. Hopefully Granny wouldn't talk through the ceremony, but I wasn't holding my breath on that. At the first sound of music, my gaze locked on the door swinging open off to the side.

"Good God," Connor murmured when Mary stepped out, looking like a pink puffball. Next to him, Dylan chuckled.

Savannah had told me they'd given up on trying to rein Mary in on her bridesmaid's dress and accessories, finally telling her she was free to outfit herself as long as she stuck to the pink theme, and did she ever. I'd never seen so many ruffles and feathers on a dress. Her hair was a bright pink, and she had one of those fascinator things on her head, also all pink, including the foot-long feather growing out of it.

The photographer had a look of pure bliss on his face as he snapped picture after picture of her while she walked toward us. She paused about halfway down the aisle and posed for him. I could only shake my head as I smiled. Savannah had said she was a mountain girl, and she wanted a mountain wedding, the over-the-top kind that our hometown girls had a taste for. She was definitely getting her wish with this one.

It surprised me that Autumn had been on board since she had a discerning eye and preferred classy and understated. But it wasn't like the barn was gaudy. They'd turned it into a beautiful venue for our wedding. We just had a couple of oddballs in the wedding party. Mary took her place across from Hamburger, who was staring at her as if he was seeing a vision of a goddess come to life.

Jenn walked out next, wearing a pale pink simple gown. I'd overheard her grumble one night that as a redhead, pink wasn't her color, but the whispered, "Wow," from Dylan said she looked just fine, and she did. Her gaze was fixed on her husband as she made her way down the aisle. They didn't like being away from Heather, their daughter, so I suspected they'd be cutting out as soon as the toasts were made and the cake cut.

The music changed to "A Thousand Years," and I inhaled a deep breath, hearing Connor do the same next to me. The girls had included us in choosing what song they'd walk down the aisle to, and this one had been the unanimous choice. I thought the lyrics were perfect for each of our stories.

Our guests stood, blocking our view, and I wanted to yell at them to sit so I could see my bride. And then, finally, she appeared at the end of the aisle. She and Autumn stopped, letting Reb take a few pictures. Then they smiled at each other before they began their walk down the aisle.

Savannah's gaze held mine, that smile that I knew was just for me appearing on her face. I might have stopped breathing. I'd seen Savannah on magazine covers, and she always looked sophisticated, glamorous, and beautiful, but she'd always seemed untouchable in those photos. I'd seen her relaxed and happy, wearing what she called her mountain girl clothes, her hair in pigtails or a braid. I loved that side of her. But the woman walking toward me, eyes on mine, was the most beautiful thing I'd ever seen in my life.

Her black hair was pulled back, then allowed to fall down her back, and her gown was simple. I think it was satin and had an off-the-shoulders scooped neck showing a hint of cleavage, long sleeves, and hugged her body. It was the perfect gown for my mountain girl. But what I loved the most were the sapphire earrings dangling from her ears.

Connor and I had given our brides earrings to match ours as wedding gifts. I glanced at Autumn to see that she was wearing the emerald ones from Connor. Her gown was more traditional than Savannah's, and it suited her. My gaze shifted back to Savannah as she neared.

"Beautiful," Connor murmured.

"Yes, she is." He bumped shoulders with me. "They both are." I held out my hand when Savannah stopped in front of me, and she placed hers in mine. *I love you, Savvy,* I mouthed.

"What'd he say?" Granny hollered.

Savannah and I shared a grin before I glanced at Granny. "I said I love her."

Granny scrunched her eyebrows together as if that puzzled her. "Ain't that why there's this here wedding?"

"Yes, ma'am, it is."

And so my brother and I married girls we'd known most of our lives, and I would be forever grateful that Savannah and I had a second chance at getting it right.

"Tell me you're wearing a lacy white bra and panties under this dress, Savvy."

"Maybe. Or maybe I'm not wearing anything at all under my gown."

I stumbled.

Savannah laughed, snuggling into me as Connor and I danced with our brides for the bride and groom's dance. We'd hired a band out of Asheville for the evening, but later, after everyone had sampled the different flavors of moonshine lined up in shot glasses on a table in the far corner, Hamburger would take the stage with his fiddle. Things would get wild then, and Savannah and I would have our mountain wedding no other way.

I put my mouth next to Savannah's ear, nuzzling her. "Have I told you I love you, Mrs. Hunter?"

My wife sighed against my neck. "I have a last name."

"Yes, you do." She'd hated being a one-name personality. I think that more than anything had made her feel like a commodity, nothing more than a product that her mother and Jackson Marks had exploited.

As much as my wife was now in control of her life in the way she had wanted, had strived for and had made happen, she would always be mine to protect. I wasn't stupid enough to tell her that, though.

My wife. Ten years ago now, I'd thought I was doing the right thing by setting her free. Maybe I had been. We'd been kids in love, and how many of those relationships lasted? If I had it to do over, I'm not sure I would have changed a thing.

Toasts followed the bride and groom's dance, Dylan getting a bit mushy and teary-eyed when talking about the group of friends who'd always been there for each other from the first grade and how they'd welcomed him, an outsider from a big city, into their ranks.

"You... y'all... y'all all are family," he said at the end of his toast, and then he plopped down next to Jenn and grinned at her like an idiot.

Connor laughed. "Our chief has been into Hamburger's moonshine."

Jenn snorted. "Ya think?" She stood, pulling her husband up with her. "It was a beautiful wedding, but I need to get

my man home." She held out her hand. "Car keys, Chief."
He obediently dropped a ring of keys into her hand.

"Give Heather a kiss from her favorite uncle," I said.

Connor punched my arm. "I'm her favorite uncle."

I smirked at my brother. "Like she can tell us apart at six months old."

"She can because she gives me a bigger smile than she does you."

"Does not."

"Time to par-tay!" Hamburger yelled from the stage, then put his fiddle under his chin and played his foot-stomping music.

"How does he even know that word?"

Savannah leaned her head on my shoulder. "Autumn taught it to him."

"Of course she did." I took my wife's hand. "Then by all means, let's *par-tay*."

Connor and I danced the night away with our brides, surrounded by the people of Blue Ridge Valley who'd been determined to see us get our happily ever afters. There was a saying in the mountains... *If everything is coming your way, you're in the wrong lane.* There was a lot of truth to that, but I knew deep in my heart that I'd finally made it onto the right lane, where I'd stay for the rest of my life with the woman I loved.

EPILOGUE

~ *Savannah* ~

Five years later...

"WHY DOES SHE ONLY HAVE three legs, Mommy?"

I trailed my hand through the soft brown fur of the puppy, my newest rescue. "Some kids hurt her, honey."

Our three-year-old daughter looked up at her father. "You said when I was three, I could have a puppy, Daddy. I want this one."

Adam smiled in that soft way he had when looking at Emma. "And why did I say you had to wait until you were three?"

"You said 'cause I was old enough now to take care of it."

"That's right. And do you promise to take care of it?"

"Oh, yes, Daddy!" She got that sly look in her eyes when she knew she had Adam twisted around her little finger, which was often. "She can come home with me, okay? Jinx won't mind."

"I'm not so sure about that," Adam muttered, making me laugh.

"What do you want to name her?" I asked. Emma had assigned herself the job of naming the animals at the farm, and they all had her favorite cartoon characters' names.

"Wendy."

"Ah, that's a good one." My current rescue residents were six dogs, ten cats, five horses, one aged pony—named Peter Pan—two alpacas, a potbellied pig, and four goats.

"But you're going to have to let Wendy stay here for a few days until she's feeling better, okay?"

Emma blinked her baby-blue eyes at her father. "But she'll feel better with me, Daddy."

The kid knew where the weak link was, that was for sure. I shot Adam a warning look.

"Ah, Mommy's the boss at the farm, baby. Besides, it's almost time for everyone to get here. Let Wendy rest for a while. You can come see her before we go home later."

When her lips trembled, he glanced at me, raising a brow.

N. O, I mouthed to his unasked question. I would have thought he'd be immune to Emma's tears by now, but he hated to see her cry, and the little stinker knew it. Considering the news I planned to tell him tonight, my husband needed to learn how to say no or we'd have two kids running roughshod over us.

"Come on, Emma. Your cousins are here," I said at hearing the sound of an engine. I took Wendy from her.

"Is Heather coming, too?"

Adam picked up Emma. "She sure is. That might be her now."

Even though Heather was two years older than Emma, the two were best friends. Her cousins, Connor and Autumn's twins, were barely tolerated by the two since they were boys and a year younger than Emma. Cooper and Parker adored the girls, though, and followed them around like eager puppies hoping to be noticed.

Soon we'd be adding to the kid count—Jenn was five months pregnant, me six weeks, and Autumn was trying. She had told Connor, though, that if she had another set of twins, he was cut off for life. I'm pretty sure she was half-serious.

"Daddy needs a Mommy kiss." Adam slid his hand around the back of my neck and pulled me to him. He lowered his mouth to mine, and I melted into him. I would never get tired of kissing this man, and I thought when we were eighty years old and he kissed me, my toes would still curl."

"Emma needs a Mommy-Daddy kiss," our daughter said, tugging on both our ears.

Adam smiled against my lips. It was an Emma thing to demand her share of kisses. We pulled apart and Adam planted a kiss on one of her cheeks and I laid one on the other.

"Let's go swimming, baby girl," Adam said.

"Yay," Emma chirped, clapping her hands.

He reached down and gave my butt a squeeze. "Don't be long."

"I won't. Send Dax in if you see him."

"Will do."

After they left, I knelt next to the puppy and checked the bandage on her hind leg. "I'm sorry you're hurt, sweetie, but I promise you're safe now." She licked my hand.

"How's she doing?"

I glanced up at Dax. "Better. She ate a little. Maybe you can get some more food down her later."

Dax had been a godsend to the farm. We'd kept in touch after I was done with Jackson, and when Dax had learned I was looking for a manager, someone to live on the farm, he'd asked for the job. Turned out he'd grown up on a farm and knew animals.

I'd run a background check on him, learning that he'd been a SEAL before going to work for Farrant Security. Whatever his story was, he was keeping it to himself. For such a big man he had the gentlest of touches with the animals. Adam had built a small log home on the property, in which Dax now lived. I liked knowing someone was here around the clock, especially a man like Dax who knew how to keep everyone safe, so it worked out for both of us.

"Poor thing," he said, kneeling next to the puppy. He glanced at me. "Everyone's here. Go spend time with your family and friends. I'll stay with her."

"Thanks. Oh, and Emma has named her Wendy."
"From Peter Pan?"
I grinned. "Of course."

Leaving Wendy in the care of my farm manager, I headed for the creek. When I got there, the guys and kids were playing in the water, along with five of the six dogs. Tinker Bell, the ugliest dog on the face of the earth and a total scaredy cat, was curled up on Jenn's lap, her head hidden under her baby blanket. She'd been horribly mistreated, and we'd discovered that she seemed to believe if you couldn't see her face, she was safe. She was suspicious of the guys and kids, but she considered women to be harmless.

Adam had built a large creekside gazebo and next to it an outdoor kitchen. Jenny and Autumn were stretched out on lounge chairs inside the gazebo, and I joined them.

"Hey, you," Autumn said. She held up her glass of wine. "Want me to pour you a glass?"

I patted my stomach and grinned. "No wine for me for the next eight months."

"You're pregnant?" Autumn and Jenn shrieked.

"Lower your voices. I haven't told Adam yet."

As if he'd suddenly developed supersonic hearing—in spite of the noise of the dogs barking and the playful screams of the kids—Adam's head jerked up, his eyes fastening on mine. A slow smile spread across his face, and he walked out of the creek, a man on a mission. A very sexy one wearing nothing but board shorts and flip-flops. I sucked in my breath in anticipation.

"Oh boy," Jenn murmured, glancing from Adam to me with a smirk on her face.

Autumn chuckled. "Someone's in trouble." She added her own smirk. "Of the delicious kind, I think."

When he reached me, he scooped me up into his arms. "Ladies, excuse us while I have a little chat with my wife about keeping secrets."

"Uh-huh," Jenn said, laughter dancing in her eyes.

"So that's what they're calling it now, a *chat*?" Autumn said, then giggled.

"Where's Daddy taking Mommy, Aunt Jenn?" I heard Emma ask as Adam carried me away.

"Um, they're just going to have a little talk, honey. You and Heather come over here and give Tinker Bell some loving."

"A talk about what?" That was Connor, and I peeked over Adam's shoulder to see him walking out of the creek, his twin boys in his arms.

"Actually, they're going to have a little"—Autumn made air quotes—"*chat*."

"Ah," Dylan said, coming to stand next to Jenn. He squatted next to her chair and laid his hand on her baby stomach. "This kind of chat?"

"I want a chat," Connor said.

At the sound of their laughter, I buried my face in Adam's neck. "This is so embarrassing."

"Sorry about that."

I heard the male satisfaction in his voice, though. "No, you're not."

He chuckled as he brushed his fingers along the curve of my breast. "Truth."

After a short hike, Adam still carrying me, we reached our special place. We'd discovered the small waterfall not long after buying the property and had spent many hours over the last five years here. There was a cave behind the fall just big enough for the two of us to fit into, and with the water forming a curtain in front of us, it was like stepping into our own private world. It was deliciously cool on a hot summer day. We suspected that Emma had been conceived in our little cave.

Adam dropped his arm away from my legs, letting me slide down his body. He took my hand and led me along the ledge and into the cave. There was a smooth rock, and he sat, then pulled me onto his lap so that I straddled him.

"Now, Mrs. Hunter. What's this about another baby in our future? And how long have you known?"

"Well, Mr. Hunter, it's true. Emma is going—"

He crashed his mouth down on mine.

"Emma's going to have a brother or sister," I finished a bit breathlessly when he lifted his head. "I've known since this morning. I mean, I suspected it, but I wanted to be sure before I said anything. I was going to tell you tonight."

We'd been trying to have another baby for a year now, and although we hadn't voiced our concern to each other yet, I thought we'd both feared it wasn't going to happen. I hadn't wanted to get him excited, only to find out I wasn't pregnant after all.

"You said you were going to the grocery store for our cookout today."

"I did that, too. After my doctor's appointment. I was going to seduce you tonight and then tell you about the baby."

"You were, were you?" I had on a cotton spaghetti-strap top, and he slipped the straps from my shoulders, tugging the shirt down under my bathing suit top. "I think you should stick to that plan. The one about seducing me tonight. However, I'm in the mood for an early celebration."

"That's pretty obvious," I said, feeling his erection pressing against my sex. I wiggled, doing my best to torture him, smiling against his neck when he grunted.

He wrapped my hair around his fist and tugged my head back. When he could look me in the eyes, he said, "I love you, Savvy. Always have. Always will."

He said those words to me a lot, but each time a thrill shot through me. "Show me," I whispered. And as he did just that, his hands and mouth working their magic on my body, happiness filled my heart. For so many years I'd thought Adam was lost to me, never dreaming that we'd find our way back to each other. I'd believed that our story was written, that it was done. But we had found each other again, and we were writing a new story, one with a happily ever after.

"I love you, heart, body, and soul," I whispered into my husband's ear.

"Always," he whispered back. He put his hand on my stomach. "And you, too, little bean."

Acknowledgments

And here I am writing another acknowledgment, my fifteenth since my first book was published in 2014. Since then, my list of everyone I want to thank has grown to the point where I think I should have created an Excel report thingy to keep track.

One of my favorite things about this publishing business is the friends I've made around the world because of my books. I've never personally met most of you, but I love talking to you each day about books, book boyfriends, and all the other fun stuff we share with each other. You guys make my day, and I love you for it.

To the members of my Facebook reader group, Sandra's Book Salon, y'all are the best, the funniest, and sometimes the craziest book lovers ever! Almost every day you make me laugh, and I treasure every moment with you. Your support, all the shares, and other things you do to get the word out on my books means the world to me. Thank you for being so special, and just so you know, I think the world of you.

If you love a book, do the author a huge favor and leave a review. Then tell your friends there's a book they just have to read. To everyone who does these two things, thank you, thank you, thank you!!!

Jenny Holiday, my friend, my critique partner, and amazing author, what a crazy and wonderful journey we've been on. Hope it lasts forever! Miranda Liasson and AE

Jones, also friends and awesome authors, my world is better for knowing you.

Thank heavens for editors. Melody Guy and Ella Sheridan, there are not enough thank-yous in the world to say how much I appreciate you and how grateful I am for your skills in making my stories better.

To my family, my love for you knows no bounds. I know you don't understand how I can spend days inside my head, but you still let me be weird and you still love me. I love you back, so much!

ABOUT SANDRA...

BESTSELLING, AWARD-WINNING AUTHOR SANDRA OWENS lives in the beautiful Blue Ridge Mountains of North Carolina. Her family and friends often question her sanity but have ceased being surprised by what she might get up to next. She's jumped out of a plane, flown in an aerobatic plane while the pilot performed death-defying stunts, gotten into laser gun fights in Air Combat, and ridden a Harley motorcycle for years. She regrets nothing.

Sandra is a Romance Writers of America Honor Roll member and a 2013 Golden Heart Finalist for her contemporary romance *Crazy for Her*. In addition to her contemporary romantic suspense novels, she writes Regency stories.

Sign up to Sandra's newsletter to get the latest news, cover reveals, and other fun stuff:
https://bit.ly/2FVUPKS

Join Sandra's Facebook Reader Group:
https://bit.ly/2K5gIcM

Follow Sandra on Bookbub:
www.bookbub.com/authors/sandra-owens

CONNECT WITH SANDRA:
Facebook: *https://bit.ly/2ruKKPl*
Twitter: *https://twitter.com/SandyOwens1*
Goodreads: *https://bit.ly/1LihK43*

Follow Sandra on her Amazon author page:
https://amzn.to/2I4uu2Y

Made in the USA
Columbia, SC
02 January 2019